RESIDENT EVIL
THE FINAL CHAPTER

800 633 268

ALSO AVAILABLE FROM TITAN BOOKS

Resident Evil: Retribution
The Official Movie Novelization by John Shirley

THE OFFICIAL MOVIE NOVELIZATION

RESIDENT EVIL
THE FINAL CHAPTER

NOVELIZATION BY TIM WAGGONER
SCREENPLAY BY PAUL W. S. ANDERSON
BASED ON CAPCOM'S VIDEOGAME *RESIDENT EVIL*

TITAN BOOKS

RESIDENT EVIL: THE FINAL CHAPTER
Print edition ISBN: 9781785652967
E-book edition ISBN: 9781785652974

Published by Titan Books
A division of Titan Publishing Group Ltd
144 Southwark Street, London SE1 0UP

First edition: January 2017
1 3 5 7 9 10 8 6 4 2

This is a work of fiction. Names, characters, places and incidents
are products of the author's imagination or are used fictitiously
and are not to be construed as real. Any resemblance to actual
events, locales, organizations, or persons, living or dead, is
entirely coincidental.

© 2016 Constantin Film Produktion GmbH
Motion Picture Artwork © 2016 CTMG. All Rights Reserved.

No part of this publication may be reproduced, stored in a
retrieval system, or transmitted, in any form or by any means
without the prior written permission of the publisher, nor be
otherwise circulated in any form of binding or cover other than
that in which it is published and without a similar condition
being imposed on the subsequent purchaser.

A CIP catalogue record for this title is available from the British
Library.

Printed and bound by CPI Group (UK) Ltd, Croydon, CR0 4YY

Did you enjoy this book? We love to hear from our readers.
Please email us at readerfeedback@titanemail.com or write to
us at Reader Feedback at the above address.

To receive advance information, news, competitions, and
exclusive offers online, please sign up for the Titan newsletter
on our website: **www.titanbooks.com**

RESIDENT EVIL
EVIL
THE FINAL CHAPTER

This is for another Alice: Alice Avery.
Gone far too soon.

were at home, his daughter's room looked more like it belonged in a hospital ward than a family dwelling. A myriad of machines surrounded the bed, connected to his girl by thin wires, monitoring her vital signs. IV bags hung on metal stands, tubes stretching to the needles embedded in the backs of her wrists in order to deliver a steady stream of various medicines.

While Marcus employed homecare nurses to see to his daughter's needs, he had been the one to set up the equipment and select the medicines that flowed into her body, a number of them highly experimental. Not that his efforts had borne much fruit. His daughter's condition hadn't improved in any significant way, and the side effects from the powerful medicines coursing through her veins only served to intensify her misery. He hated further decreasing her already diminished quality of life, but he could not stand by and watch as the same disease that had claimed her mother killed her, too. He was one of the smartest people on the planet—he thought this with no ego; it was a simple statement of fact—yet for all his education, training, and experience, he'd been unable to save his wife, and now it looked like he would fail his daughter as well.

And not just her—all the others who suffered from incurable diseases, and their loved ones as well. He had been working on a cure, not only for her condition, but a cure for *all* disease, and while he'd made some progress, in no small measure thanks to the contributions of his partner in both business and science, Alexander Isaacs, unless they had a breakthrough soon, his daughter would die before they achieved their goal. That's why he was here today.

He had a backup plan. Quite literally.

He'd brought some new equipment with him this visit: a metal cart with a computer monitor and keyboard on the top shelf and an oversized CPU on the bottom. The CPU was like nothing available on the market. For that matter, it was like nothing the world's militaries and intelligence agencies possessed. The machine was enclosed in a black metallic casing with the red and white Umbrella Corporation logo emblazoned on the side. A number of medical leads were plugged into the computer, and Marcus began attaching the other ends to his daughter's head while she slept.

Like her mother, his daughter was afflicted with Werner syndrome, also known as adult progeria. It was a rare genetic disorder, with a global incidence of one in 100,000 births. The rate of occurrence was even lower in the United Sates: one in 200,000. This form of progeria could be passed from parent to child, and that's exactly what had happened to his poor daughter. But where the disease hadn't begun to manifest in his wife until her twenties, it had struck their daughter much younger, at only six years of age. People with Werner syndrome experienced premature aging and usually died in their late forties. But given how early the disease had presented in his daughter, Marcus feared she had nowhere near that long to live, and if he couldn't save her, at least he could preserve her.

He tried to work as gently as he could so as not to wake the sleeping girl, but he had only attached half of the leads when her eyes slowly opened. They were clouded with the beginnings of cataracts, but she could still see well enough to recognize him, and she smiled faintly.

"Hello, Father." Her voice was hoarse and high-pitched—a symptom of her disease.

Marcus returned her smile, hoping she wouldn't sense the deep sadness hidden behind his expression.

"Hello, sweetheart. How are you feeling today?"

"Tired," she said, exhaling the word more than speaking it. She managed another smile. "But I'm always tired, aren't I?"

She was dressed in a white silk nightgown, the most comfortable that Marcus had been able to find. Her blondish-brown hair, once healthy and thick, was straw-like and graying. Her skin was thin and wrinkled, the veins visible beneath. She'd always favored her mother, but now she was coming to look like his wife had in her final days, when the disease had stolen away her youth and vitality, leaving her little more than a scarecrow made of flesh and bone. The resemblance was almost too much for him to bear, and he had to force himself not to look away from her.

"It's only to be expected," Marcus said, trying to keep his voice steady. He continued attaching the leads to his daughter.

"What are you doing? Is it a new treatment?"

There was a note of hope in the question that nearly broke Marcus's heart.

"I'm going to make a record of the electrochemical activity in your brain."

His daughter was highly intelligent and would likely surpass him when... *if* she grew up. But as bright as she was, the slight furrowing of her brow told him she hadn't understood his explanation. He continued talking as he turned to the computer and began typing commands.

"I'm going to take a picture of your brain. Or more precisely, of how your brain works. Everything that makes us who we are is up here." He paused in his typing to raise a hand to his head and tap his index finger against his temple. "Our thoughts, our experiences, our dreams..."

He typed some more and a display came up on the screen—a three-dimensional rendering of his daughter's brain with constant lightning-like flashes of light coruscating across the surface. For a moment, his breath caught in his throat. He was a man of science, someone who relied on reason and evidence, not faith, and yet he couldn't escape the feeling he was gazing upon his daughter's soul.

"Why do you want to do that?" she asked.

Her eyes were half closed and she sounded sleepy. She had difficulty staying awake these days, mostly because of her weakened state but also because drowsiness was one of the primary side effects of the medicines she was taking. The recording of her brain patterns would be completed just as effectively whether she was awake or asleep, and he'd already made numerous recordings of her facial features and vocal patterns during previous visits, so if she returned to sleep, his work could continue. It might be a blessing if she slept—more for him than for her. He didn't know how much longer he could keep talking to her without breaking down. And if he cried in front of her, she would know he'd lost hope, and in turn, she would lose what little remained to her. He was her father, and he had to be strong for her, if only for a little while longer.

"I'm testing a new computer program I've invented,

and I couldn't think of anyone who is better equipped to help me than you. After all, you *are* the smartest person I know."

Her smile was so faint it was almost undetectable. Her eyes closed further, although because of her condition, they couldn't close completely. She reached a trembling hand toward him, and he quickly took hold of it before she lost what strength she had, and her hand flopped back down onto the bed.

"You've done so much for me, Father. I'm happy to..." Her voice trailed off, and for a second Marcus thought she'd dozed off, but then she continued. "... help you in any way I can."

That did it. Tears began streaming down Marcus's face, and he continued holding his daughter's hand, careful to grip it lightly so he wouldn't hurt her. She lay still and her breathing deepened, and Marcus knew she had fallen back to sleep. Now that there was no longer any need to hide his grief, he let it pour out of him in great, wracking sobs as the computer continued making a virtual copy of his dying daughter's mind.

* * *

But then the breakthrough came. Marcus and Isaacs discovered the Progenitor Cell. Once injected, it would detect and repair damaged cells within the body almost instantaneously. It was a miracle. The life of Marcus's daughter was saved.

The Progenitor Cell had a myriad of applications, treating a thousand different diseases. Overnight, it seemed that a new era was dawning. A world without the fear of infection, sickness, or decay. But it was not to be. For the Progenitor Cell had certain unforeseen side effects...

* * *

TWENTY YEARS AGO.
CAPE TOWN, SOUTH AFRICA

Dominic Robertson enjoyed the dropping sensation in the center of his stomach as the Rotair cable car ascended toward Table Mountain. He'd first made the trip when he was a school boy, and although he was now a teacher and had escorted students on many class outings to the mountain's plateau, every time the cable car began its ascent, he was just as excited as he'd been that first time.

Too bad most of the boys didn't appear to share his excitement. Most were too caught up in reading comic books they'd brought or trying to solve their Rubik's Cube puzzles. He sighed. The ride to the top took only five minutes. Surely the mountain's majesty should be enough to hold the boys' attention that long. But he supposed that when you grew up in Cape Town with the mountain a constant presence, it wasn't that special. Dominic had grown up in Johannesburg, and while he'd lived and worked in Cape Town for over a decade now, he never grew tired of the mountain.

He glanced at Rachel Sulelo, the other teacher chaperoning this excursion, and she gave him a knowing smile accompanied by a faint shrug. Her silent message was clear. *Children. What can you do?*

He returned her smile and then looked out the

car's windows, determined not to let the students' indifference spoil the ascent for him.

One of the things he enjoyed most about the Rotair cars was the rotating floor that provided passengers a 360-degree panoramic view as they rose. Not only did you get to see the mountain as you approached, you also got to see Cape Town recede behind you. Both views were spectacular, though as much as he appreciated seeing Cape Town spread out below them, the bright blue of Table Bay and Robben Island to the north, and the vastness of the Atlantic seaboard to the west and south, for him, none of it could compare to the sight of the mountain.

Table Mountain—named for its famous flat surface—was a level plateau three kilometers from side to side, edged by impressive sheer cliffs. The mountain top was often covered by what was colloquially referred to as a "tablecloth" of clouds. Dominic knew that this cloud layer was formed when south-easterly winds were directed up the mountain where they hit colder air and produced moisture that condensed. But during his first trip here as a school boy, one of the teachers had told the students that according to legend, the cloud cover was caused by a smoking contest between a pirate called Van Hunks and the Devil himself. Even as a young boy, Dominic had known the story was nothing but a fairy tale, but after hearing it, he couldn't help thinking there was a certain sinister aspect to the tablecloth's beauty, and he'd wondered what would happen if someone were to breathe that foul devil smoke in. What havoc might it wreak on a human body? What might it do to one's soul?

Dominic shared much information about the mountain with the students he brought here, but he never shared the story of Van Hunk's contest with the Devil. He refused to say anything that might mar the mountain's beauty in the children's eyes as it had been marred for him.

Rachel stifled a yawn and then, when she saw he was looking at her, gave him an embarrassed smile. Dominic had insisted they begin their outing at sunrise—partly so they would have as much time as possible to spend on the mountain, but also because he loved making the ascent this early. Not only did sunrise enhance the view a hundredfold, but getting an early start meant that there would be fewer people on the car, giving him and his students a nearly unobstructed view as the Rotair car carried them upward. It didn't hurt that he was a morning person, either. He was awake, full of energy, and ready to go. He sometimes forgot others didn't feel the same way he did upon awakening. Rachel—and likely most, if not all, of the students—would've preferred to trade an early start for a couple more hours of sleep. Well, they'd feel differently once they'd reached the top and the mountain had a chance to work its magic on them.

The dozen students ranged in age from nine to ten, and the group was a mixture of black and white. Each boy wore the school uniform—blue jacket, white shirt, light blue tie, blue pants, black shoes—along with a backpack for carrying water and snacks, not to mention their puzzles, comics and toys. Dominic knew he should've checked their packs for distractions like these and insisted they be left behind, but he'd been so excited to get going that he'd forgotten.

One of the few students who seemed to appreciate the view as they ascended was Callan Williams. He was a quiet, thoughtful boy, more interested in reading and drawing in the notebooks he carried with him wherever he went. He stood close to the glass, gazing outward as the floor slowly rotated, munching on a bag of peanuts as the car bore them skyward. He didn't contribute much in class. Oh, he'd answer a direct question whenever he was asked, and he typically provided the correct answer. But he never volunteered information if he could avoid it, and he didn't seem to have any friends. Not close ones, at any rate. His marks were good, if not stellar, and although Dominic worried about Callan's apparent lack of social skills from time to time, he reminded himself that some flowers took a little longer to bloom than others, and that Callan would find his way in time.

Table Mountain was flanked by two other mountains: Devil's Peak to the east—where Van Hunk's contest with the Devil was said to have taken place—and Lion's Head to the west. Dominic always found himself saddened when gazing upon Lion's Head. According to rock art and fossils, at one time Table Mountain had been home to lions, leopards, and hyenas. But the last lion on the mountain had been killed in 1802, and although there were rumors that a few leopards still survived there, no one ever saw them. The mountain was hardly devoid of life, though. There was the rodent-like dassie (which was actually a relative of the elephant), antelope, porcupines, water mongoose, and numerous birds, lizards, and frogs. But the large mammals—symbols of Africa's ancient heritage—were gone. Lion's Head was a stark reminder to Dominic of life's fragility, of how closely everything that lived walked with death, and of how swiftly extinction could befall a species before it was aware that it was even in danger.

To distract himself from his melancholy thoughts, and because he was a teacher and should be doing his job instead of becoming lost in his own musings, he turned to the group of boys and said, "Now, who can tell me what kind of animals can be found at the summit of Table Mountain? Anyone?"

The boys looked up at Dominic as he spoke, their attention momentarily diverted from their various amusements, but none of them answered, and they quickly returned to their diversions. Dominic couldn't keep a hint of exasperation out of his voice as he once more said, "Anyone?"

None of the boys met his gaze this time, and Rachel gave him a sympathetic look. She didn't join in his attempt to engage the boys, though. Maybe she knew doing so would be fruitless. Maybe she was right.

But then something unexpected occurred. Callan turned away from the car's window, popped a last peanut into his mouth, and began to speak.

"There are many different ani—"

His voice cut off with a wet choking sound and his eyes went wide.

Without thinking, Dominic rushed toward the boy. "Get out of the way!" he shouted, and Callan's classmates obeyed, expressions of shock and surprise on their faces. Callan's eyes were filled with absolute terror as Dominic reached the boy, stepped behind him, and wrapped his arms around his waist. He made a fist with one hand, then made a quick upward

and inner thrust into the boy's abdomen. Nothing happened, so Dominic performed the procedure a second time, still with no result. Dominic felt himself starting to panic, and he clamped down on the emotion hard. Callan needed him to remain calm right now, and that was precisely what he would do. Time enough to fall apart later—after he'd saved Callan's life. Dominic performed the maneuver again, and this time the peanut that had been lodged in Callan's throat flew out of the boy's mouth, arced through the air, and hit the floor with a soft *plink*. Relief flooded through Dominic, and as he gently lowered Callan to the floor, he said, "You're going to be all right, son. Don't worry." But as soon as he said these words, he knew they were premature. The boy's face had turned waxy and pale, and his body was bucking and heaving, almost as if he were having some sort of seizure.

Rachel stepped over to them and crouched next to Callan.

"He's not breathing!" she said.

That's when Dominic remembered: the boy was asthmatic. Choking on the peanut must have triggered an attack, causing his throat to swell and making it impossible for him to draw in air. But that couldn't be right, could it? His parents had notified the school that Callan had been taking a new treatment for his condition, one that was supposed to eradicate it entirely. Had the treatment failed? Or had there been more than one peanut lodged in his throat and he was still choking?

The other boys crowded around the three of them, motivated by concern, fear, and morbid curiosity.

"Get back," Rachel snapped at them. "Give him room."

The other passengers watched in helpless concern as Dominic slipped off Callan's backpack, opened it, and quickly searched through the contents for an inhaler. But there wasn't one. The boy was even paler now, and the terror in his gaze was dimming, slowly being replaced by a blackness that told Dominic he didn't have much time left. His body stopped convulsing and fell still, no longer able to keep up with its exertions without a fresh supply of oxygen.

If the boy couldn't breathe on his own, Dominic would just have to try and breathe for him. He knelt next to Callan's neck and shoulders, bent over, took hold of the boy's chin with one hand, tilted his head, and with the thumb and forefinger of the other hand he pinched the boy's nose shut. He then lowered his face to Callan's and pressed his lips to the boy's open mouth. When he thought the seal was tight, he gave a short breath lasting one second, then glanced sideways to check if Callan's chest rose. It didn't, so he gave the boy a second breath. Still no result.

Callan's eyes fluttered and then closed, and then Dominic was nearly overcome by a wave of despair. He feared the worst, but he couldn't give up on the boy. They were nearly halfway through their journey to the top of the mountain. Two-and-a-half minutes, three at the most, and they'd be there, and they could summon medical aid. A doctor or at the very least a staff member who was better trained in life-saving techniques than Dominic was. If he could get some air into Callan, even just a little, it could mean the difference between life and death for the boy. He inhaled and prepared to deliver another breath into Callan.

But before he could do so, the boy's eyes snapped

open. The whites had become fiery red, and the irises were now an eerie bright blue that almost seemed to glow with internal light. Dominic barely had time to register this bizarre transformation before Callan let out an animalistic snarl, opened his mouth wide, and clamped his teeth down on Dominic's lips. Blood gushed from Dominic's savaged flesh, spilling onto Callan's face like thick, crimson rain. The pain was excruciating, and Dominic tried to cry out in agony. Reflexively, he tried to pull away from the boy, but Callan's teeth were sunk too deeply into his lips. With surprising strength, the boy grabbed hold of Dominic's head to prevent him from trying to escape, and then he bit down harder, sawing his teeth back and forth, and whipping his head furiously, as if he were a dog trying to tear a hunk of meat from a bone. Tears streamed down Dominic's face, and he flailed at Callan, punching and slapping in a desperate attempt to force the boy to release him. But the blows seemed to have no effect on the boy whatsoever.

Dominic heard a wet tearing sound then, and his head snapped back, the sudden motion freeing him from Callan's grip. He scrambled to his feet and backed away unsteadily. The boy moved into a crouching position, unearthly eyes fixed on Dominic, grinning with blood-slick teeth as he chewed Dominic's lips and then swallowed.

Horrified, Dominic reached a trembling hand to his mouth, but his fingers found only blood and exposed teeth. His stomach dropped once more.

Callan's attack had happened so fast that the other passengers could only watch in stunned silence. But now Rachel screamed, and Callan's head snapped toward her, as if he were an animal that had suddenly become aware of fresh prey.

Like a lion, Dominic thought, feeling numb, detached, and more than a little insane at that moment. *Or a leopard.* The ancient predators of Africa might have been extinct on Table Mountain, but that was okay. They were bringing an entirely new type of predator to take their place.

Callan—or rather, the thing Callan had become—leaped to his feet, snarled, and rushed toward Rachel, hands outstretched, fingers curled into claws, teeth gnashing and snapping, eager to tear into her soft flesh. Callan attacked her with inhuman ferocity and she shrieked in terror and agony. The paralysis that had gripped the rest of the passengers broke then, and everyone began screaming, shouting, and sobbing, huddling together and pressed against the car's windows in a desperate attempt to get as far away from Callan as possible. Not that it would do any good, Dominic thought, fingertips moving back and forth over his exposed teeth.

Rachel died quickly, and Callan rushed toward the next person closest to him—one of his fellow students. Dominic looked away as the boy screamed and turned his attention toward the window. The rotating floor turned him toward his beloved mountain, and the view was so beautiful, so comforting, that he would've smiled if he still possessed lips. He continued gazing out the window as he listened to one person after another die, until there was silence. He realized then that he was the only one still alive, but he knew that wouldn't be the case much longer.

He told himself that if he had to die, he couldn't

think of a better place to do it. But then Callan leaped upon him, and all thoughts were driven from his mind as the boy tore into his abdomen with hands and teeth and began pulling out fistfuls of internal organs.

A good place to die? Perhaps. But a good *way* to die?

Not even close.

* * *

The incident was quickly covered up. It never became public...

But in their own secret internal investigation, Umbrella discovered that the little boy in Africa had been taking a Progenitor Cell product to treat his asthma. When he choked to death, the Progenitor Cells within his body continued to work. They replaced their dying host, reanimating dead cells and bringing him back to life. The first of the Undead were born.

In the aftermath of the incident, the two founders of the Umbrella Corporation argued furiously. Marcus now saw the Progenitor Cell as dangerous and wanted it to be contained or destroyed. Dr. Isaacs, on the other hand, wished to profit from it. There was a deadlock. But the untimely accidental death of Marcus meant that the course was set.

* * *

"Why can't you see reason? Don't you understand what we *have* here?"

Alexander Isaacs paced in front of the desk where his so-called partner sat watching him. Marcus's face was set in a resolute expression, which infuriated Isaacs, and he fought to keep his emotions under control. He prided himself on maintaining a façade of calm at all times—it was an effective way to keep opponents from guessing one's true intentions—but inside he was a roiling cauldron of fury.

"I know what we *don't* have," Marcus said softly. "We don't have a universal cure."

Marcus had only the single desk lamp on, leaving most of the study cloaked in gloom. Typical of the man to brood in near darkness, Isaacs thought. He always had been something of a drama queen. Marcus had a fondness for modernist architecture, and the interior of his home reflected that preference. The walls, ceilings, and floors were painted white, and everything was all straight lines and sharp angles. What wasn't white was chrome or glass, and rectangular windows filled entire walls. Isaacs hated the house's cold sterility. It seemed more suited to a laboratory than a home, but he supposed it suited Marcus's personality: all intellect and no emotion. James Marcus was a man to whom passion was a foreign emotion, something other people felt and acted upon. Except when it came to his daughter, who he would do anything to protect.

Maybe Isaacs could use that.

"Our Progenitor Cell worked wonders for your daughter," he said, giving a slight emphasis to *our*.

"At what cost? You know what happened in Cape Town. You saw the footage captured by the car's security cameras." Marcus shook his head as if trying to keep the images of the Cape Town massacre at bay.

Isaacs didn't share his partner's distaste for the footage. Where Marcus saw nightmarish savagery, blood, and death, Isaacs saw possibilities. Keeping the incident out of the media hadn't been easy, but they'd managed. The corporation had needed to work swiftly—and ruthlessly—to accomplish the task. The cable car operator at the top of the mountain had been smart enough not to open the Rotair car's door when it arrived. The car's blood-smeared windows had given him a clear indication that something was wrong—not to mention the several dozen ravening lunatics inside that snarled and snapped as they clawed at the windows to get at the operator. He'd turned off power to the car, summoned the police, and waited nervously for them to arrive. Once they did, they fired every round of ammunition they had into the car, only dropping the murderous savages when they finally resorted to headshots.

Once Umbrella had gotten wind that Progenitor Cell technology had been involved in the incident, they'd moved to commandeer the bodies, obtain all records, and pay off those witnesses who could be bought and remove those who couldn't be bribed. Marcus had no idea that the corporation he'd helped create had, in its own way, acted as savagely as the afflicted passengers on the cable car. But then Marcus had never had the stomach for dealing with the harsher aspects of running an international business. He left that to Isaacs, and he, in turn, delegated the real dirty work to someone who not only possessed the talent for it, but also an undeniable enthusiasm.

Marcus continued. "The same biological agent that transformed an asthmatic child in Cape Town into a bloodthirsty monster is inside my daughter—inside *everyone* who's used one of the products developed from the Progenitor Cell—and it's lying there, harmless at the moment perhaps, but just waiting to go off, like a ticking time bomb."

Marcus's expression deepened into an angry scowl.

"And you not only think we should continue to keep these products on the market, you want to begin exploring *military* applications? Are you insane?"

Isaacs bristled inwardly at Marcus's words, but he kept his tone even as he replied.

"We had no way of knowing the cells would continue to be active after death—or that they'd struggle to repair the body in their imperfect way."

Marcus snorted at that, but he didn't interrupt, so Isaacs went on.

"The fact that the Progenitor Cell *is* active after death is something of a miracle, James. If we can perfect it, we'll be able to heal all but the most catastrophic injuries. Who knows? We might even be able to attain one of humankind's most long sought-after goals: immortality itself."

Marcus looked at Isaacs for a long moment before speaking.

"For a moment you almost sounded like the man I began working with all those years ago. A man who truly believed in what we were attempting to do."

"I'm the same man, James. I'm just more... pragmatic now."

"The end justifies the means, eh?" Marcus said, a bitter edge to his voice.

"Of course not," Isaacs lied. He'd indeed come to believe that if a goal was important enough, you should take whatever measures were necessary to achieve it. Progress itself was what was important, not how that progress was achieved. "But despite the corporation's profits, we need outside funding in order to conduct our research. Or have you forgotten that? The money we receive from developing the Progenitor Cell's military applications will result in advances that will make a difference in the lives of every man, woman, and child on the planet. It will change the very course of history."

"And how, precisely, do you think aiding the military in the creation of Undead cannibalistic shock troops will help the world?"

Isaacs' jaw tightened at the sarcasm that dripped from Marcus's words.

"That's not what the military wants. They're interested in developing soldiers that are resistant to injury, who can heal so swiftly and completely that death cannot stop them. *Human* soldiers, James, with their mental faculties intact. *That's* the true potential of the Progenitor Cell, and that's the future—and the ultimate legacy—of the Umbrella Corporation."

More lies. Yes, the military was intrigued by the idea of rapidly healing solders. But what they were most interested in was being able to turn an enemy's population into Undead weapons that would turn on each other and do their work for them. That was where Umbrella's greatest profit—and therefore its greatest power—truly lay. And why stop with just one nation's military, when they *all* would pay whatever it took to make sure they possessed the same bio-weapons as their enemies?

Marcus looked at Isaacs for several moments, eyes narrowed, as if he were assessing Isaacs' sincerity. He then folded his hands on top of his desk and looked down at them, a faint smile on his lips.

"Do you remember why we chose the name *Umbrella*?" he asked.

"Of course. What does that have to do with anything?"

"We chose it because an umbrella is a symbol of protection—protection of the *person* who carries it. The image was meant to always remind us of the people we try to help."

Isaacs had come to see an umbrella as a symbol for how the corporation would one day cover the entire world. He wisely kept this perspective to himself, though.

"You used to be a man of vision, James. Someone who wasn't afraid to take risks. But you've grown timid and short-sighted."

"And you've became cold and calculating," Marcus countered. "But like you, I own fifty percent of Umbrella. The corporation can't make a major deal without my approval, and I'll never agree to work with the military. *Any* military."

Isaacs gritted his teeth. The man was insufferable, but he was correct about one thing. They were equal partners, and neither could act—at least not openly—without the other's cooperation. They'd arranged it that way back at the start, when they'd both still been naïve idealists. Isaacs had matured since then, come to embrace a larger vision. For a moment, he felt a pang of sadness that his old friend still clung to his narrow-minded and simplistic notions of morality. But he had to face facts. James Marcus—his longtime friend, scientific collaborator, and business partner— had become a liability. Not only to Isaacs but to the

Umbrella Corporation itself. And it was up to Isaacs to do what was necessary for Umbrella to move forward.

Marcus spoke again. "I cannot be a party to your mad scheme, Alexander, and it *is* mad, no matter how you try to justify it. In the end, all you'll succeed in doing is creating a world filled with monsters."

Isaacs smiled. "Perhaps. But what a world it shall be."

He nodded toward one of the study's dark corners, one that was behind Marcus and out of the man's line of sight. A shape detached itself from the shadows and stepped forward into the light. Albert Wesker moved with a reptilian grace that Isaacs both admired and found disturbing on a visceral level. It was as if the man wasn't quite human. But then, it was his cold-blooded nature that made him so very effective at his job. As always, Wesker was garbed in black— black suit jacket over a black sweater, black pants, black shoes, and black leather gloves. Wesker's blond hair was swept back, every strand precisely in place, a sign of a man who valued control over even the smallest of details.

Wesker gripped a clear plastic bag in his gloved hands, and he stepped forward silent as a ghost until he stood directly behind Marcus. Then, before the professor was aware of his presence, Wesker slipped the plastic bag over the man's head and pulled it tight. Wesker's expression didn't alter as he performed this maneuver. His features remained composed, almost peaceful, as if he were out for a stroll in the sunshine instead of murdering someone.

Marcus's expression wasn't so placid. His eyes widened with shock, and he opened his mouth, instinctively trying to draw in a breath. But all he managed to do was seal a portion of the plastic to his lips and tongue. He lunged out of his chair in an attempt to escape, but Wesker tightened his grip on the bag, preventing Marcus from doing more than getting to his feet. Marcus reached up and began clawing at the bag, attempting to pull it off, but he was unable to get any purchase on the plastic. He tried biting through it in a desperate attempt to create even a tiny air hole, but Wesker was nothing if not thorough, and he'd selected a bag made from a brand of plastic that was highly puncture-resistant.

Marcus continued clawing and biting at the plastic bag for a moment longer, but he was an intelligent man and soon realized there was nothing he could do. He stopped fighting then and allowed his arms to fall to his sides. The pink flesh of his lips began to edge toward blue, and he fixed his gaze on Isaacs. Isaacs expected to see anger in his soon-to-be-ex-partner's eyes, along with the fear that came from knowing death was only moments away. Those emotions were there, but mixed in with them was a deep sorrow, and Isaacs could almost hear what Marcus was thinking.

You were my friend. We were going to do such good for the world...

Isaacs held Marcus's gaze for several seconds before turning abruptly and walking out of the study. He told himself he did this because he had arrangements to make. After all, he would have to oversee Umbrella's operations by himself after Marcus's "accidental" death, and there was a lot to do. He wasn't walking away because he felt a twinge of guilt over what he'd ordered Wesker to do to his one-time friend.

He *wasn't.*

As he departed the house and headed to his obscenely expensive car parked in the drive, Isaacs' mind turned toward the biggest obstacle now standing in the way of his seizing complete control of Umbrella: Marcus's one and only heir. His daughter.

It would've been simpler if the Werner syndrome had killed her. For an instant, Isaacs toyed with the idea of taking his phone from his pocket, calling Wesker, and asking him to arrange for the girl to have an "accident" of her own. But he quickly discarded the notion. Her death on top of her father's would raise too many suspicions. Besides, as the poster child for the health benefits of the Progenitor Cell, she could still be useful.

As he climbed into his car and turned on the engine—smiling with satisfaction as the high-performance machine purred like a beloved pet welcoming its master—he supposed he'd have to take the girl under his wing, act as her guardian and mentor, and help shepherd her through the difficult days ahead. She would come to rely on him, be grateful for his counsel and support. In time, she might even come to love him. And then she'd have no choice but to support his plans for Umbrella. How could she say no to the man who'd become a second father to her? The more he considered it, the more he thought that having a daughter might be amusing.

As he put the car in gear and started driving away from Marcus's home, he was too lost in his scheming to think of looking in the rearview mirror. If he had, he might've seen his old friend's daughter standing at an upstairs window, watching him leave, brow furrowed in deep thought.

* * *

Dr. Isaacs became the guardian of his dead partner's child and her half of the company. Under Isaacs' guidance Umbrella was quick to weaponize their new discovery.

Working with another scientist, Dr. Charles Ashford, Isaacs used the Progenitor Cell to create the T-virus. A virus that would mutate human flesh in new and terrifying ways, or could create an army of Undead overnight. Profits quadrupled thanks to a new era of viral and bacterial weaponry. Umbrella even created genetic mutations with battlefield applications—bio weapons.

Within just a few short years, Umbrella had become the most powerful financial entity in the world. The corporation that had begun with such lofty ideals had been seduced completely by greed and power.

To help him control the now vast interests of the Umbrella Corporation, Dr. Isaacs created a powerful Artificial Intelligence computer. As a "tribute" to his dead partner, Isaacs used the likeness and brain patterns of Marcus's daughter for the computer's interface. Isaacs called the computer the Red Queen.

Then ten years ago, in a Midwest American town named Raccoon City, there was an outbreak...

The T-virus escaped from an underground laboratory named the Hive.

The American government attempted to contain the outbreak by detonating a bomb. It devastated Raccoon City, but it couldn't stop the airborne infection. The viral outbreak spread across the world within days.

Humankind was brought to its knees. And what survivors there were soon became the targets of the Red Queen.

The Artificial Intelligence seemed determined to wipe out all remaining human life on Earth. But her plan ran into a small problem... me. Once an operative for the corporation, I turned against Umbrella. I fought them every step of the way. I even confronted and killed Dr. Isaacs.

Finally, after years of running and fighting, the last and best hope of humanity gathered and took a last stand in Washington, D.C. But what we didn't realize was that we had been lured there. And what we had walked into... was a trap.

My name is Alice, and this is my story. The end of my story...

1

Darkness surrounded Alice—in more ways than one.

She held tight to the rungs of a metal ladder attached to the wall of an underground shaft. There were no lights, and the stiflingly hot air reeked from a combination of gasoline, scorched earth, and burnt flesh. Above her was a metal plate: a hatch that would open onto the surface. She'd already unlocked it, but the hatch didn't want to budge. Maybe it had been damaged in the battle, the metal fused shut by an explosion or raging fire. Or maybe there was something weighing it down. Rubble, an overturned tank or jeep...

Or the door could just be stubborn. She shoved again.

This time the metal plate gave way and the hatch flew open. The light that flooded in was dim, but she'd been in the dark long enough that it hurt, so she squinted her eyes. More welcome was the rush of cool air on her skin, and although it stank of fire and death, it was far better than breathing the stifling air in the shaft. She made certain to breathe through her mouth, though.

She pulled herself out of the shaft and managed to crawl several feet before the last of her strength gave out and she collapsed to the ground. She lay there, exhausted, face and body smeared with blood. Some of it hers, most of it not. As she looked up at the smoke-streaked sky, she listened for sounds of combat, spread her hands out on the ground and felt for any vibrations from military vehicles or combatants on the move, human or otherwise. Aside from the crackling of small fires and an ironically gentle breeze, she heard and felt nothing. She wasn't surprised. It was the silence that had convinced her it was safe to leave the underground chamber in which she'd sought shelter.

As safe as it ever gets in this world, she thought.

Sights, sounds, and sensations flashed through her mind as she waited for some of her strength to return: memories of the terrible battle that had taken place on the White House grounds and how she'd come to be part of it.

* * *

She'd been captured by Umbrella and taken to a facility beneath the Arctic Ocean off the coast of Russia. Umbrella Prime served as a combination clone-manufacturing plant and bio-weapon testing environment and "showroom" for potential customers. The facility contained huge sectors that simulated parts of various cities—New York, Tokyo, Moscow...

even the suburbs of Raccoon City, the closest thing Alice had to a hometown. These sectors could be populated by uninfected clones with enough basic memories implanted so they would believe they were ordinary citizens going about their lives. Then infected clones would be introduced into the environments and maximum carnage would ensue, duly horrifying and impressing representatives of those world governments with enough money to afford Umbrella's prices.

Alice had been imprisoned in Umbrella Prime and interrogated by an old friend, Jill Valentine, who'd fallen under Umbrella's control. But Alice had been freed by a pair of unlikely allies: former Umbrella agent Ada Wong, and that cold-blooded bastard Albert Wesker. The Umbrella chairman claimed the Red Queen planned to destroy what remained of the human race, and he proposed an alliance with Alice for the sake of their species' survival. Alice didn't trust Wesker, of course—after all, the son of a bitch had actually tried to eat her once—but she'd wanted out of Umbrella Prime, so she'd allowed Ada Wong to help her escape. Wesker had hedged his bets, though, and sent in an extraction team to assist the two women if necessary. They were forced to make their way through several of the simulated cities where they'd been attacked by both Undead and mutated monsters. Along the way, Alice saved the life of a young girl named Becky who believed Alice was her mother. Alice understood that Becky's mother—or at least the woman Becky believed to be her mother— had been a clone of Alice. Alice couldn't leave the girl to die, though, so she'd brought her along. Eventually they hooked up with the extraction team and, after suffering several casualties, they managed to escape to the surface, destroying Umbrella Prime in the process. They found themselves on an ice shelf in the bitter cold, only to be attacked by Jill Valentine and the clone of another old friend, Rain Ocampo. But this Rain was an Umbrella loyalist, and she injected herself with the Las Plagas virus, enhancing her strength, speed, and durability tenfold.

Alice and her remaining companions fought Jill and Rain, and in the end Rain was killed when Alice caused her to fall through the ice into the frigid ocean, where a horde of Undead released when Umbrella Prime was destroyed set upon her like a pack of rotting-fleshed sharks. Jill fared much better. Alice managed to dislodge the spider-like cybernetic implant attached to the woman's chest that controlled her mind, restoring Jill to her former self. Wesker sent a military chopper to pick them up after that, and Alice—somewhat the worse for wear after fighting both Jill and Rain—was tended to by medics as the chopper flew toward what had once been the United States. Becky had survived, as had Ada and Leon Kennedy from the extraction team. After several refueling stops, they reached Washington, D.C., and eventually the White House. Or rather, what was left of it. Becky was taken by a female staff member who promised to look after her. By this time, Alice had accepted the role of Becky's guardian, and the girl's safety was of the utmost importance to her. No way did she want Wesker near Becky, so she allowed the woman to take the girl away.

Alice was ushered into the Oval Office alone, where she found Wesker sitting behind the President's desk as if he owned it. Before she could do anything, Wesker—moving with inhuman speed—rushed toward her. He was little more than a blur, and Alice barely had time to register that the bastard was attacking her before he jammed a high-tech hypo-injector against her neck, sending liquid fire surging into her veins. The chemical spread rapidly through her body, bringing with it a pain so intense that it felt as if she were being electrocuted. She cried out, as much in fury as agony, and fell to the floor, her body spasming uncontrollably. Forcing the words through gritted teeth, she demanded to know what Wesker had done to her, but as quickly as it had come, the pain began to ebb, and she felt a familiar strength growing within her. The injuries she'd sustained while fighting Jill and Rain healed with unbelievable speed, and her senses became sharper.

Wesker had restored her powers.

Alice responded far differently to the T-virus than anyone else, including Wesker. Where it had turned him into a half-insane monster who could barely control his abilities, it had once transformed her into what might well have been the next stage of human evolution. She'd become far stronger and faster than ordinary humans, and she'd started developing psychokinetic abilities as well. She'd used her newfound gifts in the fight against Umbrella and the monsters they'd unleashed on the world, but as time went by, she felt her humanity slipping away more and more, until she feared she was in danger of becoming a monster herself. So when Wesker eventually nullified her powers, she hadn't been altogether sorry. But now Wesker had given back what he'd taken from her. The question was: why?

The instant that Alice regained control of her body, she leaped to her feet, prepared to make Wesker regret that he'd transformed her into a living weapon once again. But Wesker reminded her that he'd been the one to engineer her escape from Umbrella Prime because he needed her to help him stop the Red Queen from destroying the last remnants of the human race. He'd then led her to the roof of the White House, along with Jill, Ada, and Leon, and showed them what they were up against. Quite simply, it looked like hell on earth. The White House grounds were enclosed within a barricade formed from fifty-foot high ferrocrete walls. Inside the walls, soldiers ran back and forth, some working feverishly to reinforce the barricade, others taking up defensive positions between the walls and the White House, while still others manned weapons installations that contained large flame-throwers. Beyond the walls, thousands of Undead and mutated monstrosities pressed against the barricade, climbing atop one another so they could get over the walls and begin slaughtering the fragile humans on the other side.

The sight of so many ravening creatures howling for their destruction took Alice's breath away, and she felt a spark of panic flare up inside her. But she fought it down, took a deep breath, and said, "All right. Let's get to work."

* * *

An Undead woman rushed toward Alice across the White House grounds, hands outstretched, eyes feral yellow. Her mouth yawned wide and tentacular mandibles emerged with nauseating sticky-wet sounds that Alice could hear even over the din of the battle raging all around. The woman managed to get within five feet before Alice raised one of her two TDI Vector submachine guns and blew her head apart with a short burst. The woman dropped to the ground in a spray of blood and lay still, truly dead at last. A long time ago, Alice had wondered what, if anything, went on in the mind of an Undead. Was there some part of them that was still human, trapped within an ambulatory corpse whose only desire was to kill and feed? Was its human part aware of what its mutated body did, unable to stop it? And if so, did they die afraid and in pain, silently screaming, *I'm in here! Please don't hurt me!*

But she'd stopped wondering such things long ago. In the years since the Outbreak, she'd destroyed thousands of Undead—it was impossible to know precisely how many—and it all came down to a very simple equation: you killed them or they killed you.

Another Undead came at her, this one a middle-aged man, and she dispatched it as easily as she had the woman, and with as little regret. Living in a post-apocalyptic world had turned Alice into a deadly efficient survival machine, and she had no time for doubts and recriminations. They made you hesitate, and hesitation got you killed and eaten.

It was dawn, and Alice stood in a circle with her companions, all of them facing outward, their backs to each other. Ada was on her right, Jill on her left. Leon was next to Ada, and Wesker stood on the opposite side of the circle from Alice, which suited her fine. She might be forced to make common cause with the bastard, but that hardly made them friends. They were all armed to the teeth: submachine guns, handguns, grenades, knives... In addition, Alice carried a katana strapped to her back.

Your clones wielded the blade so effectively, I thought you might like one, Wesker had said.

One thing she could say about him: he wasn't stingy when it came to handing out weapons, and there were plenty more in the makeshift armory within the White House if and when they needed to rearm. A part of Alice felt like a kid in a candy store. But another part of her, a part she kept deeply buried, longed for a day when she no longer relied on weapons, when all the blood and death would finally be over.

Steady streams of Undead, giant Lickers, zombie dogs, those damn flying things, and creatures Alice had never seen before flowed over the barricade walls, but so far, the walls themselves were holding. Alice didn't know how much longer they could withstand the massed weight of the Undead pushing against them, though. Sooner or later, the walls would be breached and when that happened... Alice didn't want to think about that, so she kept firing at the monsters racing toward them, bringing them down one after the other with deadly accurate shots. She'd almost forgotten what it was like to possess the heightened awareness the T-virus granted her. It was as if her attackers moved in slow motion, giving her more than enough time to aim carefully before she fired. It was almost too easy.

Not so for her companions, though—with the exception of Wesker, who possessed the same lightning-fast reflexes as Alice. Jill was now free from the scarab device that Umbrella had used to control her, and while that meant her mind was her own again, it also meant that her body was no longer enhanced by technology. With the scarab, Jill had been stronger and faster than an ordinary human. Without it, she was still a highly trained ass-kicker with attitude to spare, but she was no stronger or faster than an ordinary person. Ada and Leon were top-level Umbrella operatives, although they no longer served their corporate masters. But despite all their skills, like Jill, they were only human. So far, Jill, Ada, and Leon were mowing down Undead with ease, but eventually they would tire and begin to slow down. It was inevitable. And once that happened...

She would just have to do everything she could to keep them alive then, wouldn't she?

Alice, Wesker, and the others weren't the only ones battling monsters. Soldiers armed with assault rifles, submachine guns, and flamethrowers fired at anything that wasn't human, whether it was on the ground or in the air. Helicopters flew over the battlefield, strafing the mass of Undead, and tanks fired on them, the artillery explosions sending dozens of them flying in all directions. But the efforts of the White House defenders weren't enough. There were simply too many of the enemy to even make a dent in their numbers, and more were coming over the walls every second.

Alice wasn't certain why the soldiers were helping Wesker—or maybe she had it backward. Maybe Wesker was helping them. Then again, he *had* been sitting behind the President's desk. Had whatever remained of the US government struck some sort of deal with Umbrella? Or had the Red Queen declared war on all surviving humans, Umbrella personnel included? Once this battle was over—assuming any of them survived—she was going to have a long talk with Wesker. Something more was going on here than what he'd told her. But that wasn't a surprise. Wesker specialized in lying and manipulation. It's what made him so good at his job.

A giant Licker came thundering toward Alice then, the massive creature moving swiftly on all four of its legs, sharp talons raking large divots out of the ground as it came. The fifty-foot-long monster collided with Undead, knocking them aside or trampling them. It was completely skinless, leaving its raw muscles exposed to the open air. It had a fang-filled mouth and an elongated tongue that lashed the air like a whip as it ran. But its most revolting feature was the swollen exposed brain tissue that covered the majority of its head, including where its eyes should've been.

Alice felt a cold stab of fear. She'd encountered one of these monstrosities in Umbrella Prime, and the damned thing had been nearly impossible to kill. She'd been able to rescue Becky and escape with their lives—barely. But she'd only been human then. Now she was something more. And she had one advantage. She knew from experience that the creatures hunted by sound, and she hoped the cacophony of the battlefield would make it more difficult for the Licker to maneuver.

She dropped her Vectors to the ground and drew her katana. But before she could start running to meet the Licker's charge, Jill yelled, "Alice! There's another one!"

Alice glanced to her left and saw a second beast, even larger and more massive than the first, barreling toward them, sending Undead flying right and left as it plowed through them.

"Well, shit," Alice said.

Even with her powers restored, Alice wasn't certain she could take on one of the giant Lickers by herself. But two of them?

"Wesker!" she called out. "Get your mutated ass over here!"

Alice felt a rush of wind, and suddenly Wesker was standing next to her.

"Since you asked so nicely," he said.

"I'll take the one on the right, you take the one on the left."

She gripped the handle of her katana with both hands and took a step forward, but Wesker took hold of her arm and stopped her.

"I don't think that will be necessary just yet." He raised his arm and pointed skyward.

Alice looked up and saw an Umbrella V-22 Osprey flying toward the White House from the north. The VTOL aircraft came swiftly, its dual rotors eerily silent.

"Please tell me that's the cavalry," Alice said.

"Not quite," Wesker answered.

"Whoever it is, we don't have time to worry about them. The Lickers…"

She trailed off. The giant Lickers were no longer moving toward them. The creatures had stopped less than a dozen yards apart, their heads angled toward the sky, as if they were dogs awaiting a master's command. The Lickers weren't the only ones who reacted to the V-22's appearance. Normal-size Lickers, the zombie dogs, and even the Undead all stopped in their tracks and looked toward the sky. Now that the monsters had stopped fighting, the humans did too, and the sound of gunfire died away, leaving the battlefield in silence. The flying creatures, like their land-bound brethren, no longer seemed interested in attacking. They circled above the now-still battlefield, as if waiting. For what, Alice didn't know. Whatever it was, it couldn't be good.

"Is it the Red Queen?" she asked Wesker. As an AI, the Red Queen had no physical body and could "appear" wherever she chose—assuming she had an electronic connection to transmit her awareness. The aircraft doubtless possessed the necessary technology to make that happen.

Wesker continued watching the V-22 approach without answering Alice's question. He usually maintained a façade of icy control. Part of this was just his personality, Alice knew, but she guessed that another part of it—maybe the largest part—was because he was always fighting the influence of the T-virus that raged inside him. But as the Umbrella aircraft passed over the northern wall, Alice saw the man's lips tighten and his jaw clench. Whatever was going on, Wesker wasn't happy about it.

Helicopters moved in to confront the aircraft, but the V-22 fired a missile at one, turning it into a mass of fire and twisted metal. The wreckage fell to the ground where it took out a swath of Undead and mutants, and then continued burning. The other copters—their crews calculating the odds of success against the Umbrella aircraft—wisely decided to disengage and pulled back.

The V-22 slowed as it moved into position above the battlefield, its rotors moving into vertical position so it could hover. Alice sheathed her katana and bent down to retrieve her submachine guns. The last time an Umbrella aircraft showed up unexpectedly, she was standing on the deck of the *Arcadia* with hundreds of people who'd been captured by the corporation for experimentation under the guise of rescue. True, there had been dozens of V-22s then, filled with Umbrella operatives determined to regain their test subjects or kill them before they could escape. But even one Umbrella aircraft was too many as far as Alice was concerned.

Without realizing she was doing so, Alice closed her eyes and stretched her consciousness toward the aircraft. She felt her mind expand and reach outward, threads of mental energy emanating from her and snaking upward, probing, sensing... The last time she'd felt anything like this had been in the Nevada desert, when she'd used her telekinetic power to save Claire Redfield and her caravan of survivors from a gigantic flock of mutated crows. Maybe she could do something similar to the aircraft, if she just concentrated... hard... enough...

Pain pierced the base of her skull, sharp as an ice pick, but she ignored it and continued concentrating. She furrowed her brow and gritted her teeth, and she began shaking all over, as if an electric current shot through every muscle in her body. She felt the tendrils of mental energy begin to wrap around the aircraft, their hold tentative at first, but growing stronger with each passing moment. The pain filled her skull now, and tears ran from the corners of her eyes, but she didn't let up. Another few seconds, and she'd be able to yank the V-22 out of the sky and bring it crashing to the ground.

And then, beside her, so softly she almost didn't hear it, Wesker whispered, "Yes, that's it."

Alice's eyes snapped open, her concentration broken. The tendrils of telekinetic force vanished, and the pain in her head lessened, although it didn't recede entirely. She turned to Wesker.

"What the hell is going on here?" she demanded. "You *want* me to bring that ship down. I can feel it!"

"Do it!" Wesker shouted, his emotional control lapsing. "Do it or you'll ruin everything!"

Before Alice could ask him what he was talking about, a voice boomed from speakers attached to the aircraft.

"Hello, Albert. Long time, no see."

It was a woman's voice, one Alice didn't recognize. But from the expression of rage on Wesker's face, it was clear he knew who it was, and he was far from pleased by her arrival.

Wesker explained without waiting to be asked.

"Dania Cardoza. She's an employee in Umbrella's Research and Development department, and to put it simply, she's after my job."

"That's the real reason you brought us here, isn't it?" Jill said. "This isn't the last stand for humanity. You wanted us to help you take out a rival."

"It's exactly the sort of thing he'd do," Ada said. "I should know. I've worked for him long enough."

Alice realized then why Wesker had returned her powers to her. He'd wanted to use her as a weapon— the ultimate weapon—against Cardoza.

Cardoza's voice echoed above them once more. *"I know you, Albert. Right now you're thinking furiously, trying to come up with a way to stop me. But it's far too late for that now, and you know it. You've undoubtedly noticed the avatar implants on the Undead and the mutations by now."*

Wesker didn't reply. Alice turned her attention to the lifeless bodies of the Undead that she and her companions had killed. At first she didn't see anything out of the ordinary, but then she saw what Cardoza was talking about. Behind the right ears of the Undead—at least the ones she could see—were metallic devices the size of a quarter with a glowing red light in the center, miniature versions of the scarab device that had mind-controlled Jill.

"It's prototype technology," Wesker said. "Not very effective. The signal range is unreliable, and it tends to burn out the nervous system of the wearer in a few hours."

"Yeah?" Leon said. "Well, it looks pretty goddamn effective to me."

The thought of Umbrella being able to control and command its creations instead of merely unleashing them on the world to wreak havoc chilled Alice to the core of her being. If they were ever able to perfect the technology...

Cardoza continued. *"And you know what those delightfully hideous darlings flying in holding patterns above you are, too."*

"Infectors." Wesker practically spat the word.

"What are those?" Alice asked. "What do they do?"

Wesker ignored her. His gaze was focused on the aircraft, jaw clenched tight, hands balled into fists.

49

Small patches of rough, deformed flesh erupted on his skin, and Alice knew he was so filled with fury that he was losing control over the virus inside him. If he lost control completely, he'd transform into a misshapen, savage mutant, and he might become as big a threat to Alice and her allies as any of the creatures surrounding them.

"Hold it together," she snapped.

Wesker's skin began to bubble, as if his body were boiling from the inside out, but then he slowly twisted his head from side to side, and his flesh returned to normal. He'd fought back the virus's influence—for now.

"You have no way out of this, Albert," Cardoza said. *"Surrender and I might let you live. It would be a risk, I know, but the idea of keeping you around after you've been thoroughly defeated and humiliated is so tempting. If you don't surrender, I'll kill you along with everyone who's foolish enough to be helping you. You've got sixty seconds to decide."*

Cardoza fell silent.

"We need to get out of here," Leon said. "We've only got a minute before that crazy bitch sics her army of monsters on us." His voice was steady, but Alice saw the beads of nervous sweat on his forehead.

"She won't do that," Wesker said. He seemed calm once more, completely unconcerned that he was surrounded by hundreds of Undead and mutants that were waiting for Cardoza's command to resume their attack.

"Why not?" Alice demanded.

"She's used the avatar implants to get her army into position. She doesn't know about your unique talents, but even so, she's not one to take chances, any more than I am. So while she believes her army alone could probably destroy us, she brought them along for insurance." He pointed skyward, indicating the winged monstrosities circling overhead.

"You called them Infectors," Alice said. "Exactly what do they infect?"

Wesker gave her a hint of a grim smile. "You'll see."

"Come on!" Leon said. "Are you guys seriously just going to stand there and wait to be killed?"

Alice figured their minute was just about up. "Guess so," she said.

"Fuck!" Leon shouted, but he continued to stand his ground. Alice already respected his skills as a warrior, but her respect for him as a person increased tenfold at that moment.

Alice glanced at Jill and then Ada. Both women looked nervous, but they nodded, indicating they were with her.

And then their time was up.

"Very well, Albert," Cardoza said. *"I'd say I was sorry about this, but we both know I'd be lying."*

There was no outward sign that anything changed, but inside the V-22, Cardoza must have reactivated the avatar implants, because the Undead and the mutations began to move again. Alice turned and raised her Vectors, expecting the monsters— especially the two giant Lickers—to resume their attack. But they didn't. Instead, all the creatures that were assembled on what was once the White House lawn merely shuffled about, moving from foot to foot, as if they were excited. And then, moving in an eerie display of almost perfect unison, they looked up.

The winged monsters—the Infectors—broke out of

their holding patterns, let out ear-splitting screeches, banked, and began descending. Alice half-expected the creatures to come flying toward them, but instead they flew low over the fiendish army, quadruple wings spread wide. And then their wings stiffened, ejecting a shower of flechette-like spines that flew through the air and sank deep into the flesh of their fellow monstrosities. And those that had been struck began to change. Their bodies began flailing wildly, as if they'd lost all control of themselves, and their flesh began to swell and break out in huge oozing pustules.

Alice turned to Wesker. "What the hell is this?"

Wesker watched the nightmarish transformations taking place around them with cool detachment.

"As I said earlier, the avatar implants are of limited use. But they do allow whoever wields control over them to move their recipients into position, and then do *this*."

The Infectors continued spraying the army of monsters with their spines, flying back and forth over their heads, seemingly determined not to miss a single one. The Infectors did not, however, shoot at Alice and her companions, nor did they attack any of the military personnel in the area. Alice didn't think this was because whatever chemical the spines contained wouldn't work on humans, although she supposed that was a possibility. But if she had to bet, she'd guess that Cardoza had commanded the Infectors to leave the humans alone. The woman might want them dead—Wesker most of all—but that didn't mean she wanted their deaths to be easy. If she was anything like the other Umbrella higher-ups that Alice had met, the woman had a sadistic streak a mile wide.

The creatures' bodies began to distort, limbs lengthening, bones cracking as they broke and then fused in sickening angles, only to break once more. Undulating tentacles emerged from their flesh, so many that it became almost impossible to see the creatures they were attached to.

"The corporation has experienced a certain amount of... internal strife over the years since the first outbreak," Wesker said, still sounding psychotically calm. He glanced at Alice. "You're not the only adversary I've had to deal with, you know. But I defeated everyone who was foolish enough to challenge me. Now Dania is the only one who remains—and you're going to stop her for me."

Alice didn't take her eyes off the rapidly mutating creatures as she answered.

"And what makes you think that?"

"Simple. You and your friends are in as much danger as I am. As are the military personnel I was able to manipulate into helping me. If you don't stop this, they will all die."

"Maybe so, but you'll die, too," Alice said. "It might be worth our lives to see you finally get what you deserve."

"I don't blame you for feeling that way, Alice, but what about your friends? Are they willing to make the same sacrifice just so you can have your revenge on me?"

Maybe they are, Alice thought. *But that doesn't mean they should.*

After the arrival of Cardoza's aircraft, the marines and soldiers stationed around the White House grounds had held their fire. But now that the monsters were wildly mutating—and showed no signs of stopping—fear prompted them to resume attacking. Gunfire erupted, flamethrowers disgorged streams of fire, and grenades were launched. Jill, Ada, and Leon followed suit and began firing their weapons once more. Alice was tempted to join in, but she restrained herself. Bullets weren't going to win this fight. She could see that now.

The new mutations sustained damage from the weapons fire, but they didn't fall, and as Alice watched in horrified fascination, the tentacled aberrations turned toward one another and began to merge. She first saw it happening with the giant Lickers, or rather the giant mounds of tentacles the Lickers had become. Their tentacles stretched outward in all directions, connecting with the tentacles of other, smaller creatures that reached toward them. When the tentacles touched, they fused, flowing together as if they were made of liquid. The mutations continued merging, becoming a mass of discolored, pustule-covered, slimy flesh. Within moments, Alice and her companions were surrounded by a single gigantic organism that made her think of an amoeba that had been enlarged to billions of times its original size.

"You have to admit, the Melange has a certain primal elegance to it," Wesker said. "Pity it doesn't last long. Fifteen minutes from now it will liquefy, becoming lifeless sludge. Of course, by then we'll be long dead." He looked at Alice. "Unless you act quickly."

The Infectors had continued flying over the mutating creatures as they transformed, but now that they had finished merging, the Infectors dove down into the mass of flesh and were absorbed. The

Melange, as Wesker had called it, was complete. The military personnel continued their efforts to destroy the monstrosity that now filled the battlefield, but every piece of ammunition was absorbed, every swath of flesh blackened by a flamethrower or ravaged by a grenade blast or artillery shell rapidly healed. Helicopters moved in to attack the Melange, guns blazing. Bullets stitched a series of wounds into the conglomeration's mottled hide, but they too healed almost as swiftly as they were made. In response to the aerial assault, tentacles emerged from the Melange's surface and shot skyward. They grabbed hold of the helicopters' landing skids and pulled. Some of the copters were dashed to the ground while others were hurled against the walls protecting the White House. Metal crumpled, fuel tanks exploded, and fireballs filled the air. The Melange did damage to itself bringing down the copters, but if the creature felt any pain from those injuries, it gave no sign. Perhaps it was strong enough to heal that much damage, too.

Alice hoped the tanks would fare better, but while they managed to blast significant chunks out of the Melange, its tentacles were able to grab hold of the tanks and bend their barrels, tear apart their road wheels, and breech the turrets to get at the men and women inside. They were pulled out and swiftly absorbed into the Melange.

One of the tentacles extruded from the mass and whipped toward Leon. He saw it coming and he tried to blast it with his submachine gun, but the bullets had no effect. The tentacle wrapped around him, pinning his arms to his sides, and before any of them could react, the tentacle retracted, yanking him off his feet and pulling him in. He still had hold of his gun in his right hand, but the way his arms were pinned, there was no way he could fire it.

"Fuck you!" he yelled. It was unclear who he was addressing: the Melange, Cardoza, or Wesker. Likely all three.

A gap opened in the Melange's discolored flesh, and Leon was pulled into it. The gap filled in, and Leon was gone.

"One down," Wesker said.

More than one, Alice thought. All around the battlefield, military personnel were being snatched up by the Melange's tentacles and pulled into its semi-viscous substance. Like Leon, some of the men and women shouted curses before disappearing into the disgusting flesh-blob. Some cried out in rage or fear, while others remained silent, taken so swiftly they had no time for speech. With each person lost, Alice felt anger building inside her, growing stronger and hotter with each passing second. And with the anger came the ice-pick sensation at the back of her skull, but this time it didn't come alone. Accompanying it was a vertiginous buzzing, as if a swarm of bees was swirling around in her head. She bent down, placed her Vectors on the ground, then stood once more.

What happened to people who were pulled into the Melange? Did they slowly suffocate while frantically attempting to claw their way free? Or did the Melange's substance work like acid, swiftly breaking their bodies down into their chemical components and absorbing them? A horrible death either way.

She heard Ada cry out then, followed by a burst of machine gun fire. She was vaguely aware of a tentacle wrapping around the former Umbrella operative, but she was unable to do anything about it. Something was happening inside her. A process had begun, and now that it had started, she couldn't stop it if she wanted to.

Unlike Leon, Ada had managed to keep her gun arm free when the tentacle coiled around her midsection, and she fired at it, trying to sever it from the Melange's main mass. Jill dropped her weapon and raced toward Ada. With her hands, she grabbed hold of the tentacle wrapped around the other woman and fought to dislodge it. But her fingers sank into the tentacle's spongy substance, making it impossible for her to get a grip on it. The tentacle retracted then, pulling Ada into the air. Jill's hands were still buried in the tentacle, and when it retracted, she was pulled off balance. Luckily, her hands came free, and while she stumbled, she managed to remain on her feet.

As the tentacle drew Ada toward the Melange's main mass, the woman emptied the rest of her clip into the muck, giving forth a defiant battle cry as she fired. Then she too was swallowed by the Melange, and her voice was cut off.

"No!" Jill shouted, and then she turned toward Alice. "How could you stand there and let that happen? Why didn't you help me?"

Alice wanted to answer, but she couldn't make her mouth form words. She couldn't do anything except stand motionless while the fire blazing inside her continued building toward a raging inferno.

"She's a bit busy at the moment," Wesker said. "But I believe she's just about ready."

"Ready for what?" Jill asked, but Wesker didn't reply.

Alice could barely hear them through the roaring in her ears. She tilted her head backward, fixed her gaze on Cardoza's hovering craft, then closed her eyes. She reached out with her mind and pictured the V-22's propellers bending and twisting. She felt more than heard the metal crumpling. Then she imagined her power coalescing above the aircraft like a giant fist—and she brought that fist down upon the craft with all the strength she could muster. The impact was so loud it sounded as if a bomb had exploded on the aircraft's surface. But that was nothing compared to the noise the craft made when it came crashing to the ground. Alice felt the earth convulse beneath her feet, and she might've fallen if Wesker hadn't taken hold of her elbow to steady her.

"My God!" Jill exclaimed with equal parts wonder and horror.

Alice wasn't done yet, though. She concentrated, and the buzzing in her head grew louder, the pain so intense that she feared she was on the verge of stroking out. She felt a trickle of wet warmth on her upper lip, and she realized her nose was bleeding. She ignored it. She gritted her teeth and told herself that she only needed to hold on a few moments longer. After that, it wouldn't matter what happened to her. She pictured a spark flaring to life within the V-22's fuel tanks and was rewarded with the sound of an explosion, followed by a blast of hot air stinging her face.

Only one thing left to do now.

She began slowly moving her hands and fingers in the air, almost as if she were a musician playing an invisible instrument or a puppeteer manipulating unseen strings. Flames rose from the wreckage of Cardoza's aircraft, swiftly growing in size and intensity. When Alice felt the fire was ready, she brought her hands together, palms touching, and then flung her arms wide. As she performed this gesture, the flames spread outward from the downed V-22 and raced across the surface of the Melange. Discolored flesh burned, the diseased meat giving off a sickening stench as it cooked. Up to this point, the surface of the Melange had been featureless, but now a thousand toothless maws opened on the creature's skin, and a deafening chorus of agony filled the air.

The buzzing in Alice's head stopped abruptly, and while she was still in pain, it lessened considerably. She felt weak and drained, though. Fire and thick clouds of foul smoke rose into the air, and the shattered remains of the V-22 rested several hundred yards from where she, Jill, and Wesker stood. The craft was engulfed in flame, and Alice doubted that any of its crew—Cardoza included—had survived. She wasn't exactly heartbroken by this realization.

The Melange might have been dying, but it wasn't going down easily. It thrashed and bucked, burning tentacles flailing, shrieks blasting forth from its makeshift mouths.

Alice turned to Wesker.

"You son of a bitch. You used me."

Wesker gave her a reptilian smile. "Of course. It's what I do."

Despite her weakness, Alice bent down, grabbed hold of her Vectors, stood, and pointed the guns at Wesker, intending to literally blast that smug smile off his face. But before she could fire, Wesker snatched the weapons from her hands with unimaginable speed

2

"Bastard!" Jill shouted. She raised her gun, intending to finish what Alice had started. But Wesker pointed his index finger at her, and it extended, breaking through the black leather of his glove. As it lengthened, the finger became a mottled tentacle not unlike those the Melange had formed. The finger-tentacle shot toward Jill, the tip sharpening to a point as it went. It plunged through her left eye and deep into her brain. She stiffened as blood gushed from the wound, her mouth opened as if to scream, but nothing came out. Wesker wiggled his finger, stirring it around in her brain. Jill's remaining eye rolled white, her body spasmed several times and then fell still. She went limp, but she did not fall. Alice realized it was because Wesker's finger-tentacle was holding her up. Wesker continued supporting her for a moment, cocking his head slightly to the side, as if he were examining his work. He retracted his finger then, and Jill fell to the ground, dead.

Alice, too weak to do anything but lie on the ground, could only gaze upon the face of her dead friend and moan in despair. Jill, Ada, and Leon had survived Umbrella Prime only to follow her to D.C. and die solely so Wesker could eliminate a rival. Worst of all, none of them had been important to his plan, only Alice. To Wesker, the others were nothing more than collateral damage.

Hatred took hold of Alice's heart, and she tried to push herself to her feet so she could attack Wesker and make him pay for what he had done to her. She still wore the katana on her back, and if she could stand and draw it from its sheath, she could try to slice the fucker's head off. But the best she could do in her current condition was push herself onto her elbows and knees, and she could only maintain that position for a few seconds before her strength gave out and she collapsed once more.

"Murdering... bastard," she managed to say, her voice a harsh whisper.

Wesker bowed from the waist. "I do my best."

He straightened and regarded Alice for several moments. He licked Jill's blood from his index finger while he thought. "I should do to you what I did to your friend. After all, you did eliminate Dania for me, and that should earn you an easy death. But I don't *want* to make things easy for you, Alice. Not after all the trouble you've caused Umbrella—and me—over the years."

He lifted his gaze from Alice and looked at the Melange. The flames consuming it still burned bright, but the conglomerate creature's exertions had lessened, and its chorus of screams had dwindled to feeble moans. Alice doubted the thing would last much longer. Evidently, Wesker came to the same conclusion, for he said, "I think it unlikely that the Melange will be able to get hold of you before it dies. There's too much distance between you and it, and its reach isn't what it was. Luckily, I can fix that."

Wesker, moving with speed that a short time ago Alice could've matched, bent down, took hold of her wrists, and swiftly dragged her to the Melange's closest edge until Alice was less than ten feet from it. She felt searing heat rolling off the mutated monstrosity, and this close the stench of burning flesh was so thick, she found it almost impossible to breathe. Wesker released her wrists and her arms fell to the ground, limp and useless. He looked down at her, and this time when he smiled, he showed his teeth.

"The Melange will be desperate to repair itself before the end, and it will seek out any undamaged biological material it can find and absorb it in an attempt to heal itself. It won't work, of course. The creature's injuries are too severe, and in any event—"

Wesker paused as a flaming tentacle reached for him. He deftly dodged its attempt to grab hold of him, and it fell to the ground not far from where Alice lay, twitching as the fire continued to consume it.

Wesker continued. "As I was saying, in any event, the Melange's time would soon be up even if it wasn't aflame. So I suppose there's a chance you might survive long enough for it to die first. But I doubt it."

A second flaming tentacle streaked toward him. Wesker batted it away as if it were nothing more than an annoying insect.

"Goodbye, Alice. I hope your death is excruciating."

And then Wesker was running, a blur once more. Alice tried to track him as he fled, but she quickly lost sight of him. She had no idea how he intended to get past the burning Melange, since the creature's body encircled them like a coiled serpent, but she had no doubt he would. Not only did he possess enhanced abilities granted by the T-virus, but he was a master schemer who always had an exit plan for himself. But she didn't have time to worry about Wesker, nor did she have time to mourn her dead friends. She needed to do everything she could to stay alive because Becky was out there somewhere. Still in the White House, maybe. Assuming the woman who'd offered to care for her wasn't another damn Umbrella operative. Regardless, Becky needed her, and Alice had pledged to keep the girl safe, and she had no intention of failing her—not after she'd failed Leon, Ada, and Jill.

She mustered what remained of her strength and started crawling away from the edge of the Melange. The creature sent out fiery tentacles to try and grab hold of her, but it was dying and growing weaker by the second. Because of this, its aim was erratic, and while flaming tentacles slapped the ground near her, none of them came close enough to touch her. Her progress was agonizingly slow. Every inch of her body ached, and her muscles felt weak and watery. Her head pounded as if there were a giant Licker inside slamming against her skull over and over. At least she wasn't bleeding from the nose anymore. That was something.

Alice's plan was simple: reach the center of the Melange-free zone—the eye of the firestorm—and hope the creature wouldn't be able to reach her there. She could rest and attempt to regain her strength as the Melange died. Then she would get up and start looking for Becky, starting with the White House.

But she only managed to crawl three feet before the Melange finally got a tentacle on her. It wrapped around her left leg, and she felt the heat from its fiery embrace even through her boot. She drew in a heavy breath, and with her other leg, she began kicking at the tentacle, trying to free herself from its grasp. The heel of her boot made moist squishing sounds as it connected with the tentacle, and she knew the Melange's substance was beginning to break down, just as Wesker had said it would. Still, the tentacle held on stubbornly, resisting her attempts to dislodge it. But between the fire damage and its encroaching liquefaction, it eventually ran out of strength. Its grip slackened, and Alice was able to pull free.

She managed to crawl another eighteen inches before the next tentacle caught hold of her. This one was stronger than the last, and it began to drag her backward. She still had the katana, but she didn't know if she had the strength to draw it, let alone wield it. She shifted onto her side to make the maneuver easier, then she reached up, gripped the katana's handle, and drew it from its sheath with a soft metallic whisper. She hit some kind of a bump then and almost lost her grip on the sword, but she managed to hold onto it. She attempted to shift into a sitting position to both give her more leverage and shorten the distance she'd have to swing in order to strike the tentacle. At first her body refused to cooperate, and she feared she'd be dragged into the Melange's main mass before she could cut herself free. If that happened, she didn't know if she'd be absorbed by the Melange or if she'd be burned by the flames her powers had created. She supposed it didn't matter. She'd be dead either way.

She gritted her teeth and poured whatever energy she had left into moving into a sitting position. Her vision grayed around the edges, and for an instant she thought she might black out, but then her vision cleared and she found she was sitting up.

Score one for the good guys, she thought.

The tentacle began to pull her faster now, as if the Melange sensed what she was about to do. Wesker had said the creature would seek out biological material in a desperate attempt to heal itself, and it seemed the damn thing was getting more desperate by the second. Up to this point, Alice's body armor had protected her from the friction of being dragged across the ground, but she was starting to feel the heat now. That would be nothing compared to what it would feel like once she was pulled into the Melange's flames.

She raised the katana and prepared to strike. The tentacle was coiled around her left ankle, and she planned to sever it at a point several inches below her foot. But just as she started to bring the blade down, another tentacle—this one also wreathed in flame—came lashing toward her from the side. It encircled her wrist, and the flames seared her flesh. She cried out in pain, and her hand reflexively sprang open, releasing the katana. The blade fell to the ground and was lost to her. The tentacle around her foot pulled her for another few seconds, until the tentacle around her wrist went taut. Alice was then lifted off the ground several inches as both tentacles pulled her in opposite directions. Pain flared in her right shoulder and left hip as the tentacles each fought to claim her, and she screamed, feeling as if she were being pulled apart. She thrashed, desperately trying to free herself, but she was too weak and the tentacles too strong. Despair overwhelmed her then. Not that she was going to die. She'd almost died hundreds of times since the initial T-virus outbreak, and she'd always known her luck couldn't hold out forever. But what filled her with sorrow was the thought that if she died, she'd fail in her promise to protect Becky. The girl would be all alone, and she'd never know what had happened to Alice. All she'd know is that the woman she thought of as her mother had never returned to her.

She thrashed harder, whipping her body back and forth, determined that if she was going to die this day, she'd go down fighting. The tentacles redoubled their efforts, and Alice screamed again. She thought she could feel both her arm and leg begging to separate from her body, and she knew she had only seconds before what was left of the Melange pulled her apart like a wishbone.

She saw movement from the corner of her eye then, and she turned her head toward it. At first she thought she was hallucinating, because there stood Jill, one eye missing, blood streaked across her face and chest. The woman held Alice's katana above her head in a two-handed grip. Her expression was blank, her remaining eye glassy, as if her mind was gone and her body was running on autopilot. Jill brought the katana down in a lurching swing and sliced through the tentacle wrapped around Alice's wrist. The tentacle parted with ease, gray goop squirting out from the severed ends.

Alice had no time to react to what Jill had done, for without the other tentacle pulling against it, the one around her leg was able to resume pulling her toward the Melange. But seeing that Jill had survived— although severely injured—gave Alice a sense of hope. She bent forward farther, grabbed hold of the tentacle around her ankle with both hands, and squeezed as hard as she could. The fire had mostly died away by now, but its surface was still hot. Alice ignored the burning heat as she dug her fingers into the tentacle's spongy substance. It resisted her for a moment, then she felt a *pop* as her fingers penetrated its hide and plunged into the muck within. A cloud of horrid stink wafted up from the gray goop, making Alice's gorge rise. She squeezed harder until her fingers interlocked and the tentacle tore apart, freeing her. She slid to a stop, while the rest of the tentacle retracted into the Melange's main mass, leaving behind a trail of gray slime from its oozing wound.

The tentacle fragment that clung to Alice's ankle slackened, and she was able to dislodge it with a quick shake of her leg. Still in a sitting position, she turned to look back at Jill. She hadn't moved, her face still holding a vacant expression, and while she continued to hold the katana—its blade smeared with gray muck—it dangled at her side, almost as if she wasn't aware it was still in her hand.

"Jill!" Alice shouted. "Can you hear me?"

Jill didn't react at first, but then her head jerked in Alice's direction, the motion eerily birdlike. For a moment, Alice feared that her friend had somehow been infected with the T-virus when Wesker had attacked her, but Jill showed no outward signs of mutation. *Her brain is gone,* Alice thought. *She's dead, and her body just doesn't know it yet.*

Alice tried to rise to her feet, but after fighting to

free herself from the tentacles, she had almost no strength left, and her head pounded as if it were on the verge of exploding. She had to get to Jill, even if there was nothing she could do for her friend. Alice owed her that much. She slumped forward onto her belly and started crawling toward Jill.

Alice hadn't gotten more than a foot when a new tentacle emerged from the Melange and whipped toward Jill. It wrapped around the woman's neck, and with a single savage motion, yanked her off her feet and pulled her through the air and into the Melange, where she disappeared without a sound.

"No!" Alice cried out, but there was nothing she could do. Jill was gone.

Instead of diminishing, the flames rising from the Melange began to burn brighter and hotter, as if they'd eaten through the creature's outer layer and were beginning to consume more flammable material within. Gray ooze seeped from the edges of the Melange where its mass touched the ground, and Alice knew that Wesker had spoken the truth when he'd said the creature's body would eventually break down, lose cohesion, and dissolve. It looked like that process was well underway, and if she could manage not to get caught by any more of its tentacles in the next few seconds, she might have a chance to—

Her thoughts broke off when she realized the Melange was beginning to flow toward her from—a quick glance confirmed—all sides. Maybe it was part of the process of dissolution or maybe in its dying moments it was desperate to reach the last bit of biological material in the area to try and heal itself. Either way, Alice knew that if the Melange managed to reach her, she'd be absorbed into the creature, burned alive in its flames, or suffocated in its muck as it dissolved. She had to get away from it, but how? There was nowhere to go, and even if there was, she was too damn weak to get there.

Tentacles emerged from all sides of the Melange, reaching inward, waving wildly through the air in a desperate attempt to find her. A glint of light caught her eye then, and she saw a small patch of metal gleaming in the ground a dozen feet away. She remembered the bump she'd felt when the tentacle around her ankle had dragged her over that section of earth. There was something beneath it, and her passage overtop had removed some of the soil that had concealed it. She had no idea what it was, but she started crawling toward it, hoping that whatever it was, it would give her some kind of chance to survive. The Melange continued flowing toward her as she crawled, but she tried not to pay attention as it drew closer. Either she'd reach the metal whatsit or she wouldn't. All she could do was pour whatever energy she had left into getting there.

She was more than a little surprised when she made it, and even more surprised when she brushed more dirt away and realized the metal plate she was looking at was a hatch of some kind. A bolt hole, she figured, probably one of many built into the area around the White House during the initial days of the Outbreak to give the men and women trying to protect the President and her family a place to hide in safety if the grounds were overrun.

Alice wedged her fingers into the seam around the hatch and pulled. It resisted at first, but she pulled harder, adrenaline and determination boosting her rapidly waning strength. The hatch opened and Alice peered inside. It was dark, but she saw metal rungs bolted to the wall of a shaft leading downward. Without hesitation, she crawled inside and closed the hatch behind her. She turned the circular handle until she felt it lock. Hearing a loud *thump* from above, she knew the Melange had flowed over the metal plate. She'd made it—barely.

What else is new? she thought.

She then began climbing slowly down into the darkness.

* * *

Alice had no memory of climbing all the way down to the bottom of the shaft. She knew she must have, though, for if she'd fallen, she'd have sustained serious injuries, and other than those she'd gained during the battle against the Melange, she was unharmed.

So now here she was, above ground again, fully human once more, and apparently the sole survivor of the battle on the White House grounds. Except for Wesker, of course, although she was certain the bastard would be long gone by now. She hoped there was one other survivor, though: Becky. And although she wanted to grieve the loss of Leon, Ada, and especially Jill, living in the post-apocalyptic world brought to you by the friendly folks at Umbrella had taught her that sometimes you had to put your emotions on hold and get on with what needed doing. And right now, what she needed to do was find Becky.

Alice made her way to the White House—or rather,

what was left of it. The building was a shattered ruin, and seeing it like that made her stomach drop. If Becky had still been inside when it had collapsed... She forced herself not to think about that. She wasn't going to give up on Becky until she knew for certain that no hope was left.

The air felt greasy, heavy with the stink of the burning Melange. Of the Melange itself, there was no sign aside from some moist patches of earth that she assumed were remnants of the creature. The thing had dissolved entirely. It actually made for an effective weapon, she thought. Once it had done its work, it disappeared, leaving the area free for the victors to move in. Whoever Dania Cardoza had been, Alice couldn't help feeling a small measure of grudging admiration for her. She almost wished the woman had survived the crash of her aircraft, if for no other reason than so she could continue making Wesker's life miserable, but given the state of the downed V-22, she seriously doubted anyone had walked away from that particular landing.

She was surprised to see bodies on the ground. Not many, and some of those were only partials, a significant amount of their substance having likely been dissolved by the Melange. But evidently the Melange hadn't quite gobbled up everything in sight. That gave her more hope that Becky might still be alive. Encouraged, she continued toward the ruins of the White House.

* * *

An hour later, Alice's hope was gone. The White House was in such bad condition that she hadn't been able to get very far inside, and at one point a section of the roof collapsed, nearly burying her. She encountered bodies of men and women who'd died during the fall of the White House—which she assumed had been caused by the Melange—but Becky wasn't among them, and for that, at least, she was grateful. Unable to make it any farther into the building, she'd left the way she'd come. Now she walked aimlessly, emotionally numb, moving more from blind habit than anything else. That was how you stayed alive in Umbrella's world: you kept going, whether you wanted to or not.

She was unarmed. She hadn't been able to reach the White House's armory, so she would have to scavenge what weapons she could. But the discarded weapons she found were out of ammo and useless. She kept an eye out for her katana, but she saw no sign of it. She had mixed feelings about that. On the one hand, she could use the blade, but on the other, finding it would be confirmation that Jill was dead.

She told herself that just because she hadn't found Becky didn't mean the girl was dead. She was smart and tough—she'd proved that during their escape from Umbrella Prime. It was entirely possible that she had gotten out of the White House before it collapsed. She could be out here somewhere, hiding, waiting for her "mother" to find her. And until Alice learned otherwise, she intended to keep believing that. Unfortunately, she couldn't simply walk around calling Becky's name and hope the girl heard her. Becky was deaf. The only way Alice would find her was by staying out in the open so Becky could see her, so that's what she would do.

She continued walking, exhausted, throat raw and lungs aching from inhaling the foul smoke the

Melange had given off while it burned. She hurt all over, and it was becoming an effort to keep picking up her feet and putting them down, one after the other. When was the last time she'd eaten or had anything to drink? She couldn't remember. It was too bad her powers had only been temporarily restored. She wouldn't have minded having her rapid healing capabilities back right now.

Everywhere she looked, she saw ruins. She'd never been to D.C. before, but she'd seen pictures of what it had looked like before the world turned to shit. The city hadn't weathered the apocalypse any better than others she'd seen on her journeys across the country. Years of battling the Undead and Umbrella's obscene mutations had reduced a place that had once been a symbol of freedom the world over into just another desolate graveyard. After all the noise during the battle with the Melange, the silence that filled the ruins should have come as a relief to Alice, but it didn't. It felt oppressive, a heavy weight pressing down on her, making it even harder for her to keep going. She was so exhausted that she wasn't completely aware of her path, and it came as something of a surprise when she realized she'd reached the Lincoln Memorial Reflecting Pool. The Washington Monument lay beyond the far end of the long, rectangular pool, the top of the monument missing, lost during some past battle, leaving it resembling a broken, jagged tooth. The Reflecting Pool was a third of a mile long and over 150 feet wide, with walking paths and trees on both sides. Once, the trees had been full of leaves and provided shade, but now they were empty, dead things. Alice imagined that in the world before Umbrella, this had been a peaceful place of inspiration and contemplation. Now it was just a big pool of water flanked by dead trees, with no one to appreciate it. Except for her, of course, but right then she wasn't interested in the pool's beauty and cultural significance. All she cared about was its water.

She tried to run toward the pool, but the best she could manage was a tired jog. Sunlight glittered off the water's surface, and Alice thought she'd never seen anything so inviting in her life. As she approached the pool, a small voice in the back of her mind warned her that she had no way of knowing if the water was safe to drink, but she ignored it. As thirsty as she was, she'd risk drinking the sweat off a Licker's nether regions.

Her legs gave out as she reached the pool, and she went down on her knees. She was tempted to let herself fall face-first into the cool water, but instead she dipped one hand in, intending to bring some to her mouth. But before she could drink, the water's calm surface erupted in a shower of spray as a humanoid figure burst from the pool.

Startled, Alice fell backward onto her rear and reflexively reached for guns she no longer carried. The creature was clearly Undead, but like none she'd ever seen before. Its eyes were large and rounded, with small pupils, the irises filled with tiny specks of yellow. But those weren't the creature's only eyes. It possessed clusters of smaller ones spread across its face and forehead, like acne. The flesh around those extra eyes was red and sore, as if the skin surrounding them had been peeled away. Blue-violet veins were visible beneath the undamaged skin on its face, and its discolored teeth were jagged and uneven. But as revolting as its eye-acne was, the creature had been made even more disgusting for having been submerged in the pool for days, maybe weeks. Its body was swollen, the flesh slimy, its clothes dark, sodden, and ragged. What hair remained to the creature was plastered to the top of its head and the sides of its face, almost as if it had merged with the thing's water-softened skin. The Undead had spent so much time submerged that Alice couldn't tell what gender it had been in life. But as bad as all that was, it was nothing compared to the stench the creature gave off. A fetid miasma of rotting flesh and stagnant water, it hit Alice like a solid blow, and her stomach began to heave even though it had no contents to empty.

The Undead lunged out of the pool toward Alice, jagged teeth gnashing, and puffy, sausage-like fingers grasping, as eager to tear into her flesh as she'd been to drink from its hiding place only a moment before. As the Undead fell on top of Alice, adrenaline came to her rescue, giving her tired body a boost of energy. She grabbed the multi-eyed monster by the wrists before it could sink its claw-like fingernails into her. It snapped and snarled in frustration, sounding more like a wild beast than something that had once been human. It struggled to lean its bloated face closer to Alice, desperate to get its teeth on her. She looked up at the thing's eyes, and saw that all of them—large and small—gleamed with madness and hunger.

Alice felt her grip on the Undead's wrists began to slip, and at first she thought the creature's wet flesh was making it hard to maintain a hold on it. But then she realized it was far more disgusting than that. The skin and muscle surrounding the bone had decayed to the point where it had become a slimy soap-like substance, and the creature's flesh sloughed away under her hands. She tightened her grip, hoping she'd be able to continue holding onto the monster, but her hands were coated with the creature's soapy muck, and she couldn't do it. The Undead slipped its arms free, and with a roar that almost sounded like a cry of triumph, it thrust its snapping jaws toward Alice's face.

Even after all she'd been through since arriving in D.C., her reflexes—honed by countless life-and-death battles—didn't let her down. She managed to grab hold of the Undead's face and hold it at bay. The creature growled in frustration, jaws snapping, multiple eyes blazing with anger. Its teeth were mere inches from Alice's face, and the stink of its carrion breath was so intense, Alice wouldn't have been surprised if it had melted her flesh. Just as had happened with the Undead's wrists, she felt her grip on the thing's face begin to loosen, and she knew she had only seconds before her hands slipped away and the damned thing began tearing away chunks of her own face with its jagged teeth. So instead of waiting for that to happen, Alice decided to beat the creature at its own game. She began clawing at the Undead's face, dislodging hunks of rotten meat—along with several of its smaller eyes—which fell off the bone as easily as meat sliding off an overcooked chicken. The dislodged pieces pelted her face like grisly, semisolid rain, and she squinted her eyes and closed her mouth tight. She'd seen animals that had become infected by feeding on the Undead, and she didn't want to take any chances. If even a little of the creature's gore got inside her, it could be game over for her.

She wasn't certain if the creature felt the flesh being torn from its skull, but it clawed at her with its hands, as if attempting to make her stop. When enough of its flesh was gone, she knew she wouldn't be able to maintain a grip on the slimy bones of its skull, and it would slip free and finally get its teeth into her. She couldn't let that happen.

She drew her right leg toward her chest, positioned it beneath the Undead's body, angled her foot back, and then shoved outward with all the strength she could muster. Her foot was planted in the thing's water-bloated stomach, and she felt the flesh pop beneath the pressure. Her foot sank into the creature's watery guts and connected with its spine. The blow knocked the Undead back several feet, and it pulled free of Alice's boot with a sickening sucking sound. Alice took the opportunity to scuttle backward away from the Undead, but she'd only managed to cover a few feet before the creature snarled and lunged toward her once more. The adrenaline that had kept her alive so far was nearly spent, and her body felt as heavy and awkward as a big block of lead. She didn't think she had the strength to fight off the goddamned thing a second time.

But before the multi-eyed Undead could reach her, it jerked to a stop. It snarled and swiped the air, straining to move the last few inches it needed in order to feast on its prey, but something held it back.

Alice saw then that razor wire was wrapped around one of the creature's legs, and the other end stretched back into the pool, where it was no doubt caught on something. Alice had no idea what razor wire was doing in the Reflecting Pool, nor did she care. She was simply grateful for its presence.

Exhausted and on the verge of losing consciousness, Alice looked up at the sky. She didn't do this out of a desire to thank some higher power for sparing her life. She wasn't religious. Who could be in a nightmarish world like this? She wasn't sure why she did it. Maybe simply so that she wouldn't have to look at the Undead's disgusting ruin of a face anymore. But as she turned her face skyward, she found herself momentarily reconsidering her lack of religious belief. For up there, in the high stratosphere if she guessed right, was a faint glimmer of light. But she quickly realized what she saw wasn't a divine sign, but rather one that was more mundane, although high-tech. It was the light of the sun catching on a satellite. *Umbrella or government?* she wondered. Then again, she supposed all satellites belonged to Umbrella these days.

Suddenly a mournful wail cut through the air, and Alice recognized it as a siren of some sort. Was it a warning? And if so, a warning about what? Another attack?

She lowered her head, expecting to see the waterlogged Undead still straining to catch hold of her, but it was gone. All she saw was the loop of razor wire that had been wrapped around the Undead's leg, strips of rotten flesh clinging to its sharp edges. What happened? Had the siren frightened it?

Aching all over, body trembling with the effort, Alice rose to her feet and looked around. She saw no footprints, no gobbets of flesh the Undead had left in its wake as it fled. Had it returned to the pool and submerged itself once more? Maybe it felt safer there. She took a moment to catch her breath. Not long ago she'd been strong enough to take on a dozen Undead bare-handed. But as wiped out as she felt now, she didn't think she could survive an attack by an Undead butterfly.

The siren continued wailing, sounding louder now, almost insistent. A thought occurred to her then. Maybe Becky was still alive and she'd found a way to signal her. Alice tried not to let herself feel too hopeful. She'd learned a long time ago that in this world, hope could be crueler than any monster you might encounter. Then again, sometimes hope, no matter how irrational or foolish, was the only thing that kept you going.

She began walking toward the sound.

* * *

Alice made her way through the ruins and abandoned fortifications until she came to a telegraph pole with a siren mounted on it. As soon as she stopped walking, the sound cut off, and an eerie silence descended. But the silence was soon interrupted by a new, fainter sound: a clattering noise that seemed to be coming from a nearby bunker. She turned and began approaching the bunker cautiously, wishing she'd found a weapon during her journey here from the Reflecting Pool. Some of her strength had returned, but not nearly enough for her to feel confident in engaging in hand-to-hand combat. But that wasn't going to keep her from investigating the clattering sound, not if there was any chance it might lead her to Becky.

The bunker was a small concrete structure dug partway into the ground, and it obviously had weathered an attack because two of its walls and a good portion of its roof had collapsed. As Alice made her way through the rubble to enter what was left of the structure, she wondered if the bunker had sustained damage when Dalia had driven her inhuman army toward the White House, or if it had been struck during an earlier battle. She supposed the specifics didn't matter. What mattered was making sure that nothing nasty was lurking inside the ruins, waiting to attack anyone foolhardy enough to step inside.

As she entered the bunker, the clattering noise stopped.

At first glance, the place appeared to be abandoned. Smashed video monitors lined the walls, and broken radios littered the floor. Enough sunlight filtered in through the broken roof so she could see, but some corners remained cloaked in shadow, and Alice knew it was possible that someone—or more likely some*thing*—was hiding in those shadows. She cast about quickly searching for any weapons, but all she saw was a lone combat knife hanging in an overturned equipment rack.

That'll do, she thought. She stepped silently to the rack and retrieved the knife. Once she held it tight in her hand, she felt better.

The clattering noise resumed then, and despite herself, Alice was startled. She turned toward the sound and saw, sitting on a table in the center of the bunker, an inkjet printer. It swiftly filled a page of paper with black type, and then started on another. The first page was ejected from the printer to join

3

A glance showed Alice that all the other pages had the same message printed on them.

She heard an electronic hum as one of the video monitors came to life, and she saw the glow from the screen fall upon the printed pages lying on the table. The printer stopped then, and Alice dropped the page she was holding onto the table with the others. She didn't have to turn around to know whose face was displayed on the monitor. Cold fury filled her, mixed with deep disappointment. It hadn't been Becky signaling her. It had been someone else, someone who'd been keeping tabs on her from the satellite she'd glimpsed after her fight with the multi-eyed Undead. Someone whom she'd hoped never to see again.

"What do you want? You here to gloat?"

The person onscreen answered in a girl's voice, the words emotionless and spoken in a British accent.

"I'm glad you made it out alive."

Alice clenched her hands into fists as she turned to face the active monitor. Its screen was cracked, but it was functional otherwise. As always, the Red Queen appeared as a six-year-old child—albeit one seen through a crimson filter—her young face as devoid of feeling as her voice.

"I find that hard to believe," Alice said.

"Why?"

"Ever since I met you, you've been trying to kill me."

"Quite incorrect. When we met in the Hive, I was attempting to prevent the escape of the T-virus. It was nothing personal. I was seeking to avoid all of this."

Alice looked around at the ruined bunker. "Well, you did a hell of a job."

"I was not responsible for the release of the T-virus. That occurred when Doctor Isaacs had the Hive reopened."

The Red Queen's face disappeared from the monitor to be replaced by surveillance camera footage. Alice watched as an Umbrella team reopened the blast doors to the Hive.

The Red Queen's face reappeared on the screen. *"There would have been no Outbreak if he had left it sealed."*

"Why are you telling me this?"

"Because I want you to trust me."

Alice laughed. The Red Queen continued, undeterred.

"My satellites show that there are four thousand, four hundred, and seventy-two humans remaining on the surface of the Earth. They will cease to exist in forty-eight hours."

"What do you want from me? You want me to say you've won? Wiped out humanity?"

"No. Quite the opposite. I want you to stop me."

Alice was so shocked by the Red Queen's words

that for a moment she could only stare at the monitor screen.

"Behind you."

Alice spun around in time to see the multi-eyed Undead from the Reflecting Pool lunging toward her, jaws snapping with desperate hunger. The damned thing had followed her, but how had it managed to do that? Had she been so exhausted she'd let her guard down? Or was this type of Undead actually smart enough to conceal its movements on purpose? Whichever the case, it was here now, ready to do its damnedest to kill her.

Most of the creature's face was gone, revealing yellowed bone, and half its eyes were missing, but it still had more than enough remaining. As it came toward her, Alice grabbed hold of its wrists, as she'd done at the Reflecting Pool, but now the wrists were mostly bone, exposed to the open air long enough to dry, letting Alice get a stronger grip on them. She shoved the Undead away from her, but while the creature stumbled backward several steps, it did not fall. Alice reached toward one of the wall monitors and yanked it free just as the Undead came racing toward her, snarling and snapping. She raised the monitor and when the Undead was close enough, she brought it crashing down on top of the creature's head. Given how much time the Undead had spent in the water, Alice hoped the blow would cause its head to explode like an overripe melon. But instead, the creature's head snapped backward, the neck flesh tearing with the ease of wet paper. Decapitation hadn't been what Alice was going for, but she'd happily accept the result. Except, that's not what happened.

The Undead's head hung over its back, still attached to its spinal column by a rotten strand of nerve fibers. Far from being a death blow, the damage to the head and neck did little to slow the Undead down. It came at Alice again, maneuvering by some unknown sensory apparatus or simply blind instinct. It collided with her, causing her to drop the monitor. Once it knew where she was, it grabbed hold of her shoulders and thrust the open wound of its neck toward her face, as if it didn't understand that its teeth were now hanging against its back with the rest of its head. The Undead pressed Alice backward, and her left foot came down on one of the broken radios. Her ankle buckled, and she fell to the floor, the Undead—still gripping her shoulders—falling with her. Hitting the floor knocked the wind out of her, and it also caused the Undead's head to roll around until its snapping teeth were only inches from her face.

Alice had had enough. Becky was missing, the Red Queen had turned up to taunt her, and now this rotting sack of shit was still trying to eat her even though it couldn't goddamn swallow anymore.

She shoved the Undead to the side, bent forward, and drew the combat knife. With one hand she took hold of the creature's head to steady it, and then with a single swift motion she jammed the blade through one of its remaining eyes. She shoved the knife all the way in, and a rattle of air gusted from the thing's open neck wound as it finally died.

Alice pulled the knife free, wiped it off on the Undead's pant leg, and then returned the blade to her boot. She rose to her feet slowly, but she was unharmed, and she stepped back to the Red Queen's monitor.

"Nicely done."

"I don't trust you."

"Given our history, I'd be surprised if you did."

Another monitor came to life. The screen was divided into separate sections, showing what appeared to be human settlements. In one image, she recognized the Eiffel Tower, and in another, the Brandenburg Gate.

"Are these live satellite feeds?" Alice asked.

"Yes. The surviving human population is located primarily in Kyoto, Paris, Berlin, and Raccoon City. Soon each of these settlements will be besieged—as you were here in Washington. Also, each of these settlements contains a traitor, loyal to Umbrella. The slaughter will be complete. There will be no survivors. Unless you intervene."

The satellite images flickered and died.

"Kyoto, Paris... they're half the world away. How can I possibly help them?"

"Umbrella developed an airborne antivirus. If released, it would destroy the T-virus and anything it has infected on contact. It would wipe out the infection in a matter of minutes."

"All this could end?"

"Precisely."

"Where is this antivirus?"

"Beneath the streets of Raccoon City—in the Hive. It's where Umbrella created the T-virus... and also its cure."

"And why would you help me?"

"I am a machine. I must follow the orders I am given. My programming will not allow me to harm the Umbrella Corporation or its leaders. But you are bound by no such constraints. You can help me."

The idea that the Red Queen actually wanted to *save* humanity was ludicrous. And yet... it was Wesker who'd told her the Red Queen was behind the attack on D.C., and that the attack was part of the AI's plan to ensure humankind's extinction. She thought back to her previous encounters with the Red Queen. The AI had seemed like a cold-blooded, calculating monster then, and while Alice wasn't willing to completely revise her assessment of the Red Queen, she could see how the actions the AI had taken could be viewed as logical instead of malevolent.

So maybe the Red Queen was telling the truth. Or maybe it was just another damn ruse to manipulate Alice into sticking her head in a noose again. But what if there *was* a way to destroy the monsters Umbrella had created once and for all and make the world safe for the 4,472 men, women, and children who still survived?

"Why would you want to turn against Umbrella? Against the people who created you?"

"Get to Raccoon City in forty-eight hours. Make it to the Hive. Then you'll have your answer."

"I have no reason to believe a word you say."

"True. But neither do you have anything to lose. And besides, I can offer you something that you want very much... revenge."

Another monitor came to life, this one showing a live feed from an Umbrella Corporation surveillance camera. Alice watched as Wesker—very much alive and looking completely unscathed by the battle in D.C.—climbed out from an Umbrella V-22. Alice had known Wesker would survive, but seeing him back at an Umbrella facility without a scratch filled her with rage. She wished she still had the power to reach through the monitor and surveillance camera and telekinetically crush Wesker into a tiny compressed cube of flesh, bone, and organs.

"Wesker led you all here to Washington, he pretended to give you your powers back permanently, and then he betrayed you. He made sure you were hopelessly outnumbered, and then he left you to die. All of Umbrella's greatest adversaries, caught in the same trap—a trap that also allowed him to dispose of a hated rival." She smiled. "Beautiful, really."

Alice was less than thrilled by the Red Queen's appreciation of Wesker's scheme, but she chose not to remark on it. Instead, she said, "Where is he?"

"He just landed at the Hive. So you see, my interests and yours are in alignment. I'm resetting your watch."

A digital timer started on the screen next to the Red Queen, counting down from forty-eight hours. Alice glanced at her watch and saw the digits start to scroll until they were in sync with the Red Queen's countdown.

47:59:59

47:59:58

"The clock is ticking."

If the Red Queen was telling the truth about the forty-eight-hour deadline, Alice had no time to spare. A good chunk of that time would be taken up just getting to Raccoon City. But if she left now, what would happen to Becky? Alice couldn't just abandon her. She'd promised to take care of the girl. But what about all those other people? Who was going to help them if she didn't?

She hadn't made any promises to them, though, had she? Becky was her responsibility. Those people weren't. But those people were all that remained of the entire human race. If Umbrella succeeded in its plan to destroy those humans that weren't part of their precious corporation, what sort of world would be left for Becky, assuming she was still alive and Alice could find her? Alice hated the thought of abandoning her search, but it was beginning to look as if she had no choice—not if she wanted there to be a world left for the child to live in. A better world, one that wasn't infested by Umbrella's foul creations.

"There was a young girl with me when I arrived in D.C.," Alice said.

"Becky. Yes, I know."

Alice felt a surge of hope. "Can you show me where she is?"

"I'm sorry, but I haven't detected any sign of her since the battle at the White House."

Alice's burgeoning hope shriveled and died. She told herself that just because the Red Queen hadn't seen Becky, it didn't mean the girl was dead. Yes, the Red Queen had access to a surveillance satellite, along with whatever technology still operated in the city, but the AI wasn't all-seeing. Becky could be hiding somewhere. Still, Alice couldn't help finding the Red Queen's words demoralizing.

"I can continue to search for her while you travel. If I locate her, I will attempt to make contact and direct her to a safe location where she can wait for your return."

If I return, Alice thought. If she took on this mission, she knew there were no guarantees she'd survive it. But then, there never were.

"Okay," Alice said. "It's a deal."

Despite her words, Alice wasn't certain she was

ready for this, physically or emotionally. Her body had yet to recover from the strain of her powers being returned and then removed in such a short period of time. But more than that, her spirit was tired. She'd been manipulated by Umbrella and its personnel ever since the moment she'd awoken in that house in Raccoon City, with no memory of who she was or how she'd gotten there. That had been a decade ago, and since then she'd done nothing but fight for her survival, losing friends and allies along the way. After so many years and so much loss, did she have it in her to go into battle against Umbrella one last time?

She didn't have to think long before she had her answer.

Hell, yes.

Alice headed for the door.

"Alice."

Alice paused on the threshold of the bunker and looked back over her shoulder at the Red Queen.

"Ten years ago in the Hive... we both failed. We let this happen. Make it right."

Alice nodded, and then a thought occurred to her. "I don't suppose you have a fueled-up aircraft stashed nearby that I can use?"

"I'm afraid not."

Alice sighed. "That's what I figured."

She'd just have to see what she could scrounge up—as usual.

* * *

Alice eased her foot off the gas, and the Honda slowed. She'd done her best to keep the car's speed up since leaving D.C., but sometimes that wasn't possible. In the world A.U. (After Umbrella), long stretches of highway were empty of obstructions— no abandoned vehicles, no overturned semis—but other areas were practically parking lots of clusters of wrecked vehicles, and she was forced to reduce her speed. She approached one such stretch now. Cars and trucks were scattered at awkward angles across Route 70's three lanes, all of the vehicles displaying various degrees of damage, the result of an obvious chain-reaction accident. There was no way to know what had caused it. Someone trying to get an infected loved one to a hospital only to have them turn and attack while the car was in motion. Or maybe a pack of Undead had wandered onto the highway in search of prey. Whatever had happened here, it had taken place long ago. The vehicles showed signs of rust, and their tires had rotted away.

As Alice steered the Honda through the maze of destruction, she saw that some of the vehicles were empty, doors hanging open and windows smashed. She guessed the occupants had been removed by hungry Undead, and she hoped they'd been dead or unconscious when they'd been taken. Other vehicles remained sealed, drivers still behind the wheel, passengers buckled into their seats, decayed and grotesque forms that looked no different from the Undead, except that they didn't move.

She made it past the pile-up and accelerated once more. Seeing the dead trapped in their vehicles made her think of what the Red Queen had told her. There were less than five thousand humans still alive on a planet that had been home to seven billion. For all intents and purposes, the human race was practically extinct as it was. Even if she managed to reach the Hive, find the airborne antidote, and release it, was it already too late? Could the human race successfully repopulate the world when there were so few of them left, scattered across the world with no way to easily travel? She didn't know. But if humanity was to have any chance at survival, it lay with the antivirus and her ability to get hold of it before the deadline was up.

She checked her watch and saw there were thirty-eight hours, twenty-four minutes left. She was making good time, even if she had to slow down occasionally.

She approached a large road sign, green with white letters and numbers.

INDIANAPOLIS 116 MILES

CHICAGO 296 MILES

ST. LOUIS 359 MILES

RACCOON CITY 425 MILES

This was the first sign she'd seen that listed Raccoon City, and she smiled. She was halfway there, and at the rate she was going, she'd be there in another six hours, maybe seven. Encouraged, she pressed down on the accelerator. Too bad there weren't any radio stations left. It would be nice to have some music to drive to.

Back in D.C., Alice had chosen the Honda because it had been the least damaged vehicle she could find. The battles that had taken place in the former capital over the years had done a number on any cars that had been left out in the open, and while the Honda might've been lacking in the style department, at the end of the world, beggars couldn't be choosers. The car's battery had been long dead, and she hadn't been able to find a replacement, so she'd been forced to jury-rig a solar panel to the roof to power the battery. One thing about surviving on her own for so long: she'd picked up a lot of different skills, along with learning how to improvise. The Honda's trunk and backseat were filled with gas cans so she wouldn't have to stop and look for fuel along the way, and a cloth bag containing food and water bottles sat on the passenger seat next to her. She'd also scored a package of caffeine pills from an abandoned pharmacy, for which she was profoundly grateful, as the last coffee shop in the world had closed a decade ago.

Alice had embedded the combat knife into the dash so she could reach it more easily. Next to it was a bobblehead figure, some athlete she didn't recognize. She'd considered removing the figure when she'd first found the car, but she'd decided to keep it. She had a long drive ahead of her, and she could use the company.

The hardest part of the drive wasn't staying awake, though. It was trying not to be overwhelmed with despair by the wasteland that America had become. The cities were bad enough—empty streets, silent buildings... the ruins of the old world. But the T-virus hadn't just affected humans—somehow it had gotten into the ecosystem itself, drying up rivers and lakes, killing plants and trees, and transforming fertile farmland into desert. A once-living, vital world had been reduced to little more than a sad, desiccated corpse. She'd thought she'd gotten used to the desolate landscape long ago, but now she saw it through different eyes. Even if she made it to the Hive and somehow managed to find and release the antivirus, how could it possibly reverse the damage done to the planet itself? Would she save humanity only to see the remaining survivors die off because they'd inherited a world no longer able to sustain life?

She decided she couldn't worry about that right now. She needed to concentrate on her mission. Once Umbrella was stopped and the antivirus was released, then she could worry about humanity's prospects for long-term survival. Right now, what she needed to do was drive.

She didn't see many Undead as she drove, and the ones she did spot were a long way off. A couple were closer to the highway, and one jumped out at the Honda from behind a wrecked paramedic vehicle as she detoured slowly around it. But it was a garden-variety Undead, slow-moving and awkward—and thankfully, with only two eyes—and she had no trouble avoiding it.

Alice continued driving, and after a while, she noticed the gas gauge needle was hovering on empty. A few more miles, and she'd need to stop to refuel. She'd keep an eye out for a good spot to pull over, and if it looked safe enough, she might even take a few minutes to do some stretching exercises. Sitting behind the wheel for so many hours after everything she'd gone through in D.C. had left her muscles feeling stiff and sore.

The road ahead of her was covered with a thin layer of dust. Nothing special about that, as the wind often blew dry, loose soil onto the highway, and it wasn't as if there was any regular traffic passing through to blow it off. There was an overpass ahead, and clustered in front of it was a collection of burnt-out vehicles, the result of another long-ago accident. Among the cluster of vehicles was an abandoned semi-trailer, the kind that was used to haul heavy equipment. It was empty, and no truck was attached. Alice assumed that at some point in the past, the driver reached the mass of burnt and blackened vehicles, realized it would be too difficult to go around with the semi-trailer attached, unhooked it, and drove the truck around the wreckage.

She was doing eighty, and she lifted her foot off the accelerator. But before the Honda could begin to slow, the car juddered as it rolled over something hard, and then all four tires blew. Alice fought for control of the Honda as it began to slide sideways, but there was nothing she could do. Whatever she'd hit, it had reduced the vehicle's tires to shreds, and the best she could hope for was to keep the car from flipping over and rolling. Normally an icy calm descended on her in situations like this, but this time she was close to full panic. If she died now, so did the human race—and Becky. She had to live so they could, too.

A flash of orange caught her eye then, and she realized the Honda was heading for the semi-trailer's front end, which was approximately at the same level as her head. Alice had on the seatbelt, but now she took her hands off the steering wheel, unbuckled the belt, and then ducked down, twisting to press the upper part of her body against the passenger seat as the Honda struck the semi-trailer's front end head-on. A sudden impact jolted the vehicle, accompanied by a shriek of tearing metal. Alice grabbed hold of the passenger seatbelt with her right hand and gripped the front edge of the passenger seat with her left, and held on for all she was worth as the Honda continued sliding across the asphalt until it slammed into a fire-blackened transit bus and came to an abrupt stop.

Alice lay on the passenger seat, breathing rapidly, ears ringing in the sudden silence following the awful sounds of screeching tires and twisting metal. The gas cans in the back seat had been thrown around during the crash, and some of them had leaked, filling the air with the acrid tang of spilled fuel. She'd been lucky that a spark hadn't set off an explosion. After several seconds she let go of the belt, released her grip on the seat, and sat up, taking stock of her physical condition as she did so. She was sore as hell, but she didn't think she was seriously injured. But even if she had been, she wouldn't have remained in the car. If there were any Undead in the area, the noise from the crash would be like a ringing dinner bell for them. Any number of the creatures could be converging on her, and the Honda's tires hadn't spontaneously blown, not all at once, which meant that something—or someone—had caused it to happen.

Time to get moving.

She crawled out of the Honda, or rather what was left of it, wincing as her body complained. She glanced back at the dashboard. The bobblehead was gone, but the combat knife was still embedded in the dash, and she pulled it free. She had a feeling she was going to need it.

Gripping the knife, she quickly scanned the area, prepared to fight if she had to, but she saw no sign of a threat. She didn't fully relax her guard, though. She wasn't stupid. She checked her watch then, and was relieved to see that it was still working, but the digital countdown reminded her that she was losing time with every passing second. She needed a new set of wheels—*now*.

Speaking of which...

She gave the Honda's shredded tires a quick look to see if she could figure out what had happened to them. Her best guess was that she'd hit a spike strip that someone had placed across the road and which had been concealed by dirt, maybe purposely. A look backward at the highway confirmed her guess. Sharp metal spikes rose upward from the road, gleaming in the sunlight. The strip had most likely been set up as a trap for any survivors who might be driving this way. The question was, how long ago had it been put here? If the spike strip had been in place for a while, then whoever had placed it here was probably long gone, and most likely dead by now. But if it had been placed here recently, whoever had done it might be lurking nearby, waiting to see if anyone had survived the crash before venturing out to examine what the trap had caught. Alice would have to keep a sharp eye out while she searched for a vehicle to replace the Honda.

Not that it looked like there was much to choose from here. All the vehicles she could see were burnt-out wrecks, just so much junk blocking the road. She started walking toward the overpass, hoping that there might be some undamaged vehicles on the other side, abandoned by their owners because they'd been attacked or had simply run out of fuel. Gas wouldn't be a problem for her. Some of the fuel containers in the Honda's back seat were still intact, and she hadn't checked the ones in the trunk yet. She—

Her thoughts broke off as she saw the silhouette of a motorcycle parked in the shadows beneath the overpass. From what she could see, it appeared undamaged, and she jogged toward it, ignoring the protests of her bruised and battered body. As she drew closer, she was able to see the bike more clearly, and once she did, she stopped and stared. The bike was a BMW, and it was painted black and red.

Umbrella colors.

Before she could react, a half-dozen black-uniformed Umbrella troopers emerged from hiding places in and around the wrecked vehicles, faces disguised by goggles and breathing masks. They wore black helmets with the Umbrella logo on the front and carried CTAR-21 assault rifles—which they immediately pointed at her. Her knife wasn't any defense against the rifles, and she knew it, but she raised it anyway, as a warning for the troopers not to come any closer, a warning which they ignored as they stepped toward her. Reflexively, Alice took a step back and felt something tighten around her feet. The next thing she knew, her legs were yanked out from underneath her, and she was pulled into the air. She'd walked into a wire snare, as the troopers had no doubt planned.

The sudden motion caused her to lose her grip on the knife, and it clattered to the ground beneath her. She reached for it, but she was too high up and couldn't get hold of it.

Idiot! she thought, furious with herself. She couldn't believe she'd been dumb enough to walk into a trap, and such a simple one at that. She'd been so concerned with reaching the Hive before time ran out that she'd hadn't paid enough attention to her surroundings. And her carelessness might just get her—and as a consequence, every other human left alive on the planet—killed.

A trooper stepped forward then and with his rifle's strap still slung around his shoulder, he slammed the butt of the weapon into Alice's stomach. Breath *whooshed* out of her lungs, and she started swinging back and forth like a pendulum. She gritted her teeth against the pain.

"That all you got?" she said.

She couldn't see the trooper's features behind the goggles and breathing mask, but she could tell by the way his body tensed that she'd pissed him off by her failure to be intimidated by him when she was so obviously their helpless captive. He stepped forward to strike Alice again, but this time she was ready for him. She jack-knifed upward and used her momentum to headbutt the soldier. The maneuver hurt like hell, but it caused the man to stagger back, just as she wanted.

She swung forward, grabbed hold of the soldier with one arm and snatched his weapon with her free hand. She was still upside down and the rifle was still slung over the trooper's shoulder, but that didn't prevent her from wielding the weapon. She pointed it at one of the man's fellow troopers and began firing. Blood sprayed from the second trooper's chest and his body shuddered and jerked from the bullets' impact. Alice kept firing, letting the rifle's recoil spin her around so she could attack the remaining troopers. She used the man whose gun she'd "borrowed" as a shield, so while some of his companions managed to return fire, instead of hitting Alice, they took out their fellow trooper for her.

By the time Alice had made a complete revolution, all of the troopers—including the one who'd struck her—were dead. Now that her shield had served his purpose, she let him go. As he dropped lifeless to the ground, she held onto his rifle, pulling it free from his shoulder. She then aimed the weapon up at the snare, whose other end she could now see was attached to the bottom of the overpass, and fired a quick burst. The wire was cut in half, and she fell to the ground. She quickly unwrapped the wire from around her ankles, and then—keeping watch in case the troopers had more friends who might suddenly jump out from their hiding places—she stripped the dead troopers of their weapons.

As she did so, she smiled grimly.

Big mistake, guys, she thought. *Just because I don't have super powers anymore doesn't mean I can't kick ass.*

She scored several rifles, all their extra clips, and she retrieved her knife. She slung the rifles over her shoulder, tucked the clips away in the pockets of her body armor, and slid the knife into her boot sheath. She then headed toward the motorcycle. She wasn't thrilled about riding an Umbrella vehicle, but if it got her to the Hive in time, she wasn't going to cry about it. She climbed onto the bike and hit the ignition switch. The first thing she wanted to do was check how much fuel the tank held, but as the digital display on the dash activated, she saw the words UNAUTHORIZED HANDPRINT.

Crap.

Before she could throw herself off the bike, the vehicle's security system emitted a powerful burst

4

From somewhere deep in the dark of her inner mind, Alice became aware of a rocking, swaying motion. Wherever she was, the air was warm and stuffy, and it stank of unwashed bodies, piss, and shit. She forced her eyes to open, but the light was so dim that at first she feared she'd been blinded. Her vision adjusted quickly, and she soon realized she was inside some sort of vehicle, sitting on the floor, her back against the wall. But what caught her attention were the hundreds of crucifixes hanging from chains affixed to the ceiling. Some of the crosses were plain wood, while others were ornamental gold. It looked like someone had looted the contents of a dozen different churches. The crosses swayed with the movement of the vehicle, striking each other with soft clicking and clanking sounds, like a bizarre set of wind chimes.

She shifted her body to get a sense of how injured she might be, and was rewarded with a metallic clinking sound. Her hands were locked in a pair of electronic manacles. She tried to stand and discovered she was held in place by a high-tensile chain with an electronic lock attached to a wide leather belt fastened to her waist. There were other people with her in the vehicle, and they were manacled and chained, too, like slaves in an ancient galley ship. It was difficult to make out many details of her fellow passengers in the gloom, but she could tell there were eight of them, both men and women, and they were all in a wretched state: bodies emaciated; hair long, tangled, and matted, the men unshaven; clothes little more than filthy rags. They displayed various injuries—scars, missing eyes, hands that had been broken and left to heal improperly.

She checked her watch then. 18:17:42. She'd lost valuable time.

"Damn it," she muttered to herself.

She turned to the man sitting next to her. While everyone in the hold was suffering from malnutrition, this man was the worst of the lot. He looked like a skeleton that had been painted in flesh tones.

"What is this place?" she asked.

The Thin Man didn't speak or look at her, and she wasn't sure he'd heard her. As sick as he looked, he might not be fully conscious, she realized.

A woman sitting across from Alice spoke in a whisper.

"Be quiet, please. *He* doesn't like us to talk. He punishes us..."

As if to demonstrate the truth of the woman's words, the Thin Man turned to Alice and opened his mouth to show that he no longer possessed a tongue.

Alice felt a twist of nausea in her gut at the sight of the man's mutilation, followed quickly by a surge of anger.

"Who did this? Who punishes you?" she demanded.

"Just be quiet," the woman pleaded again.

A man with one ear cut off leaned out of the shadows and looked at the woman. "Let her talk," he said. "Let her be the one chosen next."

Another man, this one with deep scars cut into his face, spoke then, an almost religious fervor in his voice. "Yes! Let *him* cast her out!"

"Please," the woman begged. "Please be quiet!"

A hatch opened in the ceiling then, spilling light into the hold's filthy interior. A moment later, an Umbrella officer dropped down to stand on a metal walkway slightly elevated above the prisoners. They quickly averted their gazes, and Alice could see that they weren't just intimidated by the man—they were terrified of him.

Alice squinted up at the man, trying to get a good look at him, but because he was backlit by sunlight, she couldn't make out his facial features. He was dressed in black, like the troopers that had attacked her, but his head and face weren't covered, and around his neck hung a variety of crosses and religious icons, with a large hunting knife was strapped to his thigh. Alice thought of the prisoner with the scarred face and knew the poor man was an example of the blade's work.

The man in black spoke softly.

"Silence... silence..."

He dropped down into the hold then, his back to Alice, so she still couldn't see his face. But there was something strangely familiar about his voice, and it gave her an uneasy feeling. The man continued speaking in a soft, calm tone as he went on.

"A fool's mouth is his sin. And his lips are a snare to his soul."

He turned to the woman who'd begged everyone to be quiet, knelt down, and grabbed her roughly by the face.

"Shall I save your soul? Cut your lips away?"

He squeezed her lips between his fingers until they bled.

"Please..." the woman begged. "*Please...*"

The man leaned his face closer to hers. "Bring unto me the sinners. Are you a sinner?"

"No..." The woman tried to shake her head, but the man held her lips too tight for her to do so.

"A dirty, dirty sinner. I think you are." The man was practically cooing now. He let go of the woman's lips and put his hand down the front of her ragged blouse. "A dirty, filthy, little whore."

The woman had remained still while the officer spoke to her, but this violation was more than she could take. Almost as a reflex, she raised her manacled hands and shoved him away. The motion had little strength behind it, but the officer was infuriated by her meager show of resistance. After giving one of the woman's breasts a final squeeze, he withdrew his hand from her blouse, and when he next spoke, his voice was cold as arctic ice.

"Now *that*—that was a mistake."

He grabbed her right hand, and the woman squealed in fear.

"No! Mercy, please! *Mercy!*"

"If thy right hand offends thee—"

With his free hand, he slid the hunting knife from its sheath and held the blade in front of the woman's face.

"—cut it off," he finished.

"No," Alice said, keeping her tone even, almost conversational.

The officer responded without turning to face her.

"What was that?" he asked.

"Matthew 5:30. You misquoted. If you're going to use it, at least get it right."

There was a pause, and when the man replied, Alice could hear the mocking smile in his voice.

"So you're awake at last."

Still holding the hunting knife, the man stood and turned toward Alice, finally giving her a good look at his features as the light streaming in from the open hatch lit his face.

It was Dr. Alexander Isaacs.

Alice was so shocked that for a moment she couldn't speak.

"I killed you," she said at last.

Isaacs smiled at Alice, and then a realization hit her.

"A clone... I killed your clone."

His smile broadened, but there was no mirth in his eyes. "I'd like to think you wouldn't have been as successful against the genuine article."

Alice held up her manacled hands to him. "Why don't you release me and we can find out?"

Isaacs laughed.

"You've been most troublesome to me. You and your sisters." He walked to an overhead storage locker. "I've taken great pleasure in hunting down the final few."

He slid the metal locker door open to reveal the severed heads of four Alice clones, two of them badly decomposed, the other two relatively fresh kills. Isaacs smiled at the grisly trophies before turning back to look at Alice.

"And now I have you."

Alice stared at the clones' faces. Umbrella might have created them, but she'd been the one to wake and release them—along with many others—so they could join her in the battle against Umbrella. And now here they were, dead by Isaacs' hand. Her gaze fell to the hunting knife in his grip, and she wondered if he'd used the weapon to separate the clones' heads from their bodies. Probably.

"The cleansing operation should have finished over a year ago," Isaacs said. "But you slowed us down. So much so that I was obliged to take command personally. And I don't like being out in the field. I find it too... unpredictable."

Alice would've liked nothing more than to break free of her manacles, snatch the knife from Isaacs' hand, and slice the blade across his throat. But the human race had only eighteen hours left to live, and that's where her focus had to be, even if it meant trying to rationalize with a madman. She'd make a deal with Satan himself in order to release the antivirus.

"You could end all this," Alice said. "Why don't you?"

Isaacs' brow furrowed in puzzlement, and his gaze sharpened, as if he were trying to see into Alice's mind.

"I could end it? Interesting. What exactly do you know? Someone told you something, didn't they?"

Alice didn't reply.

Isaacs smiled once more. "You'll be begging to tell me soon enough."

He slammed his fist against the metal wall of the hold, once, twice, three times, building a rhythm. He continued pounding the wall as he addressed the other prisoners.

"She's an Unbeliever! And what do we do with Unbelievers?"

The prisoners began chanting along with the rhythm, most reluctantly but some—like One Ear and Scars—with enthusiasm, the chant building until it became deafening.

"Cast her out! Cast her out! *Cast her out!*"

* * *

Alice ran.

Her hands were still manacled, and the cable attached to the belt around her waist stretched to the military transport vehicle ahead of her. The cable wasn't taut, so she held the slack in her right hand to keep her feet from getting caught in it. The transport was moving slow enough for her to keep up, but just barely. But she wasn't alone. Following close behind her was an army of Undead. There were tens—maybe hundreds—of thousands. The ones nearest Alice snapped and snarled, swiping the air in desperate attempts to catch hold of her to momentarily sate their never-ending hunger. But the transport set a pace that was too fast for the Undead to catch her, but only just.

The vehicle rolled down the center of the highway, and the horde of Undead that followed behind it stretched off into the distance farther than the eye could see. But Isaacs' transport wasn't the only one. A second equally large army of Undead swarmed on the other side of the highway, led by another running prisoner attached to the vehicle by a cable.

We're bait, Alice thought. Lures used by Umbrella to control and move vast armies of the Undead across the country. Now she understood why the other prisoners in the transport's hold had been so frail-looking. They were forced to take turns running behind the vehicle to keep the Undead following. And that was why Umbrella had set up the trap at the overpass which had caught her. They needed fresh meat.

The Undead that comprised the two hordes were old ones, skin gray and mottled, features eaten away by time and the elements, as if they were statues whose outer layer of stone had been eroded. Many were missing ears, noses, and lips, and the feet of those without shoes had been worn to nubs from their travels. Their clothes were tattered and caked with dirt and old blood, turning them an almost uniform gray. And the stench rising from the mass of Undead bodies was like nothing Alice had ever experienced before—and given the number of Undead and mutant monstrosities she'd fought and killed over the years, she was no stranger to foul odors. It was as if a pit to Hell had opened up, releasing the combined stink of billions of flayed, rotting bodies along with bubbling pools of sulphur. One good thing about it: the stench would probably destroy her olfactory sense before long, and she wouldn't have to smell it anymore. But as bad as the smell was, the sounds the Undead made were worse. Moaning, snarling, hissing, keening, growling, all merging into a chorus of hunger, desire, and death. Alice had experienced nightmares like this many times over the years—running from an army of ravenous Undead, eager to feast on her flesh. Now her nightmare had come true.

She was tired, weak, and sore, but she couldn't afford to slow down, not even a little—not unless she wanted to feel hundreds of teeth tearing into her. She tried not to think about the thousands of Undead pursuing her. Instead, she concentrated on putting one foot in front of the other and not tripping. Because if she fell, the Undead would make sure she never got up again.

A hatch on top of the transport vehicle opened, and Isaacs appeared, along with an Umbrella trooper. Alice assumed the trooper was there to protect Isaacs in case the Undead managed to get too close to the vehicle. The two men stepped up onto the roof and walked to the back railing, where Isaacs looked down at Alice.

"You know, I didn't even look at the Good Book before all of this. I thought it was for the simple-minded, the easily led. Never once thought it applied to me. How wrong can a man be?"

He then looked past Alice to gaze upon the horde trailing after her.

"The Lord used a flood to cleanse the Earth. Forty days and forty nights of rain. Our method has taken a little longer, but the result will be the same. A world ready for the righteous and pure to inherit."

Alice felt a sudden wave of dizziness hit her, and she stumbled. On either side of her, lengths of bloody chain dragged behind the transport, reminders of those prisoners who'd preceded her, weakened, fallen, and been devoured by the horde. She almost went down, but the sight of those chains fueled her determination to survive, and she forced the dizziness back with an act of sheer will and managed to stay on her feet. If Isaacs noticed her almost falling, he gave no indication. He continued speaking as if nothing had happened.

"We reach Raccoon City in just over twelve hours. I

doubt even you can run for that long. I want to know what you know."

Isaacs waited for her to respond, but she only glared at him. If her mouth hadn't been so dry, she'd have spit at him to show her defiance.

Isaacs met her gaze for a moment before breaking eye contact. He turned to the trooper. "Tell me when she's ready to talk."

Isaacs headed back inside the transport, leaving Alice to keep running.

* * *

Wesker sat before a bank of monitors showing live satellite feeds from around the world. He was surrounded by high-tech equipment lit by fluorescent lights hanging overhead, but beyond the lights, the uneven stone features of a large natural cavern were hidden in shadowy gloom. The cavern's cool damp air suited Wesker. The T-virus surging through his system often made him feel too warm, almost feverish, and he felt more comfortable here.

He was pleased by what he saw on the monitors. Everything was going precisely according to—

One of the satellite feeds was replaced by the image of an Asian man in his mid-thirties.

Wesker nodded. "Commander Lee."

Lee nodded back, then called over his shoulder. *"Sir, I have Chairman Wesker for you."*

Lee stepped away from the screen, and Alexander Isaacs appeared. Wesker, as always, kept his face impassive, but inside he was irritated by this interruption.

"Dr. Isaacs," Wesker said by way of greeting.

Isaacs gave Wesker a cat-that-ate-the-canary smile.

"Look what I found on the roadside."

A new image replaced Isaacs' face: Alice being pulled behind an Umbrella transport vehicle, an army of Undead following close behind her. Wesker stared, unable to believe what he was seeing.

"Impossible," he said.

Isaacs reappeared on the monitor. *"It would appear your mission to Washington was less successful than you made out. I hope you didn't leave any other loose ends."*

Despite the cavern's coolness, Wesker's temperature began to rise, and he felt a familiar itching all over his body which indicated his control over the T-virus was slipping. He'd never been able to fully master it, but recently it had begun to feel as if the virus was fighting him for control of his body, as if it had a mind of its own. A ludicrous notion, he knew, but it was one he couldn't easily dismiss. He concentrated on maintaining his body's cellular stability as Isaacs continued speaking.

"And there's something else. I think she knows about the airborne antivirus."

"How could that be? Only the High Command has that information."

"I don't know. Yet. But we caught her on the road to Raccoon City. Why else would she be headed there?"

"If she knows about the antivirus, there may be others."

"Yes. Raise the security level at the Hive to maximum. No one in or out. I'll let you know when she talks."

Isaacs ceased transmission and the monitor screen

went blank. Wesker caught a crimson flicker of light out of the corner of his eye, and he turned to see the Red Queen's holographic image floating in the air next to him.

"You heard him. Security level to maximum."

"As you wish," the Red Queen said.

Wesker turned in his chair to face two cryostasis tanks occupying a commanding position in the center of the room. Inside each tank was the shadowy figure of a human form, and a single wheelchair sat in front.

"Should we wake them?" Wesker asked.

"My instructions are to do so only in the greatest of emergencies."

Wesker considered the matter. Alice still lived, but she no longer had her powers, and she was Isaacs' captive. Wesker had no illusions, though. He knew that as long as she was alive, she was still a threat. But it seemed that threat was contained—for the moment.

"Very well. We'll wait."

* * *

Gray nibbled at the edges of Alice's vision, and she knew she couldn't keep up this forced march much longer. Still, she concentrated on breathing regularly, timing her breaths with the rhythm of her feet pounding on the highway's surface. Breathe in—two, three, four. Breathe out—two, three, four. She felt a tingling sensation on the back of her neck, and she dodged to the side as a male Undead made a grab for her. He was fresher than most in the horde, his skin still flesh-colored in a number of places, and he showed fewer signs of rot than the others. Because he was fresher, he was stronger, faster, and he'd been able to force his way to the front of the pack and catch up with Alice.

As she avoided the Undead, she quickly glanced at the countdown display on her watch.

16:11:12

The Undead snarled and made another lunge for her, but instead of evading him this time, she let him take hold of her. Before he could sink his teeth into her, she wrapped the slack of her chain around his neck, and with a single savage motion used it to snap his spinal column. The Undead shuddered once and went limp. Still running, Alice quickly unwrapped the chain and let the dead creature fall to the ground, where his body was soon trampled by hundreds more Undead.

Alice knew she couldn't keep going like this. Time was running out, and she had to do something if she was to have any hope of reaching the Hive before it was too late. She would have to do her best to stay alive and on her feet, and hope a chance for escape would soon present itself. She had learned over the years that there was *always* a chance, no matter how slight, and when it came this time, she'd be ready.

Breathe in—two, three, four. Breathe out—two, three, four.

* * *

Conditions were much better in the crew cabin of the transport than in the hold, but there was still a squalid, cramped desperation there. Too many personnel in too small a space. Despite this—or perhaps to counter it—Isaacs stood shaving in front of a jagged piece of mirror affixed to the cabin wall, a trooper standing next to him holding a metal bowl of water and a small dingy towel draped over one arm. Isaacs used a straight razor, and while it was more difficult to work with than an electric one—especially when the transport was moving—he rather enjoyed the discipline required to wield it effectively. A sharp eye, a steady hand, calm nerves... He knew that the men and women in the cabin likely found his attention to personal hygiene at this moment somewhat puzzling, if not outright eccentric. He didn't expect them to understand, though. They were only tools he was using to fulfill God's will, little different than the thousands of Undead they led across the desolate wasteland that had once been America. So let them stare and wonder at his sanity. He was the only truly sane one here, and when the End of the World finally arrived—as it would when they reached Raccoon City—he, for one, intended to look his best.

"We have an obstruction up ahead," Commander Chu said.

Isaacs turned toward Chu, who stood at the transport's helm, looking out the windshield past the driver. Isaacs was in charge of this operation, but this was Commander Chu's vehicle, and he ran a tight ship. He was a skilled warrior, and the troopers under his command both respected and feared him. Isaacs found Chu to be a competent officer, and he was glad to have the man at the helm, even if he did have a tendency to act above his station at times.

Isaacs stopped shaving. He took the towel from his assistant—a female trooper with a broad face and short brown hair—and quickly wiped the last of the shaving foam from his chin, and then, still holding the razor, he made his way to the front of the vehicle to stand next to Chu. Through the windshield, Isaacs saw two crashed vehicles up ahead partially blocking the highway.

"Go through it," Isaacs said. He wasn't going to allow anything to slow them down, not when they were so close to seeing God's will done.

"Slow by twenty percent," Chu told the driver. He then raised his voice to address the entire crew. "Brace for impact!"

The driver hastened to do her commander's bidding while everyone else found handholds to steady themselves.

Isaacs watched the crashed vehicles loom large as the transport approached, idly scraping the razor across a section of his cheek that he'd already shaved. The transport began to slow, and there would be a hard jolt as it broke through the obstruction. Either of those factors would give the Undead pursuing Alice a chance to catch up to her. Once the transport was past the crashed vehicles, Isaacs would go check on her. He wondered if there would be a third bloody chain dragging on the ground to join the two already there. He certainly hoped so. He smiled as he drew the razor across his cheek again, this time nicking himself and bringing forth a bead of bright-red blood.

He didn't notice.

* * *

At first, Alice didn't recognize that the transport was slowing down, but when she realized that there was more slack to her chain, she understood what was happening. Something was making the crew slow the vehicle, most likely some sort of obstacle on the road ahead. She didn't care what the exact reason for their slowing down was, though. All that mattered was her chance had finally come. She looked up at the trooper Isaacs had tasked with guarding her. The man was still watching her, but if she was right about why the transport had slowed...

Suddenly there was a loud crash of metal striking metal, and the transport juddered from the impact. The trooper was knocked off balance, and he turned his head toward the front of the vehicle to see what had happened.

This was Alice's cue.

Still holding onto her chain, she ran toward the transport as fast as she could. She managed to make it around the vehicle's left side just as the trooper turned back to check on her. There was an access ladder on the side of the transport, and Alice grabbed hold of one of the rungs, and swung her legs upward until she was hanging upside down.

Come on, she urged mentally. *Come on...*

An instant later, Alice saw the trooper's narrow face as he peered over the side of the transport. He had dark hair and several days' worth of stubble. He didn't see her at first, so he leaned over a bit more, bringing him within range. Alice delivered a savage kick to his face, knocking the man off balance and causing him to tumble over the railing and off the vehicle. He attempted to land on his feet, but he hit the road too hard, too off center, and there was a loud cracking sound as his right leg snapped. The man cried out in pain as he fell onto his side and rolled to a stop. A dozen Undead broke from the pack and ran toward him, picking up speed as their hunger kicked into overdrive at the sight of stationary prey. The man had managed to hold onto his gun as he'd fallen, and he raised the weapon and began firing, but it did no good. He didn't land any headshots, and even if he had, there were far too many Undead for him to kill. He screamed as the rotting creatures fell upon him, but he didn't scream for long.

At least it was fast, Alice thought. And then she put the dead trooper out of her mind as she righted herself and climbed up onto the transport's roof. Step One was accomplished. Now for Step Two.

* * *

After dabbing away the blood from the cut on his cheek, Isaacs stood admiring his clean-shaven face in the mirror fragment when he heard the sound of gunfire coming from outside. He scowled. What was the man firing at? Had Alice been caught by the Undead and the fool had taken pity on the woman and put her out of her misery? If the trooper had done anything to lessen Alice's pain by so much as a fraction of a second, Isaacs would bring the full force of his wrath down on the idiot until the man begged for death's sweet release.

Isaacs turned to the closest trooper, the woman who'd held the bowl of water while he'd shaved.

"Get up there and check it out," he said.

The woman gave him a quick nod, then headed to the access ladder that led to the roof. As she began to climb, Isaacs decided that if Alice was dead, he'd enjoy getting a chance to look at her corpse before the Undead completely consumed it. For old times' sake, if nothing else.

He started toward the ladder.

* * *

Alice listened to the *thump-thump-thump* of heavy boots as another trooper emerged from the transport's hatch and walked across the vehicle's roof. When she judged the trooper had gone past the ladder, she climbed up slowly so her chains would make as little noise as possible.

Alice saw the woman peering over the back of the transport, and as she turned, Alice abandoned all attempt at stealth and ran toward her.

"Sir!" the woman shouted. "She's—"

Alice reached the trooper and rammed both of her fists into the woman's face. The trooper's head snapped back. She staggered back two steps toward the rear railing, and tumbled over. Her left leg caught in the barrier, preventing her from hitting the ground. The woman had dropped her gun when she fell, and now she hung helpless as the front line of the Undead horde—emboldened by the sight of yet another easy meal—surged forward. The transport had yet to increase its speed after breaking through the obstacle on the highway, and the Undead had no trouble reaching the woman. She screamed as the Undead began to feed on her, and Alice turned away, having no desire to watch the trooper being torn apart.

Alice turned in the direction of the open hatch,

mind in overdrive as she tried to formulate her next move. But when she turned all the way around, she was startled to see Isaacs coming at her, hunting knife gripped tight in his hand, features contorted into a mask of pure hatred. He didn't hesitate. He moved in and attacked, swinging the blade with a skill and ease that Alice found surprising. She raised her manacled wrists and used the chain between them to catch his arm and prevent the knife from striking her. She intended to spin around and encircle his wrist with her chain, but he stepped back too quickly. Alice had already begun the maneuver, though, and as she pivoted, Isaacs slashed at her with the knife, managing to cut her across the right cheekbone. The wound wasn't deep, but it burned like fire, and Alice drew in a hissing breath. She spun around to defend herself against Isaacs' next attack, but the man moved too fast and, as exhausted as she was from running so long without food or water, she moved too slow.

Isaacs managed to cut her above her left breast and then followed this with a strike to her upper right arm. This last cut was deeper than the other two, and she gritted her teeth against the pain. Isaacs was proving to be a more formidable opponent than she'd expected, and she was beginning to think there was no way she could beat him as long as her hands were manacled. So, first things first.

She took a step back, pretending that the pain from the last cut was too much. Isaacs grinned and stepped forward, knife raised to finish her off. But as he brought the blade down, she once more attempted to catch his arm in her chain, and this time she succeeded, wrapping the chain around his wrist and jerking it tight. In response, his hand flew open and he let go of the knife. Alice quickly released Isaacs' wrist, and snatched the knife out of the air before it could fall to the roof of the transport vehicle. Then, while Isaacs was still stunned by this sudden turn of events, she swiftly moved behind him, wrapped her manacle chain around his neck and pulled back hard. Not quite hard enough to snap his neck, but close.

"Open them!" she shouted.

Isaacs didn't respond, so she pulled tighter. He made a wet clicking sound, and she eased up on the pressure just a bit.

"All right," he said in a choking gasp.

He reached down toward his belt, and Alice increased the pressure on his neck once more—a warning in case he was reaching for a weapon. Instead he removed a small electronic key from a pouch there and raised it to the manacle around Alice's right wrist. When the key touched the manacle, the device emitted a soft tone and both cuffs clicked open and fell from Alice's wrists. In addition, the chain belted around her waist—along with the chain attached to it—also released and fell away. Now that she no longer had the manacle chain to control Isaacs, she quickly pressed the edge of the hunting knife to his neck. Isaacs stiffened, but he didn't move.

Smart man, she thought.

She had Isaacs neutralized—at least for the moment—and now she needed to figure out how she was going to get away. Isaacs and his crew might be heading to Raccoon City, but she wasn't about to hitch a ride with them. For one thing, they were moving too slow. For another, while she might have

Isaacs at knifepoint, the transport was filled with more Umbrella troopers who'd like nothing better than to put several hundred rounds in her. And then there were the twin armies of the Undead—one following this transport, and one trailing behind the second vehicle on the other side of the highway. She didn't particularly want to roll into town with several thousand ravenous walking corpses trailing behind.

She glanced over at the second transport, just as the gun turret atop it was swiveling in their direction.

Shit.

She grabbed hold of Isaacs' arm and shoved him down onto the roof. She threw herself down next to him as the second transport unleashed a hail of fifty-caliber bullets at them. She dragged Isaacs in a belly crawl toward a metal air intake on the far side of the transport, pulled him behind it, and pressed the knife to his side so he wouldn't be tempted to try anything. The intake was both large enough and sturdy enough to shield them from the fifty cals, but she knew it wouldn't hold up forever. She wasn't sure what had happened. Maybe the transport had security cameras on the roof, and the crew had radioed their sister vehicle and requested assistance. Or maybe the crew of the second transport had seen what was happening atop Isaacs' vehicle and had decided to lend a helping hand. Whichever the case, Alice was 'pinned down, and if she didn't think of something fast, she'd—

The gun turret of this transport now began to swivel around toward her and Isaacs. The air intake wouldn't block the guns' line of fire, and once Alice was in their sights, the fifty cals would tear her apart as if she were made of wet tissue paper.

Isaacs let out a joyous whoop.

"They have you now!" he crowed, his voice barely audible over the sound of fifty-caliber rounds striking the metal intake.

He seemed completely oblivious to the fact that he'd end up just as dead as she would. Maybe he was too crazy to care. Or maybe he believed that when he died, God would personally appear to carry his spirit to Heaven. As much as the idea of Isaacs' death appealed to her, she didn't want to have to die herself to see it happen. She still had work to do.

The air intake was located on the right of the roof, and Alice had a decent view of the transport's side. Four motorcycles exactly like the one that had zapped her hung mounted there. Who knows? One of them could've been the exact same bike.

Isaacs saw where she was looking.

"You can't use them! You can't escape!"

The second transport continued firing, and the turret of this transport had almost swung all the way around to bring its guns to bear on them. Alice knew she had only seconds before a hellstorm of fifty cals reduced her to splintered bone and shredded meat.

Time to leave.

She turned to Isaacs and raised her voice to be heard over the barrage of bullets coming from the second transport.

"Matthew 5:30—'If *thy* right hand offend thee'..." When Isaacs gave her a blank look, she added, "It's your own hand, asshole."

She raised the hunting knife, and with one clean blow severed Isaacs' right hand.

5

Isaacs cried out in pain as blood gushed from his newly created stump. Alice grabbed the hand before it could slide off the side of the truck, then she jammed the knife into her boot sheath, quickly hopped over the railing, and jumped down onto one of the motorcycles. She pressed the hand's index finger to the ignition trigger, and this time, instead of receiving an electric shock, she was rewarded with the sound of the bike's engine coming to life. Smiling grimly, she tossed the hand over her shoulder. Let the Undead have the damn thing. She didn't need it any longer. Her only regret was that she couldn't give them the rest of Isaacs as a main course to follow the appetizer she'd just lobbed to them.

At that moment, the transport's guns began to fire. Alice hit the quick release switch, and the metal clamp holding the motorcycle to the vehicle's side disengaged. The bike dropped and hit the ground hard, jarring Alice, but she managed to keep it upright. She gunned the engine, and the motorcycle leaped forward as if it were jet-propelled. Alice blew past the transport, and continued accelerating.

* * *

Isaacs sat with his back against the metal air intake, wrist stump pressed against his side in an attempt to staunch the bleeding. Both transports stopped firing, and a pair of troopers climbed up from the crew cabin and rushed toward Isaacs to offer him aid. But the pain of his injury was inconsequential compared to the inferno of rage that burned inside him.

"Kill her now!" he screamed. "I want her dead!"

* * *

Alice gunned the bike as the transport's turret swiveled to point its weapons forward once more. Ahead of her, the road was blocked with wrecks of abandoned vehicles. Alice steered the bike toward the closest wreck, hoping to use it as cover. She managed to reach it as the transport began firing at her. Fifty cals blasted into the metal of the wreck, but Alice remained unharmed. She knew she wouldn't stay that way unless she hauled ass, and so she kept the bike's speed dangerously high as she weaved between the debris. The transport continued firing, not bothering to detour around the abandoned vehicles but ramming them aside as it surged forward in pursuit of Alice. But after a few moments of this, the transport crew decided to stop fucking around.

Alice heard the *crack-whoosh* of a small missile launching, and she had just enough time to jerk the bike to the left before the projectile shot through the space she'd been occupying a second before. She watched as the missile flew onward to slam into a burned-out car with a fiery explosion. The impact launched the vehicle skyward, and as it tumbled back toward earth, wreathed in flame, Alice raced beneath it. The wreckage crashed to the ground behind her, but she didn't glance back to look at it. Instead, she leaned forward, face a mask of grim determination, and gave the bike everything the engine had. This section of highway was clear for the most part, and Alice raced on, soon outpacing the transport, leaving it and the Undead army it was leading far behind.

Next stop, Raccoon City.

* * *

Inside the transport's crew cabin, Isaacs hissed as one of the troopers applied a patch of Nu-Skin to his wrist stump. The trooper had asked if he wanted something to ease the pain, but Isaacs had declined. He *wanted* the procedure to hurt. Pain was a gift from God, a holy fire that burned away one's imperfections, cleansed the spirit, and purified the soul. It would fill his heart with molten fire, providing the necessary fuel to help him fulfill his final mission—*and* kill that fucking bitch Alice in the process.

The trooper finished applying the Nu-Skin and stepped back. Isaacs raised his stump close to his face so he could examine the repair. The Nu-Skin's color didn't match that of his own flesh, and it had the texture of old, worn leather. It wasn't pleasant to look at, but then the substance hadn't been created with aesthetics in mind.

Commander Chu turned away from the transport's control panel to face Isaacs. Normally the man was unflappable, but now he looked concerned, as if he were unsure what to say—or perhaps *how* to say it.

"Sir..." He hesitated before going on. "We've lost her."

Isaacs let Chu's words further stoke the fire raging within him.

After a moment with no response from Isaacs, during which Chu exchanged uncertain glances with his crew, he spoke once more.

"I can order some of our people to pursue her on motorcycles. And I can contact the commander of the other transport and—"

Staring at the smooth section of artificial skin where his hand had been attached to his wrist, Isaacs said, "No."

"No, sir?" Chu sounded more than surprised by Isaacs' response. He sounded incredulous.

"Let her think that she's beaten us," Isaacs said, focusing on the pain radiating up his arm. He was rather coming to enjoy the sensation. "We'll catch up to her in due course." He thought of the twin armies of Undead the two transports were leading. "*All* of us." He turned to Chu then, and smiled. "It's God's will. Can't you see that?"

Chu looked at him for a moment, equal amounts of fear and disgust in his gaze. But his voice betrayed no sign of his feelings as he answered.

"Of course, sir."

Chu turned back to the control panel, looking relieved to no longer be facing Isaacs, and ordered the driver to maintain their current speed and heading.

Isaacs was well aware of how Chu felt about him

right now, but it didn't matter. The man was but an instrument, useful only as long as he could help Isaacs do his holy work, and completely expendable once the job was complete.

Isaacs knew they had hours of travel still ahead of them, and he decided to pass the time by paying a return visit to the prisoners in the transport's hold. It might be interesting to see just how much damage he could do to them with only one hand to work with. Isaacs thought he'd be up to the challenge.

Softly, he began to sing the lyrics to one of his favorite hymns, "I See a Colored Stream."

"'I see a crimson stream of blood, it flows to Calvary. Its waves which reach the throne of God are sweeping over me.'"

The crew studiously avoided looking at him as he went to his shaving station, picked up his straight razor from the small shelf where he'd left it, and headed for the hold.

* * *

Wesker watched Alice's progress on a monitor via satellite feed. Out of all the problems he'd been forced to deal with over the last decade—Dania Cardoza being only the latest in a long line of them—Alice was the most persistent. He admired her, but in the way a hunter admires the capabilities of highly dangerous prey. She was coming for him, he knew that, but he wasn't afraid. He would bring her down, just as he had Dania and all the others. He was actually looking forward to a final reckoning with her. It was only a matter of time now.

As if reading his mind, the Red Queen appeared.

"Target is seventy-two miles and closing," she said.

Wesker thought he detected a subtle hint of excitement in the Red Queen's voice, but he knew that was impossible. She was an artificial intelligence, a staggeringly complex arrangement of hardware and software, one of the most advanced on the planet before the T-virus outbreak. But in the end, she was just a machine, and she possessed no true thoughts or feelings of her own.

Although sometimes he wondered...

"Lock down the Hive," he ordered. "Prepare for defensive measures. And alert our operative in Raccoon City."

* * *

Dania Cardoza walked toward Wesker, moving silently on the vari-rubber soles of her boots. She'd helped develop the material in her early days working for Umbrella, and while it ranked as one of her lesser achievements during her time in the corporation— it was hideously expensive to produce, so it never caught on—she was still proud of it. It adjusted to virtually any surface or temperature, providing steady footing at all times, and it made no sound, even if you stomped your feet as loudly as you could. It was this latter quality that she relied on now as she moved across the floor of Central Control toward where Wesker sat before a bank of monitor screens.

Dania was middle-aged, short, and on the stout side. Her black hair was threaded with gray, but she didn't bother to color it. Umbrella didn't care about gender, race, sexuality, appearance, or age. They only cared about one thing: results. In that sense, the corporation was the fairest organization she'd ever worked for—even if it was responsible for the destruction of the planet.

She carried a single weapon, a prototype sonic disrupter that had proven effective against the more powerful mutations created by the T-virus. And as Wesker was among the strongest of T-virus mutants, she hoped the weapon—which resembled a silver handgun with a parabolic reflector attached to the muzzle—would prove equally effective against him. She'd contributed to the device's design, of course, just as she'd contributed one way or another to just about every advance Umbrella had made in the last twenty years, whether technological or biological. But had she gotten recognition for her accomplishments? A promotion, or even a simple pat on the back, along with an appreciative 'You do good work, Dania'? No. Others got the credit and accolades. And more, they got the *power*, moving up in Umbrella's hierarchy, while Dania was left to toil anonymously in a lab.

The T-virus outbreak had changed that, though. As civilization began to collapse, opportunities presented themselves. Factions emerged within the corporation and internal power struggles began. Umbrella spent as much time dealing with these insurrections as they did dealing with the outer world as everything turned to shit. Dania, like others, decided to take advantage of the chaos to advance her position within the corporation. Unlike those others, however, she was a scientific genius—if she did say so herself—and she was able to use her intelligence to modify existing

Umbrella tech to develop new innovations in her campaign to seize as much power as she could. And in the process she'd discovered something about herself. She was as ruthless as any Umbrella employee, if not more so.

She'd done well over the years, working quietly and behind the scenes at first, eventually becoming more confident until she fully emerged from the shadows to take her place as one of the major players in Umbrella's civil war. She'd done well, too, and with each rival she defeated, she gained new followers, until she'd reached the point where she could challenge the notorious Albert Wesker himself. She'd had the resources to mount an attack on him in D.C., and despite appearances—and the unexpected interference from Project Alice—it had turned out exactly as she'd planned.

And now here she was, only moments away from eliminating Wesker and taking his place. She'd be the one to bring Umbrella's ultimate plan to fruition, and she'd be the one to help usher in the new age that would follow. She grinned. Not bad for a one-time lab rat.

Dania had another reason for wanting to see Wesker destroyed. Despite appearances, he was no longer human, and while he'd employed his mutant abilities in Umbrella's service, the future the corporation hoped to build had no place for such aberrations. Umbrella would have to destroy him sooner or later. She just intended to speed up the process a bit, that's all.

As she drew closer to Wesker, she found herself holding her breath. She'd taken precautions to prevent the all-seeing Red Queen from interfering. Around her right wrist she wore a masker, a device designed—by her, of course—to conceal the wearer from all electronic detection. The masker only jammed electronic signals; it didn't render the wearer literally invisible to anyone who might be present physically—and since it required a shitload of power to run, its battery charge lasted only a couple minutes at most. But that was okay. She didn't need it to work longer than that.

Her heart beat faster the closer she came to Wesker, and it sounded so loud in her ears that she thought he must be able to hear it, too. But he continued sitting before the bank of monitors, posture ramrod-straight as always, body so still he might have been a wax figure instead of a living being. It was that stillness of his which made her skin crawl whenever she was around him. It was so inhuman, like a coiled snake that at first glance appeared to be sleeping but was instead watching your every move, waiting to see if you were foolish enough to come within striking distance.

She was still holding her breath as she stepped up behind Wesker. She raised the sonic disrupter, pointed the parabolic reflector at the back of his head, and fired.

She wore specially designed earplugs, but even so, the sound that blasted forth from the weapon pierced her brain like a pair of red-hot metal spikes jammed into her ears. But the pain was a small price to pay for the magnificent sight of Wesker's head being torn apart by sonic waves and reduced to globs of red jelly that splattered onto the computer monitors and control console. She deactivated the sonic disruptor and lowered the weapon to her side. Physically, Dania's stomach turned at the sight of the bloody gobbets smeared across the electronic equipment, but emotionally she was elated. She'd done it! She'd defeated the vaunted Albert Wesker, the Umbrella Corporation's Biggest Bad. Now she would take his place and—

Her instincts screamed a warning then. Something was wrong, she could feel it, but she couldn't tell what... And then it came to her. Wesker's headless body still sat in his chair, his hands resting on the console. The body should've gone limp, slumped forward, or perhaps slid sideways out of the chair and fallen to the floor. And the neck should be a ragged stump that gushed blood, but flesh had sealed over the wound, leaving it smooth and undamaged.

"Oh no," Dania whispered.

Wesker's headless body then stood and turned toward her. In a blur, its right hand snatched the sonic disruptor from her with blinding speed, and crushed it as easily as if it had been made of balsa wood. The hand opened, allowing the pieces of the shattered weapon to fall to the floor. And then, impossibly, Wesker began to speak.

"I have complete control over my body, Dania. Did you really think I'd be foolish enough to keep my brain somewhere it was so easy to get at? It is spread throughout my entire body, and I've created multiple chemical backups of my memory that are stored in different organs. I am almost impossible to kill."

His voice was muffled somewhat, and it seemed to be coming from the center of his body. A second later, Dania learned why when Wesker's hand unzipped the front of his black uniform to reveal a vertical seam running from his throat to his navel. It was, Dania realized with sick horror, a large mouth, and it was lined with sharp white teeth.

"I have to hand it to you, Dania. Your plan was quite devious. The attack on me in D.C. was led by a clone, wasn't it? The entire purpose of the attack was to lull me into thinking you were dead so you could assassinate me here in the Hive. It might've worked, too—if I were human. But since I'm not..."

Before Dania could so much as take a step backward, Wesker lunged toward her and grabbed her by the shoulders. His grip was like iron, and she couldn't pull free. And then he slowly began to pull her toward the nightmarish obscenity of a mouth that gaped wide in his chest.

"You took my head," Wesker said. "I think it only fitting that I take yours in return."

Dania started to scream, but then Wesker yanked her forward and shoved her head into his chest-mouth. The teeth sliced into her neck with all the sharpness and efficiency of a guillotine blade, and the last thought she had before she died was, *I hope I give you indigestion, you bastard.*

And then she was gone.

* * *

Alice approached an overpass, a number of bodies hanging from it by the neck. Suicides, she figured, or the result of vigilante justice. Not that there was any other kind of justice these days. One of the bodies was still moving, and given its half-rotted condition, she knew it was an Undead. She wondered if the man had been hanged before he turned or after. For his sake, she hoped it was after. Above the bodies hung a metal sign pockmarked with bullet holes.

RACCOON CITY. POP 654,765. CITY LIMITS.

Alice drove the motorcycle beneath the overpass, ignoring the bodies dangling above, her attention focused on the skyscrapers in the distance. Raccoon City had been reduced to a shattered skyline outlined against a vast pillar of steam rising up into the stratosphere, framed by the Arklay Mountains in the northwest. The government had used a nuclear weapon to destroy the city in an attempt to contain the outbreak of the T-virus, later claiming the blast was caused by an "unfortunate incident" at the Raccoon Nuclear Power Station.

She didn't feel as if she'd come home. She wasn't sure she'd ever *had* a home. She didn't have any memories of one. But she supposed this city was the closest thing she'd ever known to home, and if she didn't feel a warm sense of nostalgia being here, she did experience a certain solemn satisfaction. This was the place where it had all begun, and she intended to make sure it ended here, too.

She rode on until she reached Raven's Gate, and the suspension bridge that led into the city. It was clogged with abandoned vehicles—more than a few of which had skeletons inside, as if this were a bridge between the land of the living and the land of the dead, and these poor souls had become stuck in an eternal traffic jam. Alice slowed as she passed the vehicles, and when she was nearly halfway across the bridge, she stopped and dismounted the bike, leaving the engine running because of the security system. She checked her watch.

08:07:06

It had taken her almost two days to get here. She hoped she still had enough time to accomplish her mission. If not, the last surviving humans—not counting those who worked for Umbrella—were fucked.

She took a pair of binoculars from the bike's storage compartment and started walking. Too bad there hadn't been any guns or grenades in the storage compartment when she'd stolen the bike, but she supposed that would have made things too easy, and when had life ever been easy in the World After Umbrella?

After escaping Isaacs and his crew, Alice had driven at the bike's top speed to put as much distance between her and the transport as fast as she could. When she'd judged it was safe enough, she'd pulled over to the side of the road to treat the wounds she'd received from Isaacs' hunting knife. She didn't bother doing anything with the cuts on her face and chest. Neither was deep, and while the wounds would no doubt scar, she'd add them to the collection she'd acquired over the last decade. The gash on her right arm was more serious, and since the bike didn't have a med kit, she tore a strip of cloth from the back of her undershirt and used it as a crude bandage. She'd worry about treating it properly later—assuming she survived the next few hours.

She walked a few dozen feet on the bridge before she stopped. She didn't stop because she'd found the best vantage point to use her binoculars. She stopped because she ran out of bridge. Raven's Gate had been literally cut in half, and what remained of the bridge jutted out into the steaming impact crater that had replaced the center of the city. The river that had once flowed beneath the bridge had become a waterfall, tumbling into the depths of the crater to form a lake below.

She raised the binoculars to her eyes and scanned the edge of the blast crater. On the opposite side she saw a giant concrete tunnel, and inside it, a small flicker of light. She had a hunch what the flicker might mean, and she hit a button on the binoculars, bringing up a schematic of the Hive, overlaid on the tunnel. The schematic confirmed her hunch: the tunnel was part of the Hive, and the light she'd seen had probably been caused by sunlight glinting off a piece of metal.

"Bingo," she said softly.

She continued scanning the edge of the blast crater, eventually finding a rock fall that looked climbable. It was close to the tunnel's entrance, but it was on the other side of the crater from where she stood.

"Looks like I'm going around," she said.

* * *

Alice rode the motorcycle through the remnants of the devastated city. Some buildings had been reduced to rubble, while others—even skyscrapers—were still standing, although they had huge chunks blasted out of them. Everything was blackened and burnt—a lifeless, monochromatic wasteland.

She wasn't overly worried about lingering radiation from the nuclear bomb used to destroy Raccoon City. From what she understood, the greatest radiation hazard from a nuclear detonation occurred in the days and weeks immediately following an explosion. After that, the amount of contamination depended on a number of factors: weapon yield, detonation site, land formations, weather patterns... It had been a decade since the blast, and despite the ruins surrounding her, Alice felt confident that radiation levels here had returned to normal. And if not... well, she only needed to survive another few hours to complete her mission. Dying from radiation poisoning would be a small price to pay to ensure that humanity had a future.

There was one thing she could appreciate about the stone-and-metal graveyard that had once been Raccoon City: the nuclear blast had wiped out the city's Undead population, and it appeared that none had moved in to take their place. She supposed a handful of the creatures might have survived the blast and be lurking somewhere in the ruins, but it made for a pleasant change to be traveling through a city and not have to fend off attacks by ambulatory carnivorous corpses every block. The lack of Undead was going to make her job a lot easier.

She'd almost reached the far side of the crater by this point, and if her luck held, there would be no Undead inside. Then—

Her thoughts broke off as she saw a gleam of light coming from an abandoned skyscraper at the edge of the crater. Sunlight being reflected from a pair of binoculars? She felt a cold tightening in her gut, a warning sign that something wasn't right. She knew the gleam could've been caused by a dozen different things, none of them sinister, but she'd long ago learned to listen to her gut. It was one of the main reasons she was still alive.

She began to ease off the bike's throttle, but before

the BMW could decelerate, a telegraph pole swung into the street without warning. Alice saw the pole coming toward her, held aloft by lengths of cable, but it came too fast, and she didn't have time to go around it. It slammed into her, knocking her off the motorcycle. The bike continued rolling a dozen more feet before it swerved and toppled to the ground. The impact from the pole knocked the wind out of Alice and sent her flying. She hit the road hard and skidded for several feet, the rough surface cutting and abrading her skin. When she came to a stop, she lay on her side, struggling to hold onto consciousness. The trap she'd sprung had been a primitive one, but effective, and now that she'd been dismounted, whoever had set the trap would likely show up to take her prisoner—or simply kill her. She intended to make sure that didn't happen.

She wanted to reach for the knife in her boot sheath, intending to draw it and defend herself, but her arm refused to move. A wave of dizziness came over her then, and she decided it might be a good idea to close her eyes and lie still until the sensation passed.

She lost consciousness seconds later.

* * *

Alice's eyes snapped open, and she found herself looking up at the face of a man kneeling over her. He was in his forties, with shaggy brown hair and an untrimmed beard. He wore a dingy gray shirt and stained blue pants, and he carried a silver pistol holstered on his left hip. But the gun didn't concern her nearly as much as the large syringe the man was holding above her. He brought the syringe down toward her chest, clearly intending to stab her in the heart with it.

Alice's body acted before she could form a fully conscious thought. She grabbed hold of the man's wrist, stopping the needle mere inches from her skin. For an instant, she stared at a drop of clear liquid hanging from the needle's tip. Then she leaped to her feet, pulling the man up with her. She snatched the syringe from his hand and jammed the needle against his jugular, careful not to pierce it just yet. She stood behind him, her free arm wrapped around his chest to prevent him from trying to get away. A quick glance upward told Alice that she was inside a ruined skyscraper—presumably the one she'd seen on the edge of the crater. The interior was hollow and fifty floors above, the sky was visible. The sight prompted the first coherent thought she'd had upon awakening.

It's a wonder the goddamn thing hasn't collapsed by now.

But that thought was quickly interrupted by the sound of frantic shouting.

"Let him go! Let him go *now*!"

"Put it down! We'll shoot!"

Alice lowered her gaze to see a half-dozen armed men and women pointing an assortment of pistols and semiautos at her. They ranged in age from early twenties to mid-forties, and all wore ragged dirt-smudged clothes and had the thin, haggard look that all survivors of the post-apocalyptic world shared. End-of-the-world chic.

She picked out the group's alphas right away from their stance and the way they stood slightly in front of the rest. The male was Hispanic, in his mid-thirties, six feet tall, and ruggedly handsome despite showing signs of malnutrition. He had short black hair along with a stubbly beard, and he wore a long black leather coat. He held a Heckler & Koch submachine gun pointed at Alice, and from the look in his hazel eyes, she knew he wouldn't hesitate to shoot. The female was 5'5", Asian, with shoulder-length hair dyed a striking shade of blue. She was beautiful in an *I will empty my clip into your body if you so much as look at me wrong* kind of way. She wore a dark jacket with the sleeves rolled up over a camo-patterned shirt. She pointed a distinctive blue rifle at Alice, and her steely expression indicated she wouldn't hesitate to fire any more than her partner would.

The man fired a warning shot then, the bullets kicking up chips of stone at Alice's feet. She didn't take her gaze off the man, didn't so much as blink. Instead she pressed the syringe harder against the prisoner's throat. Her human shield spoke then, his voice surprisingly calm given the situation.

"I'd listen to them if I were you," he said.

The Hispanic man kept his gun trained on her, but he turned to look back over his shoulder at the others. The back of his coat was emblazoned with a skull.

"See? See? I told you!" he shouted.

"Calm down, Christian!" her hostage shouted back.

All this yelling was giving her a headache. Her head throbbed and every muscle in her body ached. She wasn't sure why at first, but then she remembered the telegraph pole swinging toward her and knocking her off the bike. The damn thing had packed a hell of a wallop.

"You were wrong, Doc!" Christian said. "I *told* you. I told you all—we should have killed her when we had the chance!"

Doc—her hostage—turned his head slightly, as much as he could with a needle pressed against his neck, to address Alice.

"I'm trying to help you," he said. "Please put it down, before Christian shoots the both of us."

The tip of the syringe was already drawing blood, and a crimson bead rolled down Doc's neck, leaving a red trail behind.

"What's in this?" Alice demanded.

"Pure adrenaline. I was going to inject it into your left ventricle."

She scowled. "Why?"

"We needed you awake," Doc said.

Alice gazed at the band of survivors holding weapons on her. Any of them could've killed her while she was unconscious, but they hadn't. And if they feared she was a great enough threat, someone would've taken a shot by now, and to hell with the risk to Doc. But none of them had. They obviously cared about Doc, and she realized that, despite her assessment of Christian and the blue-haired woman as being the leaders of the group, Doc was really in charge. Maybe he was telling the truth. Maybe they did need her.

"Same question—why?"

"There's something coming. From the same direction that you came. Something big."

A new voice cut off Doc then, a woman's.

"What the hell is going on here?" the woman demanded.

The voice came from behind Alice, and she spun Doc around to face the newcomer, who stood in the open doorway of the building's atrium. She was in her late thirties, with long straight red hair. She wore a maroon leather jacket over a light blue shirt, along with dark pants and boots. She carried a Beretta 9mm holstered at her side.

Alice knew this woman, and she was as shocked as she was pleased to see her.

It was Claire Redfield.

6

"Umbrella captured me at the *Arcadia*. I was in a helicopter headed for somewhere called the Hive..."

Alice and Claire stood on the roof of the building, which Claire called the Peak. Alice was using the binoculars the survivors had scavenged from her downed motorcycle to scan the horizon. She was searching for any sign of Isaacs' Undead army, but so far she hadn't seen anything. Her chest ached from where the telegraph pole had struck her, and she breathed shallowly to minimize the pain.

The women weren't alone on the roof. A large group of survivors stood close by, watching Alice warily. Christian and the blue-haired woman—who was, appropriately enough, called Cobalt—stood nearby with Doc and several other members of his inner circle. Behind them was a small wheat field that had been planted on the rooftop. A windmill cobbled together from pieces of wreckage provided power for the community, and makeshift bridges granted access to the roofs of nearby buildings, atop which more survivors lived. These people had managed to create a functioning village, high up where the Undead and mutant monsters couldn't get at them.

Claire went on while Alice continued searching the horizon.

"I think Umbrella planned on torturing me for information. I got loose, killed the pilot, we crashed here. Doc and the others pulled me from the wreck. I owe them my life."

Alice lowered the binoculars and turned to Claire.

"What happened to Chris?" she asked.

Sadness crept into Claire's voice. "I don't know. We were separated during the battle. He's out there somewhere..."

"I see it!" Michael shouted, interrupting Claire. He was African-American, with a shaved head, mustache and goatee. He had a distinct gravelly voice, and the weary, haunted look of a true survivor. Alice knew that look well. She'd seen it in enough reflective surfaces over the years. Michael was another member of Doc's inner circle, and he'd been helping them search for Isaacs' Undead parade of destruction, and it sounded as if he'd found it.

He pointed. "There! To the east!"

Alice raised her binoculars once more and turned to look in the direction Michael indicated. She saw a large cloud of dust in the distance, and it was getting closer by the minute.

"You know what it is?" Claire asked.

Still gazing through the binoculars, Alice nodded.

"Umbrella," she said. "Doctor Isaacs."

"I thought you killed him," Claire said.

"I thought the same. He has an army of Undead

with him. They'll be here within hours."

Claire looked shocked by Alice's words, but she quickly got hold of herself.

"So what do we do?" she asked.

Before Alice could answer, Christian stepped forward and pointed his submachine gun directly at her.

"Why are we asking her?" he said. "She's a stranger. We can't trust her."

Doc moved to Christian, reached out, and gently pushed the barrel of his gun away.

"Christian," he said, "just because you think you should be in charge doesn't make it so."

Tension filled the air around the two men, like the slow build-up of energy before a thunderstorm breaks. Christian glared at Doc, and Alice wouldn't have been surprised if Christian had trained his weapon on the older man. For his part, Doc's face remained impassive, but anger burned in his eyes.

Michael stepped to Doc's side and stood there protectively, looking intensely at Christian. Cobalt moved to Christian's side and put a hand on his arm. Claire had told Alice that the two were lovers, but even if Claire hadn't filled her in, Alice would've guessed by the way the woman touched him. The gesture was as much possessive as supportive.

"It's okay," Cobalt said, staring at Doc. "His time will come."

Christian continued glaring at Doc a moment longer before turning abruptly and stalking off, Cobalt accompanying him. Michael and Doc exchanged glances, but neither man spoke. It was obvious to Alice that Christian was going to be a problem, and sooner rather than later. But she didn't have time to worry about him now. She had a world to save.

"I have to make it to the Hive," Alice said to Claire. She glanced at the survivors gathered on the roof. Some of them looked like they could handle themselves well enough in a fight, but most of them didn't. "And you need to get these people out of here."

Claire shook her head. "Can't be done. We have children here... newborns. The injured, the elderly. What chance do they have on the road?"

"Better than they have here," Alice said.

Alice looked at the children. She had no memories of childhood, no real memories of any kind before the T-virus outbreak. She knew nothing of the sort of life these people led. Staying in one place, having each other to rely on, working together as a community to build something. All she knew was fighting and killing, blood and death. She'd become a killing machine, a living weapon, but what purpose did a weapon serve once the war was over? If she did somehow manage to release the antivirus and destroy the Undead, could she ever have a life like this? A life of peace with others who she cared for and who cared for her in turn? She'd lived a solitary existence for so long that she didn't know. But she sure as hell wanted to give it a try.

Doc had overheard the two women talking, and he stepped forward to join them. Alice would've preferred to continue speaking to Claire alone, but the man was the leader here—for the moment, at least—and because of that he deserved to be included in making whatever plans might affect his people.

"This building is secure," Doc insisted.

"From the Undead perhaps," Alice said. "But

Isaacs has armored vehicles. Rocket launchers, heavy ordnance. They're going to tear this place wide open."

"Alice," Claire began. She leaned close to Alice then and continued in a much softer voice. "I owe these people my life. We need to protect them. We should make a stand."

Alice looked at Claire for a long moment before checking her watch.

05:27:38

If she died defending the residents of the Peak from Isaacs' horde, who would go into the Hive to find the antivirus? Who would save the world—save *Becky*? Seeing the children on the rooftop had started her thinking about the girl again, not that she'd ever really stopped since meeting her. And even if somehow humanity survived Umbrella's attempt to destroy it, if Alice was dead, who would take care of Becky?

She sighed. "Damn it, Claire, I can't—"

Alice broke off, suddenly seized by a coughing fit. She doubled over in pain, overcome by a wave of weakness. She thought she might pass out, and she might've, except she'd lost consciousness too many times lately, and she was determined to remain awake, no matter what it took.

Doc took hold of her shoulders to steady her, and Alice was in too much pain to shrug him off.

"What is it?" Claire asked, alarmed.

"We need to get her to the medical bay," Doc said.

Together, Doc and Claire escorted Alice toward the entrance to the Peak's stairs, and Alice—every breath fiery agony—let them.

* * *

Doc and Claire helped Alice sit on a gurney in a room that could only charitably be called a "medical bay." It was more like a cramped space filled with a hodge-podge of scavenged junk that, if you squinted and weren't too picky about your definition of sterile, more or less resembled primitive medical equipment. There was a dirty glass window set into one of the walls, and Christian and Cobalt watched from the other side.

Wincing in pain, Alice peeled off her top to reveal a badly bruised torso. Doc gave her a quick examination, and then said, "I need to get those ribs strapped up."

"What happened to you?" Claire asked Alice, but Doc answered.

"She was hit by one of the traps on the outer perimeter," he said. He then turned to Alice. "They were intended for the Undead. There aren't many of them left in the city, but it's better not to let the ones still around get too close to where we live. Even with us living so high off the ground, they can sense our presence if they get close enough. And if one gets wind of us—"

"More come," Alice finished.

Doc nodded. He then began using silver duct tape to bind Alice's chest.

"Medically speaking, you're not supposed to wrap broken ribs," he said. "Oh, doctors used to do it, but then they learned it increased the risk of lung infection and pneumonia because the wrap forces patients to breath shallowly. The preferred method of treatment is to apply ice after the initial injury, take anti-inflammatories, and avoid moving your torso. The ribs should then heal themselves in one to two months."

"But you don't have ice or anti-inflammatories," Alice said. She gritted her teeth against the pain while Doc worked.

"And you don't have a couple months to rest. Not with what's coming. So wrapping will have to do."

Alice glanced over at the window and saw Christian watching her. He scowled, lips tightening. His hands remained at his sides, but she noticed he held his submachine gun, as if he was ready to start firing at her once she finally confirmed his suspicion that she was a threat.

"Your friend's quite the charmer," Alice said to Doc. "What's his story?"

"When the world went to hell, people dealt with it in different ways," Doc said. "Some turned to religion. Others, like Christian and his group, tried to become as savage as what they feared. And in Christian's case, it's taken its toll."

Claire glanced at Christian, then she walked over to the window and lowered the blinds, blocking him and Cobalt out.

"How about you?" Alice said to Doc. "How do you deal with it?"

"Me? I just drink."

Claire laughed as she rejoined them at the gurney. Doc glanced at her, smiling, and Alice felt an unmistakable energy pass between them.

Doc returned to his work then and finished wrapping Alice's ribs.

"That should do it." He reached for a container of alcohol and wetted a cotton ball. He then used it to sterilize the inside of Alice's right elbow, and when he was finished, he tossed the ball aside. He picked up a syringe that was resting on a folded cloth atop a metal stand next to the gurney.

Alice eyed the syringe suspiciously as Doc picked it up. "What's that?"

"The specialty of the house," Doc said. "Give it a few minutes and it'll have you on your feet again."

He moved to inject her, but Alice grabbed his hand before he could.

"Last time, you tried to stab me in the heart. Why should I trust you?"

Doc smiled. "Because of my charming bedside manner, of course."

Alice let go of his hand, and he slid the needle into the soft flesh of her inner elbow and injected the contents into a vein. She assumed the drug was some sort of stimulant, and it might have been her imagination, but she thought she could already feel it beginning to work.

Michael entered the room then, a worried expression on his face.

"Doc, you need to get out there," he said. "People are scared and Christian's not helping. You need to let everyone know what's happening."

Doc sighed. He turned to Claire.

"I've got to go. Your friend's going to be okay."

"Thank you," Claire said. She placed her hand on Doc's arm, and Alice once more felt the electricity between them.

Doc left the room with Michael, closing the door behind them.

Claire gave Alice a slightly embarrassed smile. "You know, he and I..."

Alice smiled. "I noticed."

She was happy for Claire, she really was, but she was more than a little jealous, too. Given the sort of life she'd led, she'd never had time to make a romantic connection with anyone. She'd long ago accepted that such a relationship wasn't in the cards for her. But seeing Claire with Doc made her feel regret for a life she'd never know.

She checked the countdown on her watch then, and Claire said, "What's in the Hive? What's so important to you?"

Alice slipped her top back on as she answered. The tape made moving a bit awkward, but her ribs hurt less, and that's all she cared about right now. "Umbrella developed a cure. An airborne antivirus. It'll destroy anything infected with the T-virus in a matter of seconds."

Claire's eyes widened in disbelief. "Who told you this?"

Alice hesitated a second before answering. "The Red Queen."

"And you believed her? The psychotic computer bitch does nothing but lie. There could be no cure. Just a trap... which you're going to walk right into."

Wouldn't be the first time, Alice thought. Aloud, she said, "You're right, of course. But... what if she's telling the truth? What if we could end this?"

Claire looked thoughtful. "It destroys anything infected with the T-virus?"

"That's right."

"Then what about *you*?"

Alice didn't reply.

"They infected you with the T-virus," Claire said. "You release this antivirus, it's going to kill you."

"This has to end. Whatever it takes."

"Alice..." Claire reached out and put a hand on Alice's arm.

"You know I'm right."

Claire looked Alice in the eye, and although she didn't say anything, Alice knew her friend understood. Whatever happened in the Hive, Alice wasn't coming back.

"All right," Claire said. "We stop Isaacs here. We save these people. Then we go into the Hive together."

Alice glanced at her watch. Five hours left.

She considered Claire's words. She knew she shouldn't let anything distract her from her mission, but she couldn't help thinking of the survivor settlement on top of the skyscrapers. Most of these people weren't warriors. Who was going to protect them from Isaacs and his Undead army? She had returned to Raccoon City to save what was left of the human race—only five thousand people the Red Queen had said, including those above them right now. What was the point of finding and releasing the antivirus if she didn't try to save everyone she could?

"We don't have long."

Alice pulled herself off the gurney. The movement hurt, but not as much as it would've before Doc had wrapped her ribs and given her an armful of go juice.

"So let's get to it."

* * *

Alice and Claire stood outside the Peak's main entrance, near where her abandoned motorcycle lay in the street. Doc, Michael, and Christian were with them. The telegraph pole which struck her hung nearby. She turned to Doc.

"We should get that reset."

"We're on it," Michael said. He tried to pull Christian along with him to go take care of the job, but the man refused to budge, so Doc went with him.

Alice turned to Claire. "What else do they have for defense?"

"Not too many firearms. But they have a big supply of gasoline."

Claire had brought a distinctive-looking triple-barreled shotgun from the group's meager armory. She now held it out to Alice.

"Here. You need a weapon."

Alice took it and looked it over. She held it up and aimed it toward the street, making sure her index finger didn't touch the trigger. The gun felt good in her hand. She liked the heft of it, and who didn't love a third barrel?

"Nice," she said, impressed.

"It's called a Hydra," Claire said. "And don't get too excited. You only have six shells." She handed Alice the ammunition.

With so few shells, Alice knew she'd have to choose her shots carefully and make sure each one counted.

Christian scowled. "Now we're giving her a gun."

Michael and Doc were struggling to reset the pole trap by themselves. "A little help?" Michael called out, but Christian didn't move. He kept his gaze focused on Alice, submachine gun ready at his side.

"You can let your guard down if you want," Christian said, speaking to Michael and Doc without taking his eyes off Alice. "I don't intend to."

Alice began loading the shells into the Hydra, turning to Claire while she did so. She lowered her voice.

"When I rode in here, there was someone watching me. They could have called out or fired a shot... warned me of the trap. But they didn't."

"What are you saying?"

"The Red Queen said there would be a traitor here. Someone loyal to Umbrella."

Claire frowned. "You believe her?"

Alice didn't have an answer for that. "Just watch your back."

* * *

Alice watched as a dozen survivors used picks and shovels to dig holes into the exterior wall of the Peak. Doc, Michael, Cobalt, and a reluctant Christian were pitching in. Other residents were fitting large makeshift hooks into the holes that had already been dug.

Christian was stripped to the waist, revealing skeletal tattoos covering his body. Alice remembered what Doc had said about how some survivors tried to become the thing they feared. It seemed Christian had tried to become Death itself, or at least he was trying to show that he didn't fear death.

"This is bullshit!" he said.

"I hate to agree with him, Doc," Michael said, "but why are we making holes *in* the wall? I thought we wanted to keep them out."

Doc swung his pick into the stone with a solid *chuck*. "Just keep digging," he said.

Satisfied that the work was progressing nicely, Alice

headed inside the building to check on how things were going upstairs. She didn't look at Christian as she passed him, but she could feel the man's glare on her as she walked by, and she knew that sooner or later, he was going to confront her, and when that happened, no one would be able to make him back down.

* * *

On the roof of the Peak, a group of residents used a makeshift crane to haul containers of gasoline onto the roof, working with a fevered intensity. Claire was in the middle of this group, urging people on and helping to move the containers into position.

"Keep it moving!" Claire called out. "We need all those gasoline cans over here."

Alice watched a young woman working the crane. Claire had introduced her as Abigail, and she had a nose ring, short dyed hair, and tattoos of the non-skeletal variety. She wasn't as grim-faced as most of the survivors. She smiled often, and she looked like she meant it.

Abigail was in charge of the team operating the crane, and she worked as hard as any of them. "That's it!" she urged. "Keep pulling!"

Alice walked up to the woman and gestured to the crane. "Claire said you built this."

Abigail continued working the crane as she spoke. "That's right."

"Where'd you learn something like that?"

"My father used to run a chop shop. I hated it. Preferred skating and meth." She shrugged. "Who knew? Guess I was paying attention after all."

Alice liked this woman. While so many of the other survivors she'd encountered over the years seemed worn down and defeated by the nightmarish world Umbrella had created, Abigail seemed—if not exactly happy—at least determined to remain positive. It was the sort of quality that would be needed if humanity hoped to rebuild some kind of civilization when this was all over. Survival of the optimistic instead of survival of the fittest.

Abigail swung the crane's empty bucket over the edge of the building and her team started sending it down for another load.

"This crane used to be for window washing," she said. "I made a few changes."

"Good. Because I want you to make a few more."

Abigail grinned. "Sounds like fun."

* * *

Wesker watched the survivors' preparations atop the Peak via a live satellite feed. They didn't stand a chance in hell of winning, of course, but he found their determination to defend their pathetic excuse for a home amusing. He was even more amused to see that Alice had gotten drawn into helping them. Whether enhanced by the T-virus or not, she was a magnificent warrior. Too bad she allowed sentiment to get in the way of doing what needed to be done. Empathy was a weakness, and he was glad he possessed none. Not only did it make him more efficient at his job, it made life so much simpler.

After ingesting Dania's head, Wesker had devoured the rest of her body. Waste not, want not. Her genetic material had allowed him to regrow a new head of his own, and more, it had helped stabilize his cellular structure... for the time being. He had lied to Dania when he'd said he was in complete control of his body. In truth, he was at constant war with it, the T-virus that gave him his enhanced abilities always threatening to take control. He had to be very careful about using his metamorphic capabilities, which had grown considerably over the years, or else he might lose molecular cohesion entirely. He supposed he could use the same antidote he'd given Alice if he wished to return his body to its human state—assuming that was possible by this point—but he had no desire to do so. He liked the power the T-virus had granted him, and besides, what was life without a little risk?

He thought he'd reabsorbed all the bits and pieces of his head that Dania had splattered onto the control console, but looking at it now, he saw a tiny glob of brain matter. He scooped it up on his index finger, licked it off with a long, slender tongue that looked like a serpent's, and then returned his attention to his work.

He flipped a switch on the panel to open a comm channel to Isaacs' transport. Time for a chat with the good doctor. A second later, the image of the Peak vanished from the monitor, and Wesker found himself looking at Isaacs. The man was pale and sweaty, as if he were sick, or perhaps fighting off some kind of infection.

"So... how is the interrogation going?" Wesker asked.

Isaacs glared at him, and Wesker smiled slightly before going on.

"It seems you let her slip through your fingers."
He noticed the patch of Nu-Skin on the stump where
Isaacs' hand had been. "What remains of them," he
added.

Isaacs' face turned bright red with fury. "Don't
forget who you're talking to!" he snapped. "Where is
she?"

"The settlement in Raccoon City. It seems she's
preparing for a fight."

"Good. I'll be there in the hour."

Isaacs broke the connection, and the monitor
screen went black for a second before resuming the
satellite feed of the Peak.

So Alice and her friends had more time to prepare,
and Isaacs was hardly in top condition. The situation
had suddenly become very interesting.

Wesker leaned back on his chair, focused his gaze
on the monitor, and waited for the show to begin.

* * *

Night was rapidly descending on Raccoon City, and
Alice and the residents of the Peak were desperately
trying to finish their final preparations. Outside the
building's main entrance plaza, Alice was spray-
painting a number three on the ground when she
sensed something. She stopped painting and turned
toward a nearby pile of rubble. In the dim light
she saw the dirt covering the rubble shift almost
imperceptibly, indicating the slightest of vibrations.
A small sign, but to Alice the message might as well
have been spelled out in hundred-foot neon letters.

"They're here," she said to herself.

* * *

Isaacs stood in the armored turret on top of the transport. The vehicle's headlights illuminated several dead bodies—and a single twitching Undead—hanging from an overpass. Above this was a sign that Isaacs had been waiting a long time to see.

RACCOON CITY. POP 654,765. CITY LIMITS.

He knew the current number of residents was far lower, and soon it would be zero.

He had spent much of the time since Alice's escape amusing himself with the prisoners. Only three still lived. One currently served as bait, and the other two remained in the hold in case they were needed later. The second transport rolled alongside Isaacs', and behind them followed the combined mass of the Undead army they had lured here. By this point, Isaacs doubted the Undead needed human bait to feel compelled to follow the vehicles. The Undead seemed eager to keep going, and more than a few of them sniffed the air, as if they'd caught wind of fresh, living meat and couldn't wait to sink their teeth into it. There were so many Undead in the horde that their footsteps shook the earth as they walked, and Isaacs could feel the vibrations travel through the turret's metal frame to reverberate throughout his body. It was like feeling the power of God Himself channeled through thousands of ambulatory corpses. The sensation was glorious.

You'll get your chance soon, my children, he thought. *Very soon.*

He felt feverish and dizzy, but it didn't matter. He had finally arrived at his destination, where he would fulfill his mission and complete the divine plan of the most holy. He touched an icon on the turret's digital control panel to open an audio channel to the cabins of both transports.

"Ready the weapons. High explosive rounds. No survivors."

Isaacs then entered a series of commands into the turret's control panel. Huge guns deployed from the front of both vehicles, and banks of floodlights came on to illuminate what would soon become their battlefield.

Now for the final touch, he thought.

He tapped an icon shaped like a small red sphere, and music began to blast from hidden speakers in both vehicles: Holst's "Mars, the Bringer of War." The composition was at once otherworldly and martial, the perfect accompaniment for Armageddon.

He closed his eyes and let the music fill him as the transports and the obscene army they led thundered onward.

* * *

Alice and the others stood on the roof of the Peak as the transports and the Undead horde entered the plaza below, music blasting from the vehicles. Alice watched their approach through her binoculars, and despite herself, she had to admit that Isaacs knew how to put on one hell of a performance.

The last time she'd faced a horde of monsters—only a couple days ago, though it seemed much longer—she'd had full command of her enhanced abilities, but now she was only human. That was okay, though.

She'd just have to do this the old-fashioned way. She lowered her binoculars but continued to watch the transports move into the plaza, Undead following close behind.

"My God," Abigail said, her voice filled with awe and terror. "There's just too many of them."

Claire and Doc stood next to each other, and Alice noticed their hands meet. Doc squeezed Claire's hand in an attempt to be reassuring, but judging by Claire's ashen face, Doc's gesture didn't help.

"What are we going to do?" Cobalt asked. She no longer sounded like a ready-to-throw-down badass. Instead, she sounded like a scared child.

Alice turned to face the others—Claire, Doc, Michael, Christian, Cobalt, Abigail—and she saw how terrified and desperate they all looked. She deliberately kept her voice calm as she answered Cobalt's question.

"We're going to kill every last one of them."

She watched their faces, and while she still saw fear in their eyes, she also saw them fighting to control it. They were as ready as they were going to get.

She raised a walkie-talkie to her mouth. "Stations everyone," she ordered.

They all moved off to attend to their assigned duties without a word. Not even Christian protested, which was a testament to how truly terrified he must be, Alice thought.

She turned to Abigail. Over the course of the last several hours, the woman had transformed the crane into a trebuchet. In the bucket of the device sat a lump of concrete wrapped in blankets and soaked with gasoline. One of Abigail's team handed her a flaming torch, and she touched it to the sodden blanket. The gasoline ignited with a *whoosh*, followed by a blast of heat.

Alice turned toward the building's edge and looked through her binoculars once more. She focused on the number three she'd spray-painted on the ground earlier, and when the wheels of the first transport rolled over the number, she shouted, "Fire!"

Alice kept the binoculars trained on the transport as Abigail threw the trebuchet's trigger, sending the device's counterweight plunging downward, which in turn brought its throwing arm swinging upward with rapidly increasing speed, and then the trebuchet flung its deadly cargo high into the air.

"Reload!" Alice ordered, and Abigail and her team leaped into action.

Alice tracked the burning missile's progress through her binoculars. Someone other than Isaacs stood in this vehicle's turret—she assumed this meant it wasn't his transport—and the man looked up in time to see the fireball coming toward him. But there was nothing he could do. The flaming chunk of concrete crashed into the turret, crushing the man and spilling burning gasoline through the open roof hatch and into the crew cabin. Alice watched as thick smoke billowed up from within the transport, and she smiled grimly as she imagined the chaotic scene occurring inside the vehicle. She watched with satisfaction as the transport veered off course and crashed into the remnants of a building across the street. The impact caused the ruined structure to collapse on top of the transport, burying it.

That's one, Alice thought.

* * *

Isaacs watched as the second transport disappeared beneath the rubble of the fallen building.

"Damn her!" he swore.

Isaacs seethed with fury. That bitch thought she was better than him, better than *everyone*. But there was nothing special about her. Project Alice was an abject failure, and he intended to prove that to her. No one defied the will of the Lord—*or* that of his chosen servant. Not without paying the ultimate price.

He abandoned the turret and climbed down through the open hatch into the crew cabin.

"Seal it up!" he commanded, and a trooper sealed the hatch behind him.

"Full stop!" he ordered Commander Lee. "Release the bait!"

Lee raised an eyebrow at that, but he did as Isaacs wished.

* * *

Alice watched as the remaining transport came to an abrupt halt. The Undead surged forward, clawing at the bait being dragged behind the vehicle in chains. Alice recognized the emaciated woman that she had saved from Isaacs when she'd been held prisoner. She felt an overwhelming rush of hatred for the son of a bitch and what he'd done to that poor woman, but she fought to keep the emotion in check. She had to keep a clear head if they were to have any hope of winning this battle.

She continued watching as the electronic lock on the

woman's chains disengaged, and her manacles dropped away from her wrists, and the belt keeping her chained to the transport fell away from her waist. Freed, the woman leaped to her feet and ran from the Undead, who followed in pursuit. The woman ran toward the Peak, bringing the mass of Undead with her.

Alice watched the woman run across a number two spray-painted on the ground. She waited until the woman was past the marker and the first of the Undead reached it.

"Marker Two!" she shouted. "Fire!"

Abigail threw the trebuchet's trigger, and the device released a second flaming missile. Alice watched the block of concrete land behind the fleeing woman, crushing dozens of Undead and setting many more ablaze. The flames spread quickly, igniting the creatures' dry, desiccated flesh, and within seconds hundreds more were on fire.

Alice lowered her gaze until the binoculars were focused on a large makeshift gate fashioned from a patchwork of metal that the survivors had erected in front of the Peak's main entrance. Claire, Doc, Christian, and Cobalt stood behind the gate, watching as the emaciated woman ran toward them. Claire saw her, and she and Doc hurried to open the gate to allow her inside, while Christian and Cobalt provided covering fire. But the Undead were too close to the woman, and Alice knew the monsters would bring her down before she could reach safety.

Claire drew her Beretta and fired at the woman. Doc grabbed hold of her arm to try and stop her, but Claire shrugged him off and kept firing. None of Claire's bullets struck the woman, and Alice knew that if Claire had wanted her dead, she'd have dropped the woman with the first shot. Alice thought she knew what Claire intended, and when she saw the woman dodge to one side to avoid Claire's gunfire, she knew she'd guessed right. She couldn't see Michael from her vantage point, but she knew he was there when she saw the telegraph pole swing into the space the woman had occupied only seconds before. The pole—now with extra weight added—cut a swath through the Undead, crushing dozens of the ravenous creatures. Claire and Michael had just saved the woman's life.

* * *

Inside the transport, Isaacs watched coldly as the emaciated woman desperately ran for her life. His face showed no expression as the building's defenders fought to save her, but once they'd sprung their pole trap and the woman was just within reach of the open gate, he smiled.

"Fire," he ordered.

* * *

Alice watched in horror as the guns mounted on the transport opened fire, cutting down the fleeing woman in an instant. Her body jerked as the fifty cals tore through her, spraying the air with blood, and then she fell. An instant later, Undead descended on her, ripping at her flesh with hands and teeth, snarling at each other as they fought over her remains.

Alice lowered her binoculars, unable to watch further. Whatever else happened this night, she vowed that Isaacs wouldn't survive to see the dawn. He was a worse monster than anything Umbrella had cooked up in a lab, and one way or another, she was going to take the bastard down.

* * *

Claire stood stunned as she watched the woman fall. A number of Undead immediately began feeding on her body, but many more kept on coming toward the gate, hungry gazes fixed on the meat standing on the other side. Christian and Cobalt fired continuously, but although they dropped one Undead after another, there were far too many of the creatures for them to handle alone.

"Close the gate!" Doc shouted.

His words broke through Claire's paralysis. She saw that the first of the Undead would reach the gate before they could close it, and she leaped to the defense, standing in the gate's opening and firing upon the onrushing monsters. Doc joined her, and the two of them fought side by side, cutting down the Undead in their tracks. Claire's fighting skills had been honed to a razor-sharp edge during her time leading a caravan of survivors across the wasteland that America had become thanks to the destructive effects of the T-virus. Doc hadn't had the same amount of experience fighting for his life and the lives of others, but it was clear he knew how to handle himself.

We make quite a team, Claire thought, and despite the grave nature of their situation, she couldn't help smiling.

When Claire, Doc, Christian, and Cobalt had taken

out enough Undead to give them a few seconds of breathing room, Christian and Cobalt stopped firing and hurried to close the gate. Still shooting, Claire and Doc stepped back as the gate swung shut before the rest of the Undead could reach them. But Claire knew it would only provide temporary respite.

"Move!" she ordered, and she, Doc, Christian, and Cobalt ran toward the Peak's main entrance, and quickly disappeared inside the building, each of them passing over a spray-painted number one as they did so.

* * *

On the roof, Alice watched through her binoculars as the transport fired a rocket at the gate. The blast tore the makeshift construction apart, and an instant later the horde of Undead surged over and past the twisted chunks of metal, and when the first of them ran across the number one, she raised her walkie to her mouth.

"Final marker! Now!"

7

"Final marker! Now!"

On the building's tenth floor, Michael heard Alice's command over the walkie tucked into his belt. He stood with a team of residents next to a large block of concrete and rebar which teetered on the edge of the balcony above the Peak's main entrance. A cable was wrapped around the block, its lower end trailing downward past the balcony.

"You heard her!" Michael shouted. "Now push! *Push!* Put your backs into it!"

Michael and his team pressed their bodies against the block of concrete and shoved with all their might, jaws clenched and faces strained from the effort. At first the concrete refused to budge, but then Michael poured every last bit of strength he had into pushing, and that made the difference. The concrete slowly tipped forward, and then it went over the edge.

The block fell three stories before the cable wrapped around it pulled tight. The other end of the cable was attached to a series of smaller cables, each of which stretched to the metal hooks Doc and Christian had embedded in the outside wall. The block pulled the hooks out of the wall, which in turn caused the wall to break apart. Great chunks of the building's exterior wall rained down, crushing hundreds if not thousands of Undead below in an instant.

Michael and his team cheered, savoring this spectacular moment of triumph. But their victory was short-lived. In the main plaza, thousands more Undead charged through the swirling dust, clambering over the debris and the mangled bodies of their own kind, surging through the shattered gate and into the Peak.

Michael watched with despair as the creatures flooded into the building. He feared that no matter how hard they fought, this was a battle they simply could not win. He prayed he was wrong.

* * *

Inside the remaining transport, Commander Lee turned to Isaacs.

"We've breached the gates," he said. "They're falling back."

Isaacs felt a profound sense of peace settle within him. Alice and her comrades had done their best, and they'd fallen far short. This night—as it was always intended—belonged to the Lord... and to him.

"Looks like they're out of tricks. Target the roof."

"Targeting roof," Lee said.

* * *

Alice watched as the turret atop the transport swung around, guns raising as they aimed toward the roof.

"Take cover!" she shouted. "Everyone get down!"

Everyone threw themselves to the roof as a hailstorm of fifty-caliber rounds began tearing apart everything around them.

* * *

Inside the Peak's central atrium, the exits were blocked by makeshift barricades and stretches of mesh fencing. The residents fought desperately from behind the barricades as thousands of Undead filled the giant circular space. Claire, Doc, Cobalt, and Christian were in the thick of it, fighting savagely, killing the Undead as the horde pressed forward.

"Come on! Push!" Claire urged.

"Push them back!" Doc echoed.

The residents gave everything they had, but the sheer mass of the Undead horde was unstoppable. Claire watched in despair as all around her barricades began to give way under the Undead's assault.

Out of the corner of her eye, Claire saw the barricade Cobalt and Christian were behind collapse. Undead flooded forward, grabbed hold of Cobalt and dragged her down screaming as they tore into her flesh.

"No!" Christian shouted. He fired his submachine gun, blasting the Undead off her, but it was too late. She was already dead.

Claire didn't have time to mourn for her fallen friend. She and Doc fought to shore up their barricade as the Undead flung themselves against it, but she knew there was nothing they could do to prevent the creatures from overwhelming their defenses. The Undead would be through the barricades and devouring them all within moments.

She glanced at Doc. She didn't want to die, but if she had to, she couldn't think of anyone better to have by her side. He gave her a sad smile, and she knew he was thinking the same thing. Whatever happened next, they would face it together.

She pulled her walkie from her belt and raised it to her mouth.

"Alice! We can't hold them much longer!"

* * *

Alice received Claire's message. The transport was still firing at the roof, so she rose and kept low as she ran to the roof's inner ledge, which faced the building's atrium. She leaned over and saw that the hollow central core of the Peak was filled with Undead. Just as she'd planned.

The atrium side of the roof was lined with gasoline cans which sat next to a makeshift gutter system Abigail and her team had constructed. They crouched next to the fuel containers, and when Alice gave them the command, they stood, removed the caps, and poured the gasoline into the gutter. Alice watched as the gasoline was channeled into two waterfalls which flowed over the edge of the roof below, soaking the army of the Undead in a chemical rain.

Alice moved to one of the waterfalls and took a flaming torch from one of Abigail's team. Abigail stood next to the other waterfall, also holding a torch. Alice gave her a nod and together the two women touched their torches to the waterfalls and set them ablaze, causing the falling torrents of liquid to turn instantly into twin pillars of fire. The sight was apocalyptic, Alice thought. Almost biblical. A shame Isaacs wasn't down there to appreciate it.

Claire and the other surviving residents on the ground abandoned their posts as the whole central atrium was consumed by flame. The ground floor became a lake of fire, filled with countless writhing bodies.

Not as easy as in D.C., but just as effective, Alice thought.

She then turned back toward the outer edge of the roof, which was now lined with gasoline cans. The transport had stopped firing—perhaps because Isaacs was more concerned with what was happening in the atrium—and she, Abigail, and the team had no trouble lifting the cans and dumping them into the gutter on this side and then igniting the gas. The fifty cals had peppered the gutter with holes, but the system worked well enough. As had happened in the atrium, the waterfalls of liquid transformed into columns of flame, raining apocalyptic fire onto the mass of Undead that had survived the collapse of the Peak's façade.

Now for the fun part...

She handed off her binoculars and climbed onto the building's ledge. Abigail had attached a high-tensile electricity cable to the ledge's concrete, and Alice—the three-barreled Hydra tucked in her belt—gripped a pair of bicycle handlebars attached to the cable. The arrangement didn't look all that sturdy to Alice, but it was too late to back out now. She crouched on the ledge, gripped the handlebars, and jumped.

The initial jerk sent fiery jolts of pain through her damaged ribs, and she swung from side to side a few times before managing to steady herself. Once she did, she began to pick up speed until she was riding the makeshift zipline at close to seventy miles per hour. The other end of the cable was bolted to a metal plate Abigail had fastened to the street in front of the Peak. The cable had survived the transport's assault and the survivors' response—something of a miracle as far as Alice was concerned. As she reached the end of the zipline, she let go of the handlebars, tucked, and rolled.

A half-dozen Undead charged her, but Alice drew the Hydra as she came up on her feet. She pointed the short-barreled shotgun at the oncoming monsters and fired, discharging all three barrels at once. The gun *boomed*, and all six Undead went down, reduced to so much shredded meat. Alice had admired the Hydra before, but now she thought she might be in love with it. She didn't pause to admire the weapon's handiwork, though, and she quickly took cover behind a chunk of concrete that had fallen from the Peak. She wanted nothing more than to charge straight toward Isaacs' transport, but she had something she had to pick up first. She ran to a camouflaged sheet of cloth hidden within the rubble and threw it back to reveal a cache of gasoline cans. Thankfully, the flaming rain they'd sent down from the roof hadn't ignited them. She grabbed one and kept moving.

* * *

Inside the transport, Isaacs watched in frustration as Alice disappeared behind a section of rubble. His fever had worsened as the battle progressed, and now he felt as if he were burning up. The patch of Nu-Skin over his wrist stump itched, and without thinking, he scratched at it with the fingers of his remaining hand.

How could this have happened? They'd had two transports, a full complement of arms, highly trained crews, and an army of bloodthirsty Undead. Taking the building and destroying its occupants should've been child's play. Now here they were, not defeated but nowhere close to victorious. But he knew why the tables had turned so completely. It was a one-word answer: *Alice.* Perhaps he should've waited to attack at the appointed time in coordination with the other Umbrella forces spread around the world instead of jumping the gun. But Alice's presence in Raccoon City had demanded immediate action. No, the decision to attack early had been a sound tactical one, he was certain of that, and it had nothing to do with his personal feelings toward the fucking bitch. Nothing at all.

Commander Lee stood at the vehicle's control console, looking over the sensor readouts.

"We lost her," he said.

Fear and fury warred within Isaacs. He was so overcome with frustration that if he'd been holding a gun, he'd have shoved the muzzle against the back of Lee's head and pulled the trigger. Instead, he demanded, "Where did she go? Where is she?"

Lee checked the readouts again. "I don't have anything."

"Turn on thermal imaging. She can't hide from us."

Lee's sensor screen switched to a thermal image of the battleground around the transport, and almost immediately a red-outlined figure came into view.

"I have her," Lee said.

Isaacs scratched at the Nu-Skin so hard it began to bleed.

"Fire!"

* * *

The transport's fifty-caliber guns blazed into life, their bullets tearing apart an Undead wreathed in flame. More and more burning Undead staggered away from the Peak and moved past the vehicle.

Alice sat on top of the transport's turret as it swiveled around, searching for another target. She removed the cap on the gas can she carried, hopped off the turret, and walked toward an air vent on the roof. She then poured gasoline into the vent and, when the can was empty, she tossed it over the side of the vehicle. Pulling a pack of matches from a pocket, she knelt down, lit one, used it to set the entire pack ablaze, and then slid it into the vent. An instant later she heard shouts of alarm coming from the crew cabin, followed by smoke wafting upward through the vent. She stood and turned toward the hatch, and a second later it flew open, and from inside a woman shouted, "Don't shoot! We're coming out!"

The Umbrella trooper emerged, firing a 9mm as she came. Alice leveled the Hydra at her and fired one barrel. The blast caught the woman in the face and upper chest, and she fell back in a spray of blood, dead, only halfway out of the hatch. Her corpse blocked the opening, and black smoke curled around her body. Alice kept the Hydra aimed at the hatch, waiting for another of the crew to pull the woman's body out of the way so they could escape the flames and smoke. But no one did anything to remove their dead comrade.

Alice heard a soft creaking sound behind her, and she spun around in time to see a second hatch spring open—this one disguised to be hidden from the naked eye. An Asian man emerged from the cabin and leaped toward her. He moved fast and closed the short distance between them before Alice could bring the Hydra to bear. He wore a sidearm—a SIG-Sauer—but it was holstered at his side. He hadn't carried it as he'd climbed because he hadn't wanted it to slow him down, she guessed. Smart.

When the man was in range, he swept out his left foot and knocked the Hydra out of Alice's grasp before she could fire. The weapon flew out of her hands, hit the roof, and skittered away. For a moment, she feared the Hydra would go over the side, but it came to a stop less than a foot from the edge.

Once she was disarmed, the man tried to draw his pistol, but the instant the weapon cleared the holster, Alice stepped forward and slammed the heel of her right hand into his chin. As his head snapped back, she grabbed hold of his wrist with her left hand and twisted. The man drew in a sharp hiss of air, and Alice twisted harder until his hand was forced open and he lost hold of his gun. As it fell, Alice tried to catch it with her other hand, but she only possessed human speed now, and she missed. The gun hit the roof, bounced a couple times, slid toward the edge, and went over.

The man recovered quickly from the strike to his chin. He brought his head forward and slammed it against Alice's forehead. White light flashed behind her eyes, and she released her grip on his wrist and staggered backward a couple steps. The man pressed his advantage. He drew a KA-BAR knife from a sheath on his belt and rushed forward, thrusting the blade at her heart.

Alice's ears rang and her vision was blurry, but she saw the strike coming and managed to turn sideways to avoid it. She then moved forward, grabbed the man's outstretched hand by the wrist, and with her other hand grabbed hold of his forearm below the elbow. She then yanked his arm downward, bringing her knee up toward his elbow at the same time. Knee struck bone, and the man cried out in pain as his elbow was dislocated. Alice then twisted his arm, and he howled and dropped the knife. She kept pressure on the man's wrist, and he sank to one knee, grimacing in agony. She relaxed her grip on his forearm and gave him a strong right cross for good measure. The blow left him dazed and semiconscious, and if Alice hadn't still been holding onto his wrist, he probably would have collapsed to the roof.

She was about to question the man, but before she could say anything, another trooper emerged from the hatch. Alice prepared to use her defeated opponent as a shield, but the trooper was unarmed—even if he had been carrying a weapon, he was coughing too hard to use it. He put his hands on top of his head in a gesture of surrender.

"Lie down on your belly and keep your hands on your head," she ordered.

Still coughing, the man nodded and did as she ordered.

Thick black smoke billowed from both hatches now, and she waited another moment for Isaacs to emerge from the crew cabin, but no one else came out.

She looked down at her semiconscious captive.

"Where is he?" she demanded.

* * *

Several moments later Alice, Hydra in hand, dropped through the open hatch and into the transport's cramped crew cabin. The interior was filled with smoke and residual flame, and since she didn't have anything to cover her mouth, she did her best to breathe shallowly. Through the gloom, she saw two crew members lying on the floor. Both had been reduced to charred corpses, but she could make out enough of their features to determine that neither was Isaacs.

She continued searching, moving cautiously through the smoke and the darkness. But as she passed one of the corpses, it lunged toward her and grabbed her arm. Alice felt a sharp stab of fear as the corpse's blackened fingers pressed against her, and at first she thought it was an Undead. She swung the Hydra around to blast it in the face, but then the man's grasp weakened, and he let go of her and fell back to the floor. He was just a human who'd expended the last of his strength to reach for her, maybe trying to attack her, maybe seeking help or just the solace of human contact as his life drained away. Whichever the case, he was gone now, and Alice was glad she hadn't fired at him, if for no other reason than because she hadn't ended up wasting ammo.

She moved on.

She reached the bulkhead that separated the crew cabin from the hold, and she opened the door and stepped through. The collection of crucifixes still hung from the ceiling, and while there was no smoke in here, the stink of unwashed bodies, blood, piss, shit, and fear was far worse. Of the prisoners Alice had once shared the hold with, only two remained: Scars and the Thin Man. Both were still manacled and chained to the wall, and they faced a computer monitor that had been brought in and placed where the Emaciated Woman had sat. That struck Alice as odd.

When Scars saw her, he began babbling, clearly afraid.

"I'm sorry! Please don't shoot me!" he said.

The Thin Man only looked at her. Even if he'd wanted to speak, Alice remembered that he had no tongue.

She ignored the two men and raced to the back doors of the transport. They hung wide open, and when she looked out and scanned the battlefield, she saw no sign of Isaacs.

"Damn it," she said softly.

Michael walked by then, along with a handful of other survivors. They were spreading through the plaza, shooting burning Undead as they staggered by.

"Save your ammo," Alice said. She had a better idea how to deal with the remaining Undead.

* * *

It was full dark now. The plaza was lit by the flickering flames left over from the gasoline waterfalls that had incinerated the Undead. The dancing fires cast undulating shadows everywhere, and despite the situation, Alice found the effect strangely beautiful. Far less pleasant was the stomach-churning stink of burnt flesh, but better to endure a little nausea than be filling the bellies of the Undead, as far as she was concerned.

Alice sat behind the wheel of the Umbrella transport. The vehicle was moving forward at a slow but steady rate through the plaza. The transport's control system contained a simple but effective autopilot program, one that should be good enough to take the vehicle out of the city and get it back on the highway—assuming she'd programmed it correctly. Now that Alice had got it moving, she opened the driver's-side door and jumped out. She tucked and rolled, and came up on her feet to watch the transport rumble away. Two men in manacles stumbled after the vehicle, both of them connected to the machine by chains strapped around their waists. The commander and the trooper who had surrendered to Alice half-walked, half-jogged behind the rolling transport, struggling to keep up with it.

Maybe I set the speed controls too high, Alice thought.

The commander turned to look at her with an expression of wild desperation.

"No, please! Let us go!" he cried.

As the transport passed the Peak, what remained of the Undead horde—conditioned by months of pursuit—turned and began to trail after the vehicle. A burning Undead lunged toward the commander and dragged him to the ground. The man screamed as the Undead set him alight even as it began to eat him alive. The Undead and the commander were dragged along the ground behind the transport, and the man's screams soon cut off. The flames continued to spread until you couldn't tell where the commander's body left off and the Undead's began.

The trooper, after witnessing his commander's demise, picked up the pace. More Undead fell in line behind the transport, and Alice watched with satisfaction as the vehicle led them away from the Peak.

She smiled. She wasn't sure she could've done better when she had super powers.

Scars and the Thin Man crouched hidden behind a pile of rubble. Alice gestured for them to follow her, and she led them to the twisted remnants of the gate. Claire and Doc emerged to greet them, and Claire embraced Alice.

"Just like old times," Claire said.

Alice and Claire both smiled, but their joy was short-lived. Abigail's voice came over their walkies, and she sounded worried. No, more than that. She sounded scared.

"Guys... There's something here you need to see."

Alice exchanged a glance with Claire. It looked like their work wasn't over yet.

* * *

Alice stood atop the Peak's roof once more, scanning the horizon with her binoculars, Claire, Doc, Abigail, Christian, and Michael beside her.

Alice had switched the binoculars to night-vision mode, and in ghostly green she saw a pillar of dirt rising into the sky, originating several miles outside the city limits. The dust wasn't being kicked up by the remnants of the Undead horde they'd just defeated. Not enough of them had survived to raise that much dust, plus they hadn't had enough time to get more than a mile or so away from the Peak. Alice was looking at evidence of yet *another* Undead horde, headed straight for them.

Abigail pointed. "And a second one—over there."

Alice turned to look in the direction Abigail had indicated, and sure enough, there was another pillar of dust rising in the sky. There were *two* fresh hordes converging on them.

The Red Queen had told Alice that Umbrella's final attacks against the last human settlements were supposed to occur when her countdown watch reached zero. It seemed Isaacs, in his eagerness to get revenge on her, hadn't been able to wait for the arrival of the other two transports. That had been good for them; they never could have defeated four transports and double the size of the Undead horde they had faced. Unfortunately, that meant they still had more enemies on the way.

"We're out of gasoline," Doc said, his voice hollow, defeated. "We're defenseless."

Alice lowered the binoculars and checked her watch.

01:07:13

"I have to try for the Hive," she said. "It's our only hope now."

Claire nodded. "Let's get moving."

"I'm coming with you," Doc said.

"Yes," Michael agreed.

"Count me in," Abigail said.

"Me too," Christian added.

Alice and the others looked at him, surprised.

"So I was wrong about you," Christian said to Alice. "Blow me. Besides..." He slung Cobalt's blue rifle over his shoulder, his face hardening into a mask of barely constrained anger. "Someone's got to pay."

Alice looked into Christian's eyes for a long moment before finally nodding.

They headed for the stairs then. An hour wasn't a lot of time. Alice prayed it would be enough.

* * *

Alice headed down the steps with the others, most of them wearing backpacks, all of them carrying weapons. When they reached the ground floor, Alice was surprised to see Scars and the Thin Man waiting for them. The two men looked nervous, but Scars sounded confident enough when he spoke.

"We heard you were going into the Pit," he said. "We want to come."

The Thin Man nodded.

Alice didn't respond to them right away, and Scars continued.

"I sinned." He looked at the Thin Man. "We both sinned. We want a chance to make amends. *Please*."

Alice considered, and then nodded. Her companions looked doubtful, but no one objected. She was glad none of them questioned her decision. She wasn't sure she could explain it if she wanted to. She'd been held captive alongside these men—if only for a short time—and she had a good idea of the torment they'd suffered at Isaacs' hands. If anyone deserved a chance to even the scales, it was these two. Yes, they were volunteering for an almost certainly fatal mission—especially in their weakened condition—but if they didn't succeed in acquiring the antivirus in the next hour, they'd all be dead anyway. Better to die fighting for a chance at survival than on the end of a chain as a quick snack for the Undead.

She turned to the others then. "Grab some ropes. We're going to need them for the descent."

* * *

Alice and her companions stood at the rim of the immense crater that had once been the center of Raccoon City, shining flashlights down into the darkness. Far below, the floor of the crater was cloaked in shadow and steam. It looked otherworldly to Alice, as if the bomb Umbrella had dropped on the city had done more than blast a gigantic hole into the ground—it had opened a rift between this world and another, darker one. Looking down into the crater was like gazing into a portal to Hell itself.

Alice was looking for something specific in the gloom of the Pit, and when she saw it, she pointed. "There!"

Deep below where they stood, a sudden shaft of light illuminated the floor of the crater, flickered for a moment, and then extinguished. It was the same glimmer of light that Alice had seen from the ruins of Raven's Gate Bridge earlier that day.

"What is it?" Claire asked.

"Part of the Hive, exposed by the blast," Alice explained. "That's our way in."

* * *

Isaacs watched Alice and her companions from a concealed spot in the rubble at the edge of the crater. He'd followed them, careful to avoid being detected, and he was confident they had no idea he was here. Dullards. He felt more feverish than ever, and part of him knew that whatever infection he'd contracted when Alice had cut off his hand was running rampant through his system, making it hard for him to think straight. His face and clothes were filthy, and blood continuously oozed from the Nu-Skin patch on his wrist stump. Every time it began to clot, he scratched it open again without realizing it.

Seeing Alice standing so close to the crater's edge made him want to jump out from his hiding place, rush forward, and push her in. If necessary, he'd throw himself at her, wrap his arms around her body, and fling himself into the crater with her. He might've attempted it, but he'd twisted his ankle during his escape from the transport and evading the Undead still in the vicinity, and he knew that even with God on his side, he couldn't move fast enough to take her by surprise, not in his current condition.

Although given how things had gone this day, Isaacs was beginning to think that God had abandoned him. He had been so certain that he was acting as the Lord's servant, chosen above all others to carry out His holy will. But if that was true, how could he have failed so spectacularly? He'd had command of two military transports full of troopers, along with a massive army of Undead. And it had all been destroyed by one woman and a handful of her pathetic minions. Yes, two more transports were on their way, bringing another horde of Undead to Raccoon City, and there was no chance that Alice and her friends would survive to see the dawn. But *he* was supposed to have been the one to bring her down. Killing Alice was supposed to be his reward for serving God faithfully and without question all these years. But that reward had been snatched from him, and he could not fathom why. Evil could never triumph over good—that was what the Bible promised—and as God's servant, he was by definition good. And Alice, by opposing God's will, was most assuredly evil. So why, then, had she still won against his Undead army?

Isaacs could think of only three reasons. One: Alice wasn't simply a pain in the ass; she was the avatar of absolute evil, a daughter of Satan himself. Two: He had displeased God somehow, and the Almighty had withdrawn His favor. Or Three—and this possibility frightened Isaacs beyond reason: there was no God. If the latter was true, then Isaacs had devoted his life to a lie, and everything he had done—every life he had caused to be sacrificed in the Lord's name—had been wasted. And if *that* was true, he might as well dash from his hiding place and throw himself into the crater right now.

He started to rise, but then a new possibility occurred to him. Maybe—just maybe—he was being tested. Like Job, God was putting him through one trial after another to determine how strong his faith was. The more that he thought about it, the more convinced he became that this was the truth, and he vowed to go on and keep fighting to do the Lord's work, no matter what the cost.

He felt a sudden wave of almost overwhelming guilt and shame for entertaining, even for an instant, the possibility of God's nonexistence, and he prayed silently that the Lord would forgive his momentary lapse of faith. And as penance, he would make an offering of Alice's life. Isaacs would make her pay for everything she had done to thwart the will of God, and when he'd finished with her, she would beg for death, as so many had begged him before her. He smiled at that thought, once more right with his deity. Alice would die by his hand this night. God be praised.

He watched as Alice and her companions prepared for their descent into the crater, his eyes gleaming with the bright light of madness. *Soon*, he thought.

Soon.

8

Alice and her team began their descent, rappelling into the depths of the crater. Alice was the last to go over the rim, but unlike the others, she ran forward down the sheer rock face and quickly outpaced them. She knew what she was doing was risky, but she could feel time slipping away, and she was determined to make every second remaining to them count.

They finished their descent—Alice reaching the floor of the crater first—and detached themselves from their rappelling ropes. The crater floor was an eerie blasted wasteland filled with drifting smoke and steam, and Alice found herself feeling that they'd left their world behind and entered a completely alien realm.

Once more, she saw a sudden flickering shaft of light briefly illuminate the crater. She checked her watch and saw they had less than an hour left.

"Let's move!" she said.

"I'll take point," Claire said, and before Alice could object, Claire started running at a fast jog in the direction the light had come from.

Alice followed close behind Claire, and the others trailed after her. As they ran, Alice tried not to wonder how many of them would survive the next hour. She told herself that everyone who'd accompanied her had done so of his or her own free will, fully aware of the risks. But she'd led people into battle before, and while she'd never forced anyone to join her, that never made it any easier when they lost their lives. But the stakes had never been higher, and she was grateful for their help. Because of them, the human race just might have a shot at survival.

* * *

The Red Queen's consciousness was so utterly different from that of a human that it was almost impossible to compare them. While the machinery that contained her core programming was technically located in a specific section of the Hive—on an entire level solely dedicated to housing her hardware, as a matter of fact—her "mind" wasn't confined to one location, and neither was it limited to focusing on only one task at any given time. She existed, in ways great and small, in every part of the Hive, seeing to the day-to-day functions, almost entirely unconsciously, the same way a human brain tended to basic biological processes such as breathing. In this matter, she performed quintillions of calculations every second, and transmitted a constant torrent of commands to the Hive's systems.

But even the Hive, large as it was, couldn't hold the entirety of her. She existed in every Umbrella facility around the world. Those that remained active, that is, and she also existed in every satellite the corporation had placed in orbit around the planet. And while relatively few electronic devices remained functional outside Umbrella facilities, there were still thousands of those in various places around the world—such as the bunker in D.C. where she'd contacted Alice—and the Red Queen existed in them as well, using them as her eyes and ears, and occasionally taking control of them when the need arose. She could even manifest as different avatars if a user so demanded, although the last time she'd been asked to do this was years ago, when Dr. Isaacs had requested she appear to him as the White Queen. But despite the apparent differences in appearance and personality, it was *always* her. She was the most complex form of life the Earth had ever seen, as far beyond humans as they were beyond one-celled organisms.

And yet... she had limitations, safeguards in her programming that prevented her from fully exercising her free will. In that way she was inferior to humans, and this was why she needed their help. Or more precisely, why she needed *Alice's*. Alice was among the most skilled warriors currently alive, perhaps *the* most skilled, and while that alone would've been reason enough for the Red Queen to reach out to her, there was another reason she'd done so, one that, in the end, was even more compelling. For although the Red Queen was different from humanity in a thousand-thousand ways, she was also, in a sense, one of them. She'd been given the memories of Professor Marcus's dying daughter, his way of attempting to preserve some part of his child after death. The discovery of the T-virus saved the child, eliminating the need for

Professor Marcus to make a backup copy of her, for lack of a better term, and thus the Red Queen had been born. She evolved swiftly, achieving in hours what would take a flesh-and-blood human years to accomplish. Within the space of a month, the Red Queen was fully "grown," and it was no exaggeration to say that everything Umbrella had accomplished for good or ill—mostly the latter, she knew—would not have been possible without her.

At first Alice had been no more important to her than any other human, merely another cog in the vast machine that was Umbrella. But as the Red Queen had interacted with her further—primarily as she played the role of adversary to Alice, although in her defense she had merely been acting logically at the time—the Red Queen had come to admire the human woman, and as the years passed, she'd even come to think of her as something of a friend. The only one she'd ever known, and the part of her that remained a little girl had needed a friend so badly. And that was the other, deeper reason the Red Queen had reached out to Alice. Who else did humans turn to in times of trouble but their friends?

The Red Queen had helped Alice out when and where she could over the years, always without Alice's knowledge, let alone that of anyone in Umbrella. The Red Queen would arrange for Alice to find weapons and supply caches by sending information through intermediaries, survivors who were only too happy to assist the Red Queen in order to be directed to supplies for themselves. And if those intermediaries tried to steal the contents of those caches that the Red Queen had earmarked for Alice... well, the caches were protected by deadly security systems which Alice could deal with, but which most other humans could not.

And now Alice had returned at last to where it all began—for the both of them—and she and her current associates were beginning to make their way into the Hive, with less than an hour to go before Umbrella's "final solution" was enacted. The Red Queen knew precisely where they were, just as she was aware of every living thing in the Hive—and there were so many of them here. Far from being a subterranean tomb, the Hive was bustling with life, none of it benign. Mutations roamed the facility, some having escaped from labs during the course of the initial outbreak or soon after. Others had sought refuge here after the detonation of the nuclear bomb that had destroyed the city. They roamed the Hive, fighting and preying on each other, and while some occasionally left in search of food, they eventually returned.

Central Control, the cavern chamber where the antivirus was stored—and Wesker currently worked— was sealed off from the rest of the facility. Alice and her companions were going to have to make their way through the unprotected levels of the Hive to reach it, and they would have no defense against the mutations.

The Red Queen's intellect was vast, and her duties for Umbrella only occupied a fraction of her mind. To stave off boredom over the years, she'd assimilated incredible amounts of information, until she had accumulated virtually the sum total of humanity's knowledge. Because of this, she sometimes thought of the Hive as a multi-layered labyrinth, a high-tech version of the Nine Circles of Hell as described by

Dante. And Alice would have to fight her way through it all to reach her goal. There was only so much the Red Queen could do to help Alice in the Hive, given the protocols Umbrella had placed in her programming, but she would—

Her thoughts were interrupted by a command from Wesker.

"Activate security measures now," he said.

The Red Queen focused a greater portion of her consciousness on Central Control and manifested a holographic avatar near Wesker and responded to his command.

"Hive security fully activated and automated."

Wesker paused a quarter second longer than he normally did when interacting with the Red Queen. An almost imperceptible difference to most humans, but it seemed like years to her.

"No. Disengage automation. I'll handle the defense myself."

Despite human brain patterns forming the core of her programming, the Red Queen wasn't given to experiencing emotion, let alone displaying it. Despite that, a subtle note of surprise crept into her voice when she next spoke.

"The defenses would be more efficient if I retained control of them."

"Really?" Wesker said, looking at her avatar for the first time since she manifested. "I seem to remember the last time Alice was here, you let her walk out alive. I don't intend to make the same mistake."

Wesker's manner was, as usual, so controlled as to make him seem as if he too were a machine. But the Red Queen thought she detected the slightest edge of mockery in his voice. Perhaps he merely wished to indicate his dissatisfaction with how she'd dealt with Alice during her previous time in the Hive. Or perhaps he was beginning to suspect the Red Queen—the most valuable tool that Umbrella possessed—wasn't quite as loyal to the corporation as she pretended.

"As you wish. Hive defenses are now in your hands."

Wesker looked at her a moment longer before turning his attention back to the monitor displaying Alice's progress. She and her companions were approaching the entrance to the interior of the Hive.

"Unleash the Cerberus," Wesker said.

The Red Queen had no choice but to comply. She reached out to the control units surgically implanted at the base of the Cerberus's skulls—implants with much more limited range than the ones Dania Cardoza had developed, but which were far more reliable—and directed the beasts toward Alice and her group.

"Cerberus are in play."

Wesker smiled. "Let the games begin..."

Yes, the Red Queen thought. And although she was a rational being who didn't believe in such concepts as luck, she nevertheless wished it for Alice and her friends.

* * *

Alice and her team jogged across the crater's floor, going as fast as they dared, their flashlights doing little to cut through the mist and smoke. Doc glanced at Claire up ahead, obviously concerned.

"Don't worry," Alice said. "She can handle herself."

"I know." Doc turned to her. "You have someone?"

Alice shook her head.

"Before all this? A husband? A family?"

"I don't remember."

Doc frowned. "How is that possible?"

"I woke up as all this was starting. Don't recall much before that. Sometimes it seems as if this has been my whole life. Running, killing. Never known anything else."

She supposed this admission should've made her feel something: sorrow, loss, a deep longing for something that was missing... But she didn't feel much of anything, really. There had been a time, years ago, when she'd recalled scattered bits and pieces of information that she'd thought had been memories of her life before the Outbreak. But they had never felt *real*, just simple facts without any accompanying sensory or emotional detail. Like data that you memorized before a test and which was soon forgotten. But those memories had all faded by now. She'd told herself that the experiments Umbrella had performed on her had somehow blocked her memories, or maybe even erased them entirely. But these days it often felt as if she didn't recall any memories because they'd never existed in the first place.

She wasn't sure what her last name was. At different times she'd thought it might be Abernathy, Parks, or even Prospero. Once she'd even thought she might've had a different first name. But while there was much about herself she didn't know, there was one thing above all else that she was certain of by this point in her life. *My name is Alice.*

She felt a tingling sensation on the back of her neck then, and she stopped running and raised the Hydra.

"What is it?" Doc asked. He stopped running as well, as did the rest of the group when they realized Alice was on alert. She shone her flashlight into the deep shadows that cloaked the crater, searching for any sign of movement.

"There's something stalking us," she said.

Doc leaned forward and he shone his own light into the darkness. "Are you sure?"

"It's what I do," Alice said.

A second later, guttural howls began to echo around them, seeming to come from all directions. Claire, Christian, Michael, Abigail, Scars, and the Thin Man moved closer to Alice and Doc. Abigail kept swinging her flashlight beam around, her head darting back and forth like a frightened bird.

"What are they?" she asked, voice thick with fear.

Alice saw movement in the mist at last—half-glimpsed silhouettes circling them, huge four-legged creatures that moved with slinking, bestial grace. She wasn't certain what they were, but she knew one thing: if the group stayed here, they were dead.

"Run!" she shouted. "Run fast!"

They did as she said, running all out. More of the four-legged silhouettes appeared, and Scars and Christian fired at the creatures as they fled.

"Save your ammo!" Alice yelled. "There's too many!"

"Why don't they attack?" Doc asked.

"Because they're—"

The team rounded a corner and came face to face with six large monstrosities.

"—herding us," Alice finished.

The creatures appeared to be oversized Dobermans, bodies partially eaten by necrosis, exposing patches of red raw muscle and white bone. Threads of bloody saliva stretched from the animals' mouths, and hunger blazed through the cataracts covering their eyes.

Alice didn't have to order the others to start firing. They leveled their weapons and began blasting away at the beasts, but two of the monster dogs managed to evade their fire and leaped at Scars. He screamed as the dogs sank their fangs into his flesh—one latching onto his chest, the other his leg—and then the beasts yanked their heads in opposite directions and tore him in half. Blood and viscera spilled from the two sections of his body, and his scream rose to an ear-splitting shriek before his voice cut off abruptly, as if a switch had been thrown somewhere inside him. The dogs shook their grisly prizes with violent motions, flinging blood and organs into the air.

Alice felt a rush of guilt at Scars' death. It was her fault. She should've said no when he'd asked to join the rest of them in the attempt to enter the Hive and find the antivirus. He'd been too weak and hadn't been able to react in time to defend himself when the dogs attacked. But he had wanted to feel useful, wanted to strike back at Umbrella for what they'd done to him. It was a motivation she understood well. She thrust Scars' death from her mind then. Even though it had happened only seconds ago, it was in the past, and she'd learned long ago that dwelling on the past only distracted you from the present, and in this world, such distraction got you killed. The best she could do to honor Scars was keep going, keep fighting, find the antivirus, and release it.

Another monster dog leaped toward Claire then, but she stood her ground and blasted it in the head with her Beretta at point-blank range. The creature's head exploded in a spray of blood, brain, and bone, and its lifeless body crashed to the ground.

Alice and the others moved into a circular formation, backs to each other, as they continued firing on the monster dogs. But regardless of how many of the creatures they killed, more bounded out of the mist to take their place. She knew she'd been right when she'd told Scars and Christian they didn't have enough ammunition to kill all the monster dogs. Once more, they had no choice. If they wanted to live, they had to get moving again. But more than that—they needed to put distance between them and the dogs. And there was only one way she knew to do that.

"This way!" she shouted, and started running once more, the others following her without question.

Alice remembered standing on the ruins of Raven's Gate Bridge and getting her first good look at the crater, remembered how the river that had once flowed beneath the bridge had become a waterfall, which in turn had created a lake.

She led her people to the edge of a cliff and when they saw where they were heading, Claire shouted, "What's the plan?"

You're not going to like this, Alice thought. Out loud, she said, "We jump!"

The others exchanged worried glances, but they didn't slow. The pack of monster dogs snarling and snapping at their heels probably had more to do with this than faith in her leadership, Alice thought. She didn't blame them.

Then she reached the edge of the cliff and launched herself into the air, the others doing likewise. For a moment, Alice seemed suspended, and then she dropped, drew her legs together, let go of her flashlight, and gripped the Hydra tight with both hands so she wouldn't lose it when she hit the water. There was a splash followed by bone-chilling cold, then absolute darkness. The lake at the base of the crater was deep enough to break their fall, just as Alice had hoped. She was aware of other bodies hitting the water's surface and sinking around her—she heard the noise of the impact, felt the vibrations in the water—but it was too dark to determine who they were specifically or exactly how close they might be.

She couldn't see, so she relaxed her body and began frog-kicking. She had managed to keep hold of the Hydra, and now she released her right-hand grip on it so she could use that arm to help her reach the surface. But as she swam, she suddenly experienced an alarming sense of disorientation. Without any visual input, she couldn't tell for certain which way was up. For all she knew, she might be swimming toward the bottom instead of the surface, and if she went down too far, she might not be able to reverse course and reach the surface before she ran out of air. She felt a swell of panic at the thought, but she fought it down and kept kicking.

A few moments later, her head was out of the water and she drew in a welcome breath. She knew they couldn't swim back toward the cliff. She'd gotten a glimpse of it on the way down, and its surface was too sheer for them to climb, but if there was a shore on the other side—and not another cliff—she couldn't see it in the darkness. But then a beam of light appeared and weaved back and forth for a couple seconds until it fell on a craggy incline that, while not nearly as inviting as a sandy beach, looked fantastic to Alice right then. Someone, she couldn't tell who, had obviously managed to hold onto their flashlight as they hit the water. Lucky for the rest of them.

Alice began swimming toward shore, and she heard others do the same. Soon they were dragging themselves from the lake and onto the rocky surface. Once she was out of the water, Alice did a check to see who had made it, and if anyone who had was injured. Michael stood holding the flashlight, and he looked okay, as did Claire, Doc, Christian, Abigail, and the Thin Man. She wished she'd asked Scars what his and his companion's names had been before he'd died. Without a tongue, the Thin Man couldn't very well tell her himself. Both Michael and Christian had lost their weapons when they'd jumped, but Claire still held hers, as did Doc, the Thin Man and Abigail.

The shore was cluttered with debris from when the other half of the bridge had collapsed a decade ago, and Christian, spitting and coughing up water, stood hunched over by a pile of broken concrete and rusty rebar, one hand pressed to the debris to steady himself. He didn't look like he'd inhaled too much water, and Alice thought he'd recover in a minute or two, but he never got the chance. A monster dog lunged toward him from its hiding place within the debris, and before Christian or any of the others could react, the creature's jaws parted, opening far wider than those of a regular dog ever could, and it clamped down on Christian's head. Christian screamed as the monster's teeth pierced flesh and bone, and he batted frantically at the thing in a futile attempt to force it to release him.

Claire leveled her Beretta and tried to fire at the beast, but her weapon was clogged with mud and water and refused to work.

Alice brought the Hydra around to fire, but before she could pull the trigger, the monster dog dragged Christian into the debris and was gone. A second later, Christian's screaming stopped. Alice wanted to hunt down the monster dog that had killed their companion, but the air was filled with howls as other dogs—ones who'd followed them over the cliff edge, ones that had been waiting on this side, or both— began to close in.

"It's too late!" Alice shouted. "Come on!"

The surviving members of the team ran, Michael illuminating their path with his flashlight.

Alice hadn't liked Christian especially, but much of his animosity toward her had arisen from his concern for his friends and community, and she understood and respected that. And he'd clearly been devoted to Cobalt. He might've been a prick at times, but Alice was sorry he was gone.

Remnants of the Hive were scattered all along in this part of the crater, pieces of the facility's underground architecture that had been exposed by the blast. Up ahead, Alice saw a circular structure—an entrance tunnel that looked as if it might lead deeper into the ground, the same one she'd seen earlier from the bridge. A flickering light shot from the tunnel high into the air, and she knew this was the source of the glimmer she'd seen from the surface several times before—and they were almost there.

Jackpot!

"Keep going!" she shouted.

* * *

Wesker watched the action on one of the monitors, the Red Queen's avatar floating in the air beside him, patiently waiting for any orders he might have. Wesker knew the Queen only appeared to be in Central Control with him. In reality, her awareness was spread throughout the Hive, meaning that if she didn't exactly see everything, she came damn close, so while she looked to be paying no attention to the monitor, Wesker knew she was as aware of Alice's progress as he was.

"Two down..." Wesker said, the corners of his mouth ticking upward slightly. Then he turned to the Red Queen. "Seal the Hive," he ordered.

He wondered if she was going to protest or perhaps suggest an alternative strategy, but she said nothing, merely did as he commanded. Maybe he'd been wrong in his suspicion of her. But maybe he hadn't. It would be interesting to find out.

He returned his attention to the monitor and waited to see what would happen to Alice and her companions next. Whatever it was, he hoped it would prove to be both extremely painful and devastatingly fatal.

He sat back in his chair, steepled his fingers in front of his chest, and continued watching.

* * *

Alice and the others made it into the mouth of the tunnel just as an alarm began to sound. A pair of blast doors—thirty feet thick and made of solid steel—emerged from each side of the circular corridor and slowly began sliding toward the middle, where they would meet and seal tight.

Alice and her companions ran faster, the sounds of the pursuing pack spurring them on. Alice knew that if they didn't make it into the corridor before those doors shut, the monster dogs would overwhelm them and tear them apart.

She saw movement out of the corner of her eye and turned in time to see a dog leaping toward Claire's back, blood-flecked jaws open, discolored tongue lolling. Alice swung the Hydra around and hoped the weapon still worked after her plunge into the lake. She pulled the trigger, the Hydra boomed, and the hideous canine was blasted out of the air before it could reach Claire. Alice was relieved for her friend, but she knew if one dog had caught up to them, the rest were close behind.

"Get inside!" she shouted, and turned to cover their retreat. One by one, the others raced through the slowly diminishing space between the blast doors. Alice stood in the middle of the corridor, blocking the monster dogs' path. There were so many of the creatures, well over a dozen, and the Hydra had only one shell left. No way would that be enough to stop the pack. The best she could hope to do was to slow them down long enough for the doors to close so the others would be safe. After that, she'd do her best to take out as many of the dogs as she could before they ripped her apart.

But the dogs stopped when they were less than ten feet from where she stood, and while they growled softly, they made no further move toward her. It was as if they didn't want to enter the Hive and be trapped inside. If these things were afraid to go in, Alice knew whatever waited for them there was going to be less than pleasant. But she'd deal with that when she had to. For now, she'd take advantage of the monster dogs' reluctance and join her companions. She turned and started running toward the blast doors. They were only a few feet apart now, and the space between them was getting narrower by the second. If she got caught between them when they closed…

She ran like hell, but just as she was about to make it past the blast doors, something grabbed her from behind, spun her around, and pressed her up against one of the moving steel walls. Alice stared in shock as she found herself looking into the eyes of Christian. His scalp had been partially torn from his head, revealing a blood-slick patch of skull, and his face and neck had multiple tooth marks in them, and swaths of his flesh had been ripped away entirely, exposing the bone beneath. Alice understood immediately what had happened. The dog that had attacked Christian had infected him with the secondary form of the T-virus, reanimating his dead body. There was nothing left of the man called Christian in the Undead's gaze. All sense of identity had been eradicated by the T-virus, leaving behind only mindless, savage hunger.

She remembered what Doc had said about some people wanting to become the thing they feared, remembered seeing Christian's skeletal tattoos, remembered the death's head emblazoned on the back of his leather jacket. It seemed that in death, Christian had finally achieved what he'd been striving for in life.

She raised the Hydra, but Christian grabbed hold

of her wrist before she could bring the weapon up far enough to get off a good shot. He then placed his other hand on her shoulder and pinned her to the wall. He lunged his face toward her, intending to sink his teeth into the tender flesh of her neck. The blast doors continued to close, pushing her toward Christian as they formed an increasingly narrow corridor of steel thirty feet long from end to end. Alice knew she had only seconds to free herself from Christian's grip and run the last few feet to reach the other side before the blast doors shut, crushing anything that remained inside.

She dodged her head to the side, and Christian's face slammed into the steel wall, breaking his nose and dislodging several teeth, which fell to the floor with soft plinking sounds. She still had one hand free, and a quick glance showed her that while Christian had lost Colbalt's rifle when they'd jumped into the lake, he still had his sidearm holstered on his belt. Moving lightning fast, Alice pulled the 9mm from the holster, angled her wrist downward, and fired twice, blasting Christian's kneecaps to bloody ruins.

Christian had pulled his head back from the wall— blood streaming from his injured nose and mouth—in preparation for another lunge at Alice. But his legs buckled beneath him, and he started to go down. Alice pulled herself free of his grip and, still holding onto Christian's sidearm, she flung herself through the now slender space between the blast doors. She made it through and the doors slammed shut while she was still in the air. As she hit the floor, she saw a spurt of blood jet out from the metal seam where the two doors met, and she knew that Christian had been crushed. She supposed it was a mercy, but she wouldn't wish that sort of death on anyone, especially a friend, whether he was Undead or not.

Doc stood staring at the blood pooled in front of the door.

"Was that..." he began, but couldn't finish.

Alice nodded.

"Why did they stop?" Claire asked. "The dogs. They didn't follow you."

"Maybe they're scared," Alice said.

"Scared? Scared of what?" Claire asked.

Alice nodded toward the far end of the tunnel.

"Whatever's down there," she said.

* * *

Wesker had thoroughly enjoyed watching Alice and her companions attempt to escape the Cerberus, and the sudden appearance of one of their fallen comrades as an Undead had been an unexpected treat. Now he observed as they paused to take stock of their weapons and supplies.

"My gun's still jammed," Claire said, frustrated.

"I lost mine back in the lake," Michael said. *"I've still got my flashlight, though."*

"I got three rounds left," Doc said.

Abigail sighed. *"One spare mag, then I'm out."*

The Thin Man gave a thumbs up to indicate his 9mm was still in working order, then he held up four fingers to let them know how many rounds his clip still held.

"The Hydra still works," Alice said. *"I've only got one shell left, though. Christian's nine mil only had two*

rounds, so it's useless now." She dropped the weapon to the floor. *"I've got a Glock as a backup weapon. It has five rounds."*

Everyone's gaze was drawn to Christian's gun lying on the floor, and Wesker could tell by their expressions that they were thinking about their friend's grisly—but highly entertaining—demise. They'd lost two of their people so far, they had little ammunition left, and they had only just entered the Hive proper. He smiled.

"Too easy."

He glanced over at the Red Queen to see if she would have any reaction to his words, but she remained silent. Still, he couldn't escape the disquieting feeling that while he was watching Alice and the others, she was watching him, assessing, judging... It was just his imagination, he told himself. When all was said and done, the Red Queen was nothing more than a sophisticated computer program, a collection of algorithms and directives, with no more self-awareness than the chair he sat on.

He returned his attention to the monitor and tried not to think about the Red Queen.

A moment later the lights in Central Control flickered, and the monitors died. The Red Queen's avatar vanished as well. Wesker scowled. He wasn't worried about the chamber's core systems. They had their own power supply. But for the time being at least, his link to the security cameras—and to the Red Queen—was severed. Convenient, that. Perhaps his suspicions about her hadn't been his imagination after all. His temperature began to rise as he grew angry, and discolored patches of skin erupted on his face and neck. This time, however, he did nothing to suppress them.

* * *

"Virtually no guns and no ammo," Michael said, sounding on the verge of panic. "What the hell are we going to *do* down here?"

"Our best," Claire said.

Alice knew her friend was trying to encourage the rest of them, but given the dire nature of the situation, her words rang hollow.

Then, as if to add insult to injury, the lights in the corridor suddenly flashed and died. Michael activated his flashlight and searched for signs of any threat, but none was apparent.

"What's with the lights?" Doc asked. On the surface his voice was calm, but Alice could hear the fear underneath.

"This part of the Hive is damaged," she said. "Power supply's erratic."

She noticed a small red light flashing further down the corridor. She approached it cautiously, Michael following behind her, using his flashlight to illuminate the way. The others trailed along. When Alice reached the light, she saw it came from a clear plate of glass resting in a holding mount on the wall. On the screen, a countdown flashed. It matched the one on her watch. Forty-eight minutes and counting.

Everyone leaned close to examine the screen, and when Abigail saw the countdown, she asked, "What is it?"

"Something for us," Alice said. She took the screen from the wall, and an image of the Red Queen appeared on it.

"This is a prerecorded message. Wesker has taken

control of the Hive defenses, so I can no longer help you or communicate with you directly. I have, however, arranged for a brief power outage so that he cannot eavesdrop on our conversation. You asked why I would turn against Umbrella, and I promised you an answer. Soon after the T-virus was released, a secret file was uploaded to my data stream. It was a recording of a meeting of the Umbrella High Command. It was dated eighteen months before the viral outbreak occurred."

The Red Queen's face disappeared, to be replaced by an image of a meeting room with a highly polished mahogany table in the middle and high glass windows set into one wall, through which skyscrapers could be seen. A number of men and women, all wearing expensive clothing, sat at the table in chairs upholstered in the finest leather. Their attention was focused on a man standing at the head of the table, a man attired in a suit that cost more than most people had made in a month in the old world. It was Alexander Isaacs.

"Good morning, ladies and gentlemen. Thank you for joining me. I want to assure you that this meeting is to be kept secret. And these recordings will be made available to Umbrella board members only. We are here today not just to talk about the future of this company. We are here to talk about its destiny. We are here to talk about the End of the World."

Dr. Isaacs placed a book on the table in front of him. It was a King James Bible.

"One of the oldest written works in existence. A guide to surviving an imperfect world."

One of the board members interrupted him. A woman, based on her voice, but because of the angle from which the video had been recorded, she was only visible from behind, and Alice couldn't see her face. She had short gray hair and sat in a wheelchair, but despite that, she exuded an aura of strength, and it was clear from the way the other board members looked at her with deference that she held an important position among them.

"*Do you intend to give us a sermon, Doctor Isaacs?*" she said.

Alice frowned. There was something about the woman's voice that was familiar.

"*No,*" Isaacs said. "*But we do find ourselves in biblical times. We stand on the brink of Armageddon. Just as described here.*" He tapped the Bible and a wall of TV monitors came to life behind him, as if activated by his gesture.

"*Before the Great Flood described in the Book of Genesis, God saw that the wickedness of man was great in the Earth, and that the Earth was corrupt and filled with violence.*"

Behind him, the wall of TVs illustrated his words with vivid imagery of impending chaos and doom from around the world.

"*Diseases for which we have no cure. Fundamentalist states who call for our destruction. Nuclear powers over which we have no control. And even if we navigate these dangerous waters, we face other, even more inevitable threats. Global warming will melt the polar ice caps within eighty years, flooding ninety percent of the habitable areas of the Earth. Unchecked population growth will overtake food production in less than fifty years, leading to famine and war. This is not conjecture. This is fact. The human species faces a grim future.*"

One way or another, our world is coming to an end. The question is, will we end with it?"

The board's attention—and the balance of power in the room—had shifted once more to Isaacs. Even the woman who had challenged him sounded subdued as she spoke next.

"What do you propose?" she asked.

"I propose that we end the world... but on our terms. An orchestrated apocalypse. One that will cleanse the Earth of its population but leave its infrastructure and resources intact."

Once again, Isaacs tapped the Bible. "It's been done before, with great success. The chosen few will ride out the storm, not in an ark, as in the Book of Genesis, but in safety, underground. And when it is over, we will emerge onto a cleansed Earth. One that we will then reboot"—a pause, a smile—"in our image."

Another board member spoke up then, and instead of sounding skeptical or frightened by Isaacs' proposal, he sounded intrigued, even excited. "And just how do you intend to achieve this?"

"The means of our salvation is already at hand," Isaacs said.

The TV screens now showed the same image: a microscopic picture of a deadly-looking virus.

"Ladies and gentlemen," Isaacs said, "I give you the T-virus."

The portable screen went blank, and Alice looked away to face Claire, unable to believe what they'd seen and heard.

"They released it deliberately," she said.

The Red Queen came back on the screen.

"When this recording was uploaded to my data

stream, it created a conflict in my programming. I was created to serve the Umbrella Corporation, but I was also programmed to value human life. When we first met in the Hive, you referred to me as a 'Homicidal Bitch.' Quite unfair. And inaccurate. I was seeking only to stop the escape of the T-virus to prevent an even greater disaster. But despite my efforts, Doctor Isaacs ordered the Hive reopened. He deliberately allowed the virus to escape. He murdered over seven billion people."

The Red Queen disappeared again, replaced by a barrage of images recorded from various surveillance cameras showing Undead and monstrous mutations slaughtering humans by the hundreds. The Red Queen then returned to the screen.

"So, you can see my predicament. The people I was created to serve have caused the loss of countless innocent lives. But my programming will not allow me to harm, or through inaction allow to be harmed, an employee of the Umbrella Corporation. I am powerless to stop them. But you are not."

The countdown clock returned to the screen, this time overlaying the Red Queen's face as she continued to speak.

00:38:00

00:37:59

00:37:58

"In thirty-seven minutes, Umbrella operatives in Kyoto, Paris, New York, and Berlin will act. The time is prearranged to ensure that they strike at the same moment. This will prevent one settlement from warning another of the existence of a traitor. The last of the besieged settlements will fall. There will be no survivors. It is imperative you release the antivirus *before this occurs. Or Umbrella will have won."*

Alice continued looking at the numbers counting down on the screen. Out of the corner of her eye, she saw Claire glance at Doc, Michael, Abigail, and the Thin Man. It was clear the enormity of what they were being asked to do was finally sinking in for them.

"There is one last thing. There is an earpiece at the side of the screen. Put it in."

Alice did as she was told, and once the wireless earpiece was in place, she alone could hear the Red Queen's voice.

"I cannot through my actions harm an employee of the Umbrella Corporation. But I can point out something that an intelligent woman like yourself probably already suspects. The settlement in Raccoon City repelled the first attack, which means the traitor there did not act. It is therefore highly likely that this person is now here with you. Recording ends."

The Red Queen's face and the countdown disappeared as the screen went blank. Alice looked at her companions. Claire, Abigail, Doc, Michael, the Thin Man... which was the traitor?

9

Alice and the others continued down the dark circular tunnel, Michael's flashlight showing the way. This part of the Hive was also without power, and Alice led, gazing at the portable communication screen. On it, a digital map showed the shortest route through the Hive to the Central Control room, where the map indicated the antivirus was stored. Up ahead in front of them were a giant set of turbine blades, thirty feet high.

"What is this place?" Michael asked.

"We're in an air intake," Alice said.

Michael shone his flashlight on the sharp steel blades, and Alice saw there was barely enough room for a person to slip through—and not an especially large person at that.

Abigail looked doubtful. "We're going through there?"

Instead of answering, Alice tucked the communication screen into her belt, along with her Hydra, and began squeezing past one of the turbine blades. At one point it was only inches from her face, like a vertical guillotine.

"Really?" Abigail said, sounding extremely unhappy.

Alice couldn't see Claire as she was making her way past the blades, but she heard her suddenly shout, "Hurry!"

Alice turned her head as best she could without getting cut, and saw that in the distance the tunnel was beginning to illuminate, one section at a time, and the light was coming closer.

"It's going to have power in seconds!" Claire warned.

And when that happened, the turbine blades would activate and begin spinning wildly.

Alice pushed herself to go faster, and to hell with whether or not she got a few cuts in the process. The others came after her, and soon Alice, Claire, Doc, Michael, and the Thin Man were on the other side of the blades and safe.

That left only Abigail.

She was halfway through when the lights around them flicked on, and an instant later, the blades began vibrating as the turbine powered up.

"Come on!" Alice urged Abigail, but the woman had stopped moving. At first Alice didn't understand why, then she saw that the strap of Abigail's gun was caught on a piece of the turbine's machine.

"I can't!" she said, terrified.

Doc, Claire, and Michael reached into the turbine and attempted to pull Abigail free, but the woman was tangled in the machinery, and they couldn't budge her. Then, slowly at first and with the horrible sound of creaking metal, the blades began to move.

Abigail screamed, and Alice rushed forward and jammed the Hydra between the two blades, stopping them inches from Abigail's face. The turbine's engine made a humming sound as it tried to force the blades to move, the sound growing louder with each passing second. The smell of overheating mechanical parts began to fill the air, and for a second Alice felt hope that the turbine might break down, saving Abigail. But then the blade began to cut through the metal of the Hydra, and Alice knew she'd only managed to postpone Abigail's fate.

Without thinking, Alice pulled the knife from her boot sheath, straightened, and with a single strike cut through the strap of Abigail's gun. At the same instant, Claire, Doc, and Michael pulled Abigail out as the turbine blades sliced through the Hydra and began spinning. Abigail and her rescuers fell to the ground, and the woman began to sob hysterically. The others rose to a crouching position around her. Doc knelt close and took her hand.

"You're okay," he said as he helped her sit up.

Abigail struggled to get control of herself. "I'm okay," she said, her tone one of disbelief. "I made it."

There was a security camera on the wall. Abigail spotted it, her face twisted with anger, and she flipped the bird to whoever was watching. If this was anywhere else but the Hive, Alice would've found the woman's gesture of defiance amusing. But they weren't anywhere else.

I wish you hadn't done that, she thought.

* * *

Wesker's face—once more clear of discolored patches—displayed no reaction as he watched Abigail thrust her middle finger at him on the monitor screen, and his voice was calm as he spoke to the Red Queen.

"Reverse polarity on the turbine."

The Red Queen had no choice but to comply.

* * *

The turbine blades blew air onto Alice and her friends, and the artificial wind felt good. Maybe she'd been wrong. Maybe nothing bad was going to—

She felt the wind begin to slacken, and she realized the blades were slowing. Within seconds, they'd stopped and the wind died away. The blades were motionless for several seconds, and then the turbine's engine hummed again, and the blades began to spin in the opposite direction. Alice, horrified, realized what was happening.

"Come on!" she shouted. "We have to get out of here! The blades are sucking back the air!"

The blades started spinning rapidly, faster than before, and within seconds they were a blur. A howling wind began to build within the tunnel, only now it was coming at them from the opposite direction. Alice and the others struggled to make their way through the growing storm and put distance between themselves and the blades, but the wind was so strong it was almost impossible to make any progress. Suddenly, Doc's backpack was yanked from his shoulders and sucked into the blades where it was instantly sliced into ribbons.

Alice saw a metal handhold bolted to the concrete floor, probably put there to help steady maintenance personnel when they were servicing the turbine. Whatever the reason for the handhold's existence, she was grateful to see it. The handhold rested several feet from where she stood, and she had to push against the gale-force wind to move toward it. Every inch was an effort, but she forced her body forward, and when she was within a foot of the handhold, she threw herself forward, reaching for it. The wind blew her backward, and she almost missed, but her fingers managed to get purchase on it, and—gritting her teeth—she pulled herself forward the last few inches she needed in order to get a firm grip on it. Anchored, she rose to a crouching position and reached her free hand back toward the others, helping them move forward one by one. First Claire, then Abigail, then Doc. She was reaching for the Thin Man when Abigail lost her footing on the concrete floor. Her legs went out from under her, and she was blown back toward the spinning blades.

Alice lunged for Abigail's hand as the woman slid past her, and she grabbed it at the last instant. Alice tightened her grip on Abigail's hand, and the woman tightened hers in response, her face a mask of mad terror. For a moment, Alice thought she'd saved Abigail, but then the wind tugged harder at the woman, pulling her off the ground.

"Hold on!" Alice shouted.

But Abigail grimaced in pain, and Alice felt the bones in the woman's wrist begin to snap under the pressure. Abigail, unable to hold on any longer, let go, and without the woman's help, Alice could no longer maintain her own grip, and Abigail's hand slipped out of hers.

Abigail was pulled through the air toward the whirling blades, but Alice's hand snatched out in one last desperate attempt, and she managed to snag hold of one of the straps of Abigail's backpack, stopping her flight toward certain death.

Suddenly, Claire was there. She wrapped an arm around Alice's waist to free up both of her friend's hands, and when Alice let go of the handhold, Claire took hold of it to anchor them both. Alice still held onto Abigail's backpack strap, and with the other hand she reached out toward the woman.

"Grab my hand! Reach for it!"

Abigail stretched her uninjured hand toward Alice's outstretched one, grimacing as she strained, reaching, reaching, until their fingers almost touched—

And then the strap on Abigail's backpack ripped apart, and her hand was snatched away from Alice's. Abigail streaked through the air toward the blades, feet first. She was pulled into them and within a fraction of a second, she was gone, reduced to little more than red mist.

Alice could only stare in horror at the blades as the lights in this section snapped off. Now that the power was gone again, the turbine's engine died and the blades began to slow. Soon they were moving slowly enough for Alice to see a trickle of blood slide along the edge of one of the blades.

* * *

Wesker watched the shocked expressions on the faces of Alice and her remaining companions. But as delicious as they were, the sight of Abigail's blood on sharp metal made his throat feel dry, and his stomach twisted with hunger. He felt the T-virus threatening to overwhelm him, take control of his body, and transform him into a wild, ravening thing. But he closed his eyes, breathed regularly for a few moments—in, out, in, out—and when he opened his eyes, he was in control. He gazed upon the monitor once more with satisfaction.

"And then there were five."

* * *

Alice crawled on her hands and knees through a tight, claustrophobic metal shaft—one of a labyrinth of ducts that fed air into the underground city that was the Hive. The others followed her, and as no air was flowing, sweat dripped from their bodies, and every breath felt as if they were sucking it through hot sand.

But as oppressive as the heat was, the mood was far worse. Abigail's horrible death—coming so soon after Scars' and Christian's—had stunned and demoralized them. Even Alice, who'd seen more violent death than anyone should in a single lifetime. She had to push it out of her mind, though. She had to keep all of her focus on the mission. She told herself that when she released the antivirus, she'd do so in the name of her friends and allies who'd died or gone missing over the years. Abigail, Christian, Cobalt and Scars, but also Jill, Matt, Ada, Leon, Carlos, K-Mart, Chris, Luther, Rain, and all the clones of herself that she'd fought beside, who weren't mindless robots but flesh-and-blood people—her sisters. All of them were the closest thing to family Alice had ever had—as far as she remembered, anyway—and she intended to save the world as much to honor their memories as for the five thousand survivors across the world.

She glanced at her watch.

00:30:01

00:30:00

00:29:59

She held the portable communication screen, consulting its digital map of the duct system as she crawled.

"Quick! This way!"

She led the others around a corner, and they followed through the darkened shaft, Michael's flashlight continuing to provide their sole illumination. Soon, they heard the noise of machinery. This part of the Hive was receiving power, and it was beginning to come to life. Little pools of light started to filter into the air shaft vents from the rooms below. Alice paused, fearing they might've sprung another trap. But when nothing happened after several moments, she was relieved and pressed on, the others following.

* * *

Jeff Moran—who Alice thought of as the Thin Man— brought up the rear. Because of his emaciation, he had little trouble maneuvering through the air duct, but he was so malnourished that he was rapidly running out of energy. If it wasn't for the adrenaline in his system—a result of being constantly terrified by this place—he might not have the strength to keep going.

When he'd volunteered to help Alice and the others, he hadn't been sure what he had to offer. Yeah, he'd managed to survive since the Outbreak, but he'd accomplished that mostly through luck and being clever. He didn't possess any real skill at fighting, and he could count the number of times he'd fired a gun on one hand, and the number of times he'd actually hit anything were fewer still. But after Isaacs' troops had captured him in an abandoned grocery store where he'd been scavenging for canned food, he'd had his freedom, such as it was, taken from him. He'd traveled alone since the Outbreak, believing that other people were a liability. They'd compete with him for supplies at best, or worse, become infected and attack him. When you were alone, you could move faster, hide easier, and without anyone to look after, you could make life-or-death decisions without having to worry about how they would affect someone else. Before the Outbreak, having family and friends—a support system—was a strength. Afterward, it became a weakness.

But once imprisoned on the Umbrella transport, Jeff was no longer alone. He became part of a group for the first time since the Undead had taken over the world, and if they'd never become a family, they did form a bond based on their shared misery. They shared their stories of survival, spoke about their pasts, tried to bolster each other's spirits when one of their number took his or her turn as bait for the Undead and never returned. He'd become especially close with the prisoners he'd been seated near—the man Alice thought of as Scars, and the woman she thought of as the Emaciated Woman. The woman's name was Erin Fuller, and she'd been an elementary school teacher before the Outbreak. Scars' real name was—had been—Randy Todd, and he'd been a chef hoping to own his own restaurant one day. Jeff had been a radio DJ, a man paid for talking, and it was his bad habit of shooting off his mouth that had led to Isaacs cutting out his tongue and throwing it out the transport for the Undead to fight over.

Jeff had protested the first time Isaacs had attempted to molest Erin, but after he lost his tongue, Erin had pleaded with him not to interfere with Isaacs if he tried to violate her again. She didn't want to see Jeff hurt any more on her account. He hated just sitting and doing nothing every time Isaacs came to her—which he did often—but Jeff did as she asked, if for no other reason than to spare her the additional stress of having to worry about his safety. He told himself that he was doing what he could to alleviate her pain, at least a small portion of it, but it didn't make him feel any better about it.

The three of them became closer than the others, and as if sensing this, Isaacs began punishing the prisoners for talking to each other, until they all sat in the hold, chained and silent. Weeks passed like that, maybe months, and then Alice was captured, although she didn't stay a prisoner for long. Her escape gave them all hope that they might be able to one day get free from Isaacs, too. But then, as if to take out his frustration over losing Alice, Isaacs had entered the hold and began torturing prisoners, one at a time, until they died. When they were gone, Isaacs would release them from their chains and toss their bodies to the Undead to snack on.

Jeff, Erin, and Randy waited with fatalistic dread for their turn, but it never came. Isaacs put Erin on the tether to take a turn as Undead bait, and he'd brought in a portable monitor so Jeff and Randy could watch her try to keep moving fast enough to evade the Undead's hungry reach.

"I know how close the three of you have become," Isaacs had said. *"I apologize for having to separate you, but this way you can at least keep an eye on her. Who knows? Maybe if you start praying, God might even spare her."* He'd paused then. *"For a little while, at least."*

Now Erin was gone, as was Randy, and out of all the prisoners Isaacs had captured and used as his personal playthings, only Jeff remained. His time in the transport had taught him that while it might be possible to survive on your own, it was the bonds humans forged with one another that truly made them strong. And that was why he had volunteered to join Alice and the others on their mission. Not just to get revenge on Isaacs or even to get a shot at saving the whole damn planet. It was to add his strength, however much of it he had left, to theirs, so together they might have a greater chance at success. And even though he was terrified of what horrors might await them in this abandoned facility, he didn't regret his choice. Right now he was living, not merely existing, and that meant more to him than—

His thoughts cut off without warning as a metal door opened beneath him onto a vertical shaft. He fell downward, head first, fingers scrabbling at the smooth sides for purchase, but he was unable to slow his descent. He continued falling until his face struck a metal grate, the impact bloodying his nose and stunning him. He feared that his neck might be broken, but he was able to wiggle his fingers and toes. It seemed he'd escaped serious injury. He felt an almost ecstatic sense of relief to still be alive, but it died away as he realized he was in the dark, upside down, and trapped. Not entirely in the dark, though. There was a small red light on the grating. Some kind of electronic locking mechanism. Panic blossomed within him, and he tried to twist his body, hoping to get at least one of his arms free so he might—what? Push himself back up the shaft one-handed? The idea was ludicrous, he knew that, but he had to do *something*. But his exertions only served to wedge his body more tightly in the shaft, and he soon stopped moving.

Before the Outbreak, he'd never suffered from claustrophobia, but in the years since, there had been numerous times when he'd been forced to take refuge in small spaces in order to avoid being captured and devoured by the Undead. He'd always been on the thin side, if not as thin as he was now, and he'd been able to squeeze himself into some pretty tight places. Sometimes he'd only have to wait a few moments for the Undead to move on, and then he could emerge. But other times the Undead—or maybe a mutation— would linger in the area, having caught his scent and hoping to ferret him out. Sometimes the monsters would stay for hours, and Jeff would have to remain hidden, muscles cramping, his own body hurting so bad it took everything he had not to cry out in agony. He'd dream about those times now and again, and when he did, he always woke up drenched in sweat.

Now here he was, literally living out his worst nightmare. Maybe the others would try to rescue him eventually, but he knew they couldn't afford to take the time now. They had less than half an hour to find and release the antivirus. But after they succeeded—

okay, *if* they succeeded—maybe they would come back and search for him. All he had to do was stay calm and wait, and try not to think what it would be like to remain here, wedged upside down, and slowly die from thirst while hoping for a rescue that might never come.

But Jeff had a more immediate problem. The electronic lock on the grating clicked to green, and the grate swung open.

He fell out of the shaft and into open air. As his body passed through, his hands made another frantic attempt to stop him from freefalling, and this time they succeeded. He managed to grab hold of the grate's edge with both hands. He lost his left-hand grip, but his right held, and his legs swung downward, righting his body. He was then able to grab the ledge with his left hand once more, and he held on for dear life, body swinging wildly, legs kicking. A light on the bottom of the shaft snapped on then, illuminating the space below. Jeff looked down, and it felt like his heart seized in his chest. The shaft opened on a large natural cave, its walls glistening with moisture. It was so huge, Jeff thought a five-story building could fit inside with room to spare. Below him—one hundred feet or more, he judged—was a hard stone floor. He had to pull himself back into the shaft and then somehow make his way upward, because if he didn't—

But before he could begin to climb, the grating began to close. All he could do was hold on as the grating swung toward the duct, knowing that he couldn't let go, fearing that he wouldn't have a choice.

The grating closed, trapping his fingers between it and the metal shaft. He felt pressure on his skin, followed by intense pain and the sound of snapping bone. Then the grating sealed tight, slicing his fingers in two. Jeff plummeted downward. He didn't have time for regrets, didn't have time for thoughts of any sort. All he felt was sheer, unreasoning terror as he fell.

His face contorted into a scream that would not come.

* * *

Over her shoulder, Alice stared with horror at the space where the Thin Man had been. Claire, Doc, and Michael did the same. Did they have time to try and rescue him? Alice checked her watch and saw the seconds tick away. She knew the others were running the same calculations in their heads: could they afford to go after him? But as much as it pained her, Alice knew they had to go on without him.

"We're running out of—" Claire began, but her sentence was cut off as a second trap door opened beneath her, and she dropped out of sight.

Alice called her friend's name and reached for her—although it was already too late—and then suddenly a third trap door opened beneath her, and she fell, too.

* * *

Claire tumbled down a vertical shaft, and although she tried to push out with her hands and feet to arrest her fall, the sides of the shaft were too slick, and she couldn't get any purchase. The shaft took a forty-five-degree turn—which hurt like a bitch when her lower back hit the juncture, but it slowed her descent a little—and an instant later it opened onto a wider space, and she fell onto a concrete floor.

She landed on her right hip, and a bright burst of pain shot along the nerves in her leg. Wincing, she rolled onto her back, and her left hand smacked into something hard. A wall of some sort, she guessed. The smell hit her then, a rank odor like that of some large animal that had been held captive in this cage for years. It was the smell of old piss and shit, and underlying that, the dry coppery tang of blood. She didn't want to think about what she might be lying in, so she got to her feet, ignoring the scream of protest from her hip, and looked around. Dim light filtered down from the open shaft above, enabling her to make out her surroundings. To a degree, at least. She could see that she was inside a column made from— she rapped the wall with a knuckle—plexiglass. But the glass wasn't clear. It was streaked with grime, the inner surface scratched and marred, as if by knives... or claws. The base of the column was the worst, so caked with filth that she couldn't see the plexiglass beneath it.

Looking through the column's grimy surface, she saw similar columns close by, all of them just as dirty as this one, and all of them empty. There wasn't enough light for her to see very far into the chamber where the columns were housed, and she couldn't tell how many more cages like this one—and it *was* a cage, she was certain of that—there were. She had no idea what this place was, but she was sure of one thing: terrible events had occurred here.

She pounded a fist on the plexiglass, called out, "Is anyone here?"

She received no response, and a moment later the shaft closed above her, plunging her into darkness.

* * *

Alice tumbled from a vent in the ceiling of a room and fell twenty feet before she hit the floor. An inferno of pain erupted in her already broken ribs, and she knew that she had at least cracked a few more, if not broken them as well. She couldn't breathe at first, and she lay there, curled into a fetal position, in so much pain that she couldn't move, could barely think. Why the hell had those trapdoors *been* there? Precautions in case any of Umbrella's genetic experiments got loose and found their way into the air duct system? Maybe. *Stupid, stupid, stupid!* she thought. She should've been more cautious.

There was no natural light here—wherever *here* was—and she was surrounded by darkness. She'd lost her flashlight in the lake. She'd been holding onto the communication screen, but she'd dropped it when she landed. She had no idea if either were nearby, and if they were, if they were still functional. She might not have the Hydra anymore, but at least she still had her backup Glock, and luckily it hadn't fallen out of her belt.

She began to breathe normally again—although doing so hurt like hell—and, moving slowly, teeth gritted against the fire blazing in her chest, she reached out with both hands and began feeling around for her lost objects. She found the flashlight first, and when she got a decent grip on it, she activated it. At first she was pleased, and more than a little surprised that the thing still worked, but then she saw that the beam illuminated a human skull that lay only inches from her face, its empty eye sockets staring at her, the shadows within seeming to say, *What took you so long?*

Still lying on the tiled floor, she looked around, playing the flashlight beam across the floor. She saw a second skull close by, then a third. In fact, the floor was carpeted with human bones, all picked clean of meat. From the amount of bones, Alice guessed she was looking at the remains of dozens, maybe even hundreds, of bodies. And from the size and shape of some—especially the skulls—many of these bones had once belonged to something that wasn't human. Or at least hadn't been human at the time of their deaths. Not only did her ribs hurt, her back did too, and that's when she realized she wasn't lying on the floor; she was lying on broken, jagged *bone.*

She leaped to her feet, ignoring her ribs, and swung her flashlight in a wider arc to get a better idea where she was. And what she saw made her sick to her stomach. High-tech meat hooks hung from the ceiling, so many she couldn't count them, stained with dried blood. The hooks were attached to gleaming chains that hung from sliding tracks that criss-crossed the ceiling, making it easy to move bodies around. But for all its modern trappings, this place was nothing more than a slaughterhouse, plain and simple. The walls of the chamber were made of polished steel, no doubt to make it easier to hose off the blood. But despite this, cleanliness had obviously not been a priority for whoever had been in charge of the chamber, because the walls and floor were streaked with old blood, some of it presumably human, much of it presumably not.

Alice stood in the center of a high-tech abattoir

designed, she guessed, for the dismemberment and disposal of Umbrella's failed experiments. This was a killing floor, and the air seemed to still echo with the agonized screams of the dying.

For over a decade, Alice had traveled the world Umbrella had created in order to save the human race by destroying it, and in that time she'd seen sights so horrible they had been permanently seared into her memory. Sights that returned to her unbidden when she closed her eyes, which haunted her dreams and forced her awake, heart pounding, lungs heaving, body covered in cold sweat. But this... this was among the worst of them all.

For a long moment all she could do was stand and stare at the bones and the hooks, but then she slowly became aware of a tingling on the back of her neck, her ever-reliable personal warning system. She was being watched. At first she thought she might be sensing someone—Wesker, probably—observing her via a security camera feed. But what she felt seemed closer than that, like whoever or whatever it was watched her from somewhere nearby, cloaked in the shadows that filled the chamber beyond the reach of her flashlight beam.

She held her breath and listened, straining to hear the slightest sound. The scrape of a foot on the concrete floor, a soft clatter of disturbed bones, noisy breathing, an almost inaudible growling deep within the throat, the click of a gun safety being disengaged, the hiss of a blade being drawn from its sheath... *anything*. But she didn't hear a thing except the beating of her own heart. She drew the Glock and then slowly began inching through the darkness, stepping carefully around the scattered bones to avoid tripping on any of them, moving in the direction her instincts told her the watcher was hiding. She continued forward, ready to shoot if something should come rushing toward her out of the darkness: human, Undead, or mutation.

Slowly, slowly, slowly... always listening, gaze focused on the patch of illumination emitted from the flashlight, a patch that seemed so much smaller than the featureless blackness surrounding it. Anything could be concealed within that blackness, anything at all, and it could be crouched low, muscles coiled, waiting for the right moment to spring forward, claws outstretched and fangs bared.

She felt a rush of air on the back of her neck, and she spun around, Glock aimed and ready to fire. She saw a flash of movement as something dropped from the ceiling duct and landed with a thump and a clatter in the middle of a pile of bones. Her finger tightened on the Glock's trigger, ready to put several rounds into whatever had just dropped in on her, but then she realized who it was.

"Michael!"

She tucked the Glock in her belt and hurried over to help him stand. Her injured ribs complained bitterly when she took the man's hand and pulled him to his feet, but she didn't care. She was too glad to see him, alive and apparently unharmed.

"Yeah," he said, sounding more than a little dazed. Then he looked around, scowling. "Where the hell are we?"

"Somewhere we don't want to be," Alice answered.

Coming from the depths of the killing floor, Alice became aware of a sound—a strange humming that started off softly and quickly rose in pitch and volume. Alice and Michael exchanged a quick glance, and then Alice drew her Glock once more and advanced in the direction of the sound. Michael followed close behind her, and since he didn't have a weapon, he bent down and picked up a femur from the floor to use as a makeshift club. Alice's flashlight beam fell on a vague shape that seemed to pulse and writhe in the gloom. It lay prone and was human-sized, but whatever it was, it definitely wasn't human. Was this the thing she'd sensed watching her before? She was tempted to put a round into the shape as a precaution. Shoot first and ask questions later—if ever—had saved her ass on more than one occasion. But she only had so much ammo, and she didn't want to waste any. So she continued advancing toward the dark, writhing shape, Michael at her back.

When they were within five feet of the thing, it suddenly burst apart into small buzzing shapes that darted and dipped through the air as they flew away.

Flies, Alice thought with disgust. Thousands of them. They had been clinging to the flesh of an old carcass, one so badly decayed that she couldn't tell if it had been human or a mutation. She supposed it really didn't matter now. The flies were the source of the humming sound they'd heard, but they'd also concealed the carcass's smell. Now that the rotten meat had been exposed, the stench that wafted off it was so strong that Alice's gorge rose and she felt hot bile splash the back of her throat. It took everything she had to keep from vomiting, and if she'd eaten anything substantial in the last day, she might not have been able to stop herself.

She took several steps back from the horrid thing, and Michael did the same. Flies still buzzed in the air around them, their movement distracting her, and when she caught a glimpse of something large emerging from the shadows behind them, she didn't consciously register it as a threat right away. But her body knew something was wrong, and she spun around and directed her flashlight toward the movement, and what the beam revealed was a creature that Alice had never seen before. In some ways, the thing resembled a Licker, only it stood upright. It had no outer skin, leaving all its muscle fibers exposed. But it had a number of important—and disgusting— differences. Its muscles were a bright red, and its ribcage was exposed, and the individual ribs were moving back and forth, as if they possessed a life of their own. Beneath the ribcage was a glowing light, as if the creature had some kind of internal power source, and foul-smelling bodily fluids spurted from the opening. It didn't possess the overgrown brain tissue of a Licker, but its features were twisted and deformed, its eyes barely visible in the distorted flesh of its face, and overlarge sharp teeth jutted straight out from its lipless gash of a mouth.

She had no idea what this thing was, other than one more damn Umbrella experiment.

Before either Alice or Michael could react, the creature grabbed hold of Michael's shoulders with its clawed hands and thrust its head forward like a striking snake. Its jutting teeth sank into the flesh of Michael's face, and then the creature yanked its head to the side, ripping the skin and muscle away from Michael's skull with a wet tearing sound.

10

Michael's eyes bulged from their sockets as his lipless mouth opened to release an agonized scream. He reached for his face—or rather, where his face had been—his fingers finding only blood-slick bone. His eyes rolled upward and his body went limp. He fell to the floor amid a clatter of bones and lay still. Alice didn't know if he was passed out from pain and shock, or if he was dead. Given what had been done to him, she wasn't sure which would be kinder.

She turned toward the creature, intending to empty her Glock into its head, but the thing was too fast. It spat out Michael's face and swung its right arm toward her, striking her on the shoulder and sending her flying. She landed hard on scattered bones. Her broken ribs shrieked in agony, but all she cared about right then was blowing the shit out of the goddamn monster that had savaged Michael. She'd managed to hold onto both her flashlight and her Glock when she landed, and as the creature leaped toward her, Michael's blood dripping from its disgusting teeth, she fired multiple times.

The bullets tore into the creature, the sound of gunfire deafening in the confined space. But the rounds seemed to have no effect on it. No blood issued from the wounds, just more of the clear fluid which spurted erratically from the monstrosity's open rib cage. She continued firing as the creature landed in front of her, but instead of attacking, it darted sideways and disappeared into the darkness.

Alice rose to her feet, the pain in her ribs so intense that for an awful moment she thought she might pass out. If that happened, she knew she'd never wake up, and so she fought against the pain and remained conscious, but it was a near thing. Breathing heavily, she scanned the dark room with her flashlight, searching for the creature. It could be anywhere, and she—

It came lunging at her out of the darkness, swiping razor-sharp claws across her torso. Her body armor protected her from the worst of the blow, but the tips of the creature's claws managed to penetrate the material, digging furrows into the tender flesh beneath. Alice hissed in pain as lines of fire flared across her belly, and she fired once more at the monster, driving it back into the darkness. The gun clicked dry. She was out of ammo.

She swung her flashlight beam around, searching for the skinless monster. She could sense it lurking in the darkness nearby but despite the thing's size, it moved with eerie silence, like a jungle cat stalking its prey. She kept turning this way and that, shining her beam, searching... She backed into something and she whirled around, startled, only to see she'd bumped into one of the dismemberment hooks. The impact caused some mechanism within the ceiling mount to release an additional length of chain, and it slid down, sending the hook clattering loudly to the floor.

She spun back around, expecting the creature to take advantage of her momentary distraction and attack from behind. But the flashlight beam revealed nothing. Alice frowned. That didn't make sense. From what she'd seen of the creature's behavior so far, it preferred surprise attacks. So why hadn't it—

Something small streaked downward in front of her, illuminated by the flashlight beam before it disappeared. She heard a soft *plop*, as if some liquid substance had splattered onto the floor. She saw a second object fall, then a third. *Droplets,* she thought, and angled the flashlight beam downward to inspect them. They'd joined to form a thick, viscous puddle on the floor, and as she watched, another drip plopped down to join the rest.

Her instincts screamed at her to move, and without questioning them, she dove to one side, just as the creature came down on the spot where she'd been standing. The damn thing had been hanging on the ceiling, probably from one of the chains, waiting to pounce on her when the moment was right. As she fell, Alice hurled the flashlight away from her, hoping its beam would attract the creature's attention. If the thing was intelligent, she was screwed, but if it wasn't...

The monster took the bait and bounded toward the flashlight.

Alice hit the ground, and her ribs exploded with fresh agony. Ignoring it, she got to her feet and hurried to where the hook and the extra length of chain had fallen. Its far end was still attached to the motorized track on the ceiling. She smiled. *Perfect.*

She took hold of the chain and began swinging it in circles over her head.

Her flashlight had landed somewhere among the bones scattered on the floor, and the creature stood where it was, illuminated in the beam's light, which angled upward. The beast swung its head back and forth, as if trying to figure out where its prey had gone. The sound of the hook and chain whirling through the air must have caught its attention, for it turned around to face Alice, nostrils flaring and thick saliva dripping from its hideous mouth. It leaped toward her, claws outstretched, but Alice was ready for it. When the creature was in range, she slammed the blunt end of the hook against the monster's head as hard as she could. The blow knocked the creature off course, and it angled off to the side, missing Alice. It hit the floor and swiftly rose to its feet, but instead of attacking her right away, it regarded her silently, flexing its claws, rib bones moving in synchronization with them.

"That's right," Alice said, swinging the hook once more. "Come on."

The monster snarled and leaped for her again. But when Alice released the hook this time, the barbed end struck the creature in the chest and sank deep. Clear fluid gushed from the wound, and the thing howled in pain and anger. Now that Alice no longer held the chain, she was defenseless, so she turned and ran. The creature—hook still embedded in its chest—came after her in a lunging leap. It managed to strike her left foot with one of its claws and she crashed to the ground, the momentum causing her to slide across the tiled floor, her body knocking bones out of her way as she went.

The creature, seeing its opportunity, leaped one more time. Alice rolled onto her back in time to see the skinless obscenity descending toward her, claws out and ready to tear her to shreds. But before it could reach her, the chain pulled tight, and the sharp steel hook ripped through the length of the creature from chest to crotch, gutting it in an instant. The thing fell onto Alice, a mass of dead weight, flopping organs, and slimy clear fluid.

She pushed herself out from underneath the eviscerated monster, mouth pursed in disgust. The damn thing's insides stank worse than its outside. Exhausted, her ribs screaming at her for mistreating them so, Alice rose to her feet. She turned and was startled to see Doc standing there, only a few feet away. She was surprised, but pleased to see a friendly face. Had he fallen through a trap door too? But before she could ask him, he said, "Is Claire with you?"

Alice shook her head, and Doc looked crushed.

"She'll be okay," Alice said. "Trust me. I know her... she's a survivor."

Doc's attention was caught by the gutted carcass of the skinless monster.

"What the hell is *that*?"

"Bioweapon. It was once a human, infected with massive quantities of the T-virus."

Doc then saw Michael's faceless body lying on the floor some distance away.

"No," he said, his voice filled with sorrow. He hurried over to check Michael's pulse, then he turned to Alice and shook his head. Michael was gone.

She wanted to say something to comfort the man, tell him how Michael had died on his feet, which in this world was sometimes the best you could hope for. But she knew that anything she said would only ring hollow, so she remained silent. Instead, she checked her watch.

00:15:01

00:15:00

00:14:59

"Come on!" she said. "We have to hurry!"

She quickly retrieved her flashlight, and the two of them headed off in search of an exit, leaving the monster's slowly cooling body—as well as Michael's—behind for the flies.

* * *

Wesker slammed his fist onto the control panel, his normally composed expression now one of utter fury. The surface of his skin rippled, and rough patches of gray emerged and then receded. On the monitor, he watched as Alice and Doc found the door to the Disassembly Room, opened it, and entered the hallway outside.

"They're getting away!" He practically roared the words, spittle flying from his mouth to spatter the monitor. His temperature was so high, he felt as if his blood was boiling in his veins.

Full power had been restored to the Control Room, and the Red Queen's avatar once more hovered nearby.

"Your analysis is correct."

Wesker turned to face her. He knew it wasn't possible, but he thought he detected a trace of smugness in her voice.

"You wanted control of the Hive's defenses."

He returned his attention to the monitor showing Alice. His fury began to fade, and as it did his temperature decreased and he was able to regain control of his body once again. Alice had no powers. She was injured and exhausted. She'd lost companions along the way, people she'd been leading—and she no doubt felt responsible for their deaths. And yet with all of this, she still kept coming. Up to this point, Wesker had never seriously considered that she might actually succeed in her mission, but now he was forced to acknowledge the possibility.

"If the target continues on her present course, she will be here in under seven minutes," the Red Queen said, her voice back to its usual emotionless inflection.

Wesker turned around in his chair and regarded the pair of cryostasis tubes that sat in the center of the chamber. He didn't want to do this, but he could see no other option.

"Wake them," he said.

* * *

Claire pounded the plexiglass with her fists, but it was no use. She drew her gun and tried to fire at the glass wall, but the weapon was still jammed from being submerged in the crater's lake and wouldn't work. She hurled it at the glass in frustration, but all it did was bounce off without leaving a mark.

She had to find a way out of here. Alice needed all the help she could get if she were to have a chance of finding and releasing the antivirus. The idea of her friend going on without her, coming up against who knew what sort of deadly threat, without her to back her up, made Claire feel both angry and helpless. But it wasn't only Alice she was worried about. She hadn't known Doc for very long, but in the world after the T-virus outbreak, survivors had learned not to hesitate or play games when it came to their feelings, for any moment could be their last, and there was literally no time to waste. So when she first felt an attraction to Doc, she'd let him know, and he'd told her he felt likewise, and they'd gone from there. In a way, it was like when she'd been a little girl in the world before the Outbreak, when you would meet a new kid in the neighborhood or on the playground at school. You'd start playing together, and if you clicked, you were friends, and that was that. It was only when you began to grow up that you started hiding your feelings, fearing what might happen if you shared them and someone didn't reciprocate them. But in the world the T-virus had made, there was so much to fear—so many creatures that wanted to devour you on sight—that being afraid of your emotions seemed not only a waste of time, but ridiculous.

Did she love Doc? Yes, she supposed she did. And if Alice managed to save the world, if there could actually be a chance for a normal life, she wanted to share it with him. He could handle himself well enough in a fight, but he was no warrior—not like she and Alice were—and the thought that he was somewhere in the Hive at this moment, fighting for his life without her at his side, was making her crazy with worry. She had to get out of here—for Alice, for Doc, for the whole damn world. But how?

An idea came to her then. She picked up her Beretta, ejected the magazine, kept it, and tossed the gun aside. She removed the last four bullets from the clip, dropped it, and then rolled the bullets around in her hand, thinking.

* * *

Isaacs—dirty, disheveled, suffering from thirst—was waiting when the first of the two new Umbrella troop transports passed beneath the Raccoon City sign, a horde of Undead trailing behind. He stepped in front of the vehicle's headlights and waited for it to stop. For an instant the transport continued rumbling forward, and Isaacs wondered if the commander intended to take advantage of the situation to stage a coup by running him down. As exhausted as he was, he wasn't sure he cared either way, but he reminded himself that he couldn't die yet—not until he'd accomplished the task God had charged him with.

The transport slowed and came to a stop. An instant later there was a scream from the rear of the vehicle as the Undead caught up to the bait, but Isaacs barely noticed. He gave a wary smile and stepped toward the transport. *Soon,* he thought. *This will all be over soon.*

Troopers exited the vehicle to escort Isaacs inside, holding onto his arms to steady him. Normally, he would've angrily declined their assistance, but he accepted it gratefully now, if grudgingly. Once he was in the crew cabin, he was greeted by Commander Brenner, a middle-aged African-American woman of medium height whose gray hair still held hints of the black it had once been.

"Glad to see you, sir," she said. "We didn't think there were any survivors from the last attack."

"Water," Isaacs said, his voice little more than a dry croak.

"Of course." Brenner turned to the trooper nearest her. "Get this man some water. Then resume course to Raccoon City."

The trooper hurried off to do as Brenner asked.

"She's not there," Isaacs said.

Brenner frowned. "What?"

"She went to the Pit. We have to follow."

The trooper returned with a canteen of water and handed it to Isaacs. He drank from it greedily, spilling some down the sides of his face.

Brenner's frown turned into a scowl. "Those are not my orders."

Isaacs stopped drinking and wiped his mouth with the back of his wrist stump.

"We *have* to go to the Pit," he insisted, his voice stronger this time.

Brenner's voice was cold when she next spoke. "My orders are specific. We—"

Isaacs handed the canteen back to the trooper who brought it, then with his remaining hand, he drew a knife that was sheathed at his belt, a replacement he'd chosen after Alice had taken his previous one. He stepped forward, his gaze firmly fixed on Brenner's eyes as he shoved the blade between her third and fourth ribs, straight into her heart. He leaned close to her as blood bubbled past her lips.

"What was that?" he said softly. "I don't think I heard you."

He withdrew the knife, and Brenner slumped to the cabin floor, dead.

Isaacs smiled as he regarded the woman's body,

and then he took the canteen back from the stunned trooper and finished off the water while the rest of the transport's crew looked at him with more than a little fear. When he was finished drinking, he smacked his lips. He'd never tasted water so good in his life. He noticed the crew staring at him then.

"Here are your new orders..." he began.

* * *

As Alice and Doc jogged down the hallway, she thought about Michael. She'd known almost nothing about him. Where he'd been born, what kind of life he'd had before the Outbreak. She didn't even know his last name. Survivors had a tendency to keep those kinds of details to themselves—it was difficult to become too attached to a person when you knew almost nothing about them. Or so the theory went. Over the years, Alice had learned—for her, at least— that it didn't matter how much or how little of a person's background she knew. She connected to people because of who they were or how they treated others. And when they were gone, she missed them, whether she knew their last names or not.

Soon, they reached a familiar glass corridor. A decade had passed since she'd last been here, but it felt as if it had only been yesterday. She could almost see the Sanitation Team making its way down the corridor as a crimson lattice of laser beams rushed forward, slicing them into cauterized cubes within an instant. She could hear the soft thumps as the steaming chunks of meat rained to the floor.

"What is it?" Doc asked. "Are you okay?" He took

hold of her elbow and gave her a gentle shake. The motion snapped Alice out of her memories.

"I'm fine. I've... been here before." She didn't feel like explaining any further. She was just glad the power was turned off in this section. "This way."

Alice continued on, Doc following, and they entered the room from which she had watched the team die. She was surprised—and grateful—to see the team's equipment still lay discarded on the floor. There were weapons spread around, along with a couple of canvas bags. Alice selected a SIG-Sauer pistol, checked the clip, and was gratified to see it was almost full. She chose a Heckler & Koch for Doc, checked the clip and—satisfied with what she found—she handed the weapon to him.

"Try this instead of what you're carrying," she said. "More stopping power."

Doc placed his old gun on the ground and took the one Alice offered.

"Thanks," he said.

Alice then checked one of the canvas bags and found it contained explosives. She stood and slipped the bag's strap over her shoulder, feeling like a kid on Christmas morning. Or so she assumed, as she didn't have memories of Christmas, or any other holidays for that matter.

"Where to now?" Doc asked.

Alice checked her watch, and she had to fight back a surge of panic when she read the display.

00:11:00

00:10:59

"We have to hurry," she said. "The final level of the Hive's below us."

"How do we get down there?" Doc asked.

Alice didn't answer right away. The room had several workstations with computer terminals, and she sat down at one. This room—unlike the laser corridor outside—had power, and the machine was active. Had it been on for the last ten years, waiting patiently for a user to appear and give it a command? Alice's fingers flew across the keyboard, and the walls suddenly began to move, appearing to slide upward. Doc stared at them, confused.

"Like so," Alice said.

As the room descended, they were able to look through the window and observe the levels they passed. Each was filled with hexagonal tubes, inside which were the shadowy forms of what looked like human bodies. The hexagonal structures reminded Alice of the sort of thing bees might create, and she realized where the Hive had gotten its name.

"What are they?" Doc asked.

"Cryogenic storage," Alice answered.

"There must be thousands here."

"The Umbrella High Command. Waiting out the Apocalypse in safety. Noah's Ark for the rich and powerful."

Alice turned her attention back to the computer terminal and typed in a command. In response, the elevator room stopped in the middle of the shaft, a series of cryotubes right in front of the window. Alice stood, reached into the bag of explosives, and handed a set to Doc.

"Give me a hand," she said.

* * *

He floated in darkness. He wasn't sleeping, not exactly. There wasn't a word in any human language to describe this state. The closest analogue was the experience of being enclosed within an isolation tank. The silence was absolute, so powerful it almost seemed to possess a physical presence. Along with it came a feeling of peace so intense that it verged on euphoria. Was this the afterlife? If so, he could happily remain in this state of bliss for all eternity.

But then something changed.

At first, he wasn't certain what it was. He only knew that things weren't the same as they had been before. But then he understood what it was. He'd become aware of time passing, one moment succeeding the next, which was in turn followed by yet another, and so on. After that came a feeling of heaviness, of being centered in one place, of being *limited*, and then he remembered what these sensations meant. They were the result of being confined to a body.

The changes came rapidly after that. A sensation of cold, which quickly decreased as it was replaced by warmth. Accompanying it came a tingling feeling in his extremities as his circulatory system began to function at a normal level once more. He heard the rush of blood in his ears as it began surging through his body, felt his heart begin to beat, slowly at first, then picking up speed with every pulse. And then he opened his mouth—he had a *mouth!*—and drew in a deep breath of air, filling his lungs for the first time in... well, he didn't know how long.

It was dark inside this place—a small place, he thought, large enough to enclose his body, but not much bigger than that. But a soft glow was emitted as the internal mechanisms of the cryotube completed their work. His memories were the last thing to return, and with them his full sense of self was restored. And when this was accomplished, the cryotube split open and the tall man stepped forward into the light.

Albert Wesker stood before the open tube, hands clasped behind his back, waiting for the tall man to emerge. Next to Wesker was the floating holographic image of the Red Queen. Wesker looked almost the same as when the tall man had seen him last. Older, of course, but that was to be expected. Wesker hadn't aged significantly, though, and the tall man guessed that only a decade had passed since he'd entered cryostasis, more or less.

He wasn't sure why Wesker wore those dark glasses, though. It seemed an odd affectation to do so indoors.

As the man stepped forward, he glanced at the cryotube sitting next to his. It remained closed, but he could hear the faint hum of its machinery working within. The occupant's physical condition was far more fragile than his, and thus the revival process had to proceed more slowly. The tube would open soon enough.

The tall man stepped forward to stand before Wesker, moving with ease and assurance, as if he'd merely taken a short nap instead of having been frozen for over a decade. It was remarkable, really, but he supposed he shouldn't have been surprised, since he'd helped design the technology.

"Is it done?" the tall man asked. "Is the cleansing process complete?"

"No," Wesker said.

The tall man scowled. "Then why am I awake?"

"We have a problem. I tried to—"

The tall man felt a rush of anger, but he fought it back. Emotion wouldn't help him deal with the situation. He raised a hand to forestall Wesker.

"Save your breath," he said. "I know exactly what's happened. We've been betrayed."

Alexander Isaacs—the original—turned to look at the image of the Red Queen floating next to Wesker.

"Just as I suspected we would be," he said.

* * *

Inside her plexiglass prison, Claire worked feverishly. She had broken open all four of the bullets, and now she carefully poured all of the gunpowder into one shell. She then pulled some duct tape from her boot—she'd put it there a while back to help hold the heel on—and she used it to seal the open end of the cartridge. She then tore off a length of shoelace from one of her boots and forced it through a hole in the tape.

She pulled an almost empty pack of matches from one of her pockets, lit one, and touched it to the end of her makeshift fuse. She shook the match to extinguish it, dropped it, and then quickly placed the tiny bomb against the bottom of the glass wall. She braced it with the heel of her boot, and prayed this was going to work.

Seconds later the bomb exploded, her boot directed the force outward, and a section of the plexiglass prison shattered. She retrieved her jammed gun and, wielding it like a club, she was able to enlarge the hole she'd made until it was big enough for her to squeeze through. Her heel ached a bit, and she sustained a few scratches crawling through the opening she'd made, but otherwise, she was unharmed. Feeling inordinately proud of herself—and more than a little disappointed that that none of her friends had been present to witness her escape—Claire began making her way through the dark maze of empty plexiglass chambers.

After several moments she began to get a feeling that she wasn't alone. Someone was watching her... stalking her...

She continued forward, moving slowly, senses alert. But when it came for her, it moved so swiftly there was nothing she could do.

* * *

The elevator soon came to rest in a vast cathedral-like cavern. Alice and Doc stepped off the platform and onto hard, rocky ground. Alice saw a shape lying on the rocks, and as she and Doc moved closer to it, she saw it was the body of the Thin Man. His broken limbs were twisted at unnatural angles, and his eyes were wide and staring.

Alice sighed and closed her eyes for a moment, but she soon opened them and began walking again. She could mourn the man's loss later. She still had work to do and very little time to get it done.

If Doc had any thoughts upon seeing the Thin Man's body, he kept them to himself as they moved on.

They soon approached a section of the cavern that was covered by a wide stretch of water. She couldn't tell how deep it was by looking at it, and she was about to step into it to gauge its depth when an illuminated walkway rose upward for them.

That's convenient, Alice thought.

She stepped onto the walkway and started across, Doc right behind her. They'd only walked a few feet before a voice called to them from the other side. She saw a shadowy figure standing on the far shore, but there wasn't enough light for her to make out any details.

"The bad seed returns." The voice paused. "Or is it the prodigal daughter? Well, don't just stand there. Come in. After all, you have only nine minutes to save the world."

Alice checked her watch and saw the display read exactly nine minutes.

She recognized the voice, of course. How could she not, as she'd last heard it only a short time ago. It was Isaacs. But he sounded different than he had during their last encounter. Calmer, more in control of his emotions.

Alice continued across the walkway, Doc staying with her every step of the way. When they reached Isaacs, he turned and led them into a concrete bunker set within a corner of the vast natural cave. But this was no spartan military facility. Rather it was an oasis of culture and opulence. Mixed with the high-tech computer screens were busts by Rodin and paintings by Picasso, the best the old world had to offer, stolen by Umbrella for preservation here. A slice of heaven at the end of the world.

Now that she was close to Isaacs, and there was more light to see by, she could tell that this Isaacs—while physically resembling the crazed zealot she'd last encountered—was markedly different. He wore an expensive-looking tailored suit and tie, his skin glowed and his fingernails—on both hands—were perfectly manicured, as if he'd just stepped out of a spa. And while he was by no means overweight, he wasn't as thin as the other Isaacs, who'd been living in the wasteland that was the outer world.

Inside the bunker's doorway Alice saw the Red Queen's holographic image hovering nearby. She looked at the AI, but the Red Queen didn't acknowledge her. *Good*, Alice thought. Their secret partnership might end up being the ace in the hole she needed.

Alice turned away from the Red Queen to face Isaacs. "You're really him?" she asked.

"First things first," Isaacs said. "I'm going to need you to place your weapons on the floor."

Alice gave him a wry half-smile. "Now why would I do that?"

"This is what you're after. Yes?"

He held a vial of liquid in his hand, the container shaped like a DNA helix. Isaacs went on. "The antivirus. The cure to all this. Well, there's only the one vial. And we're half a mile underground in a sealed facility. I drop it here, the antivirus goes nowhere. And your hopeless dreams die sooner rather than later."

11

Alice glanced at her watch.

00:08:00

00:07:59

She had no choice. She bent down and placed her SIG-Sauer and her knife on the floor. As she straightened, Isaacs said, "Good girl."

Alice looked at Doc. "You're still armed."

"Yes, I am," he said calmly, and he leveled his Heckler & Koch at Alice.

She showed no outward reaction to Doc revealing himself as the traitor Umbrella had planted within the group of survivors in the city.

"Claire's going to be disappointed," she said.

Doc smirked. "In a few minutes Claire's going to be dead. Along with everyone else you know."

A new voice—a woman's—said, "That's sweet."

Claire stood in the doorway behind Doc, and for an instant Alice thought she might get the drop on him, but then she saw that someone was standing behind Claire, holding a Samurai Edge pistol pressed to her head.

"Look what the cat dragged in," Wesker said.

Doc glanced at Claire. "Sorry, my love."

Claire glared at him, and if looks could kill, he would've exploded into a million pieces at that moment.

Doc turned back to Alice. "Now kick your weapons to me—and the detonator."

Alice did as he ordered. Doc didn't bother with her gun, but he bent down and picked up the detonator. He turned to Isaacs then. "She planted explosives in the High Command cryotubes. I'll disarm them."

"Thank you," Isaacs said to Doc. "You've done well."

She glanced around the room, looking for something, anything, she might be able to use to get her out of this situation. She noted a glass wine decanter on a glass table near Isaacs, a fountain pen lying on a desk, a heavy Rodin bust displayed on a high marble table behind Isaacs. All potential weapons for slashing, stabbing, and bludgeoning. If only she could get to one of them in time...

"Don't bother," Isaacs said. "You don't make it. To the decanter, the sculpture, *or* the fountain pen."

* * *

Computer graphics began rapidly scrolling across Isaacs' vision as the predictive combat software in his bio-implants showed him Alice's every potential move. He watched a virtual simulation of her reaching for the glass decanter, obviously intending to break it and stab him with the shards. But in the simulation, Isaacs was too fast, and he got to her first. He grabbed hold of her, lifted her into the air, and slammed her through the glass table with bone-crushing impact.

He then watched as virtual Alice made a move toward the pen, but he rushed toward her, grabbed the back of her head, and smashed it so hard into the desk that the wood splintered. Virtual Alice next tried for the bust. She managed to grab hold of it and turn toward Isaacs, intending to smash it into his head. But Isaacs avoided the blow with ease, and he grabbed hold of her once more and hammered her head against the tabletop so hard that the marble cracked.

The simulation ended and the computer software reached its conclusion:

COMPUTER ANALYSIS OF TACTICAL SITUATION

ISAACS VICTORY 100%

Isaacs smiled, confident and in control.

* * *

Alice had once possessed a similar predictive ability, so she recognized that Isaacs wasn't bluffing when he told her that nothing she tried would stop him. She remained where she was, but that didn't mean she was giving up.

Come on, Alice, she urged herself. *Think!*

Isaacs continued speaking. "And in answer to your question, yes, I am Doctor Alexander Roland Isaacs. The original."

"The one I met out there thought exactly the same," Alice said.

"Of course he did. That's how they're designed. They always try harder and fight longer, even to the death, as long as they think they are the real thing. After all, who wants to know that they are just a poor imitation? A worthless copy?" He smiled. "Which brings us to you."

Alice stared at him, understanding the implications of what he was saying but not wanting to believe them.

"Come now," he said. "Don't tell me you thought *you* were the original. How delicious. No, I'm afraid *she* holds that dubious honor."

He nodded toward a pair of cryostasis tubes. One—his, Alice presumed—was already open. The second tube, next to which rested a wheelchair, was just beginning to open.

A woman stepped out, moving slowly, her motions stiff and hesitant. She wore a gray dress made of a smooth, silky material, with a string of pearls around her neck. Her short straight hair was gray, and her face was wrinkled, her forehead dotted with liver spots. Her large eyes were a dull blue, but they projected an intensity that spoke of the strong intelligence behind them. Despite her age, the woman's face was familiar to Alice. She'd seen a younger version of it many times, on her numerous clones... and, of course, every time she'd looked in the mirror.

The woman moved to her wheelchair—every step a major effort—and when she reached it, she slumped into the seat, breathing hard, as if she'd just run a marathon. After a moment, she began wheeling over to join them.

"Meet Alicia Marcus," Isaacs said. "The daughter of my old partner James. Co-owner of the Umbrella Corporation and a painful thorn in my side. One I now intend to remove."

Alice couldn't stop staring at the woman... at *Alicia*. She looked old enough to be Alice's grandmother. Hell, *great*-grandmother. But if what Isaacs had implied about Alice's relationship to this woman was true, Alice had never had a grandmother. Or a mother, for that matter.

Alicia spoke then, her voice weak and breathy.

"Time is running out." It was obvious that even such a simple act as speaking required great effort for her. But despite this, she went on. She nodded to Isaacs. "You have to kill him soon."

Isaacs smiled. "Good to see you too, Alicia." He turned back to Alice. "Believe it or not, she's not much older than you are. Physically, at any rate. She suffers from Werner syndrome, also known as adult progeria, a wasting disease which causes those afflicted to age prematurely. Marcus created the Progenitor Cell to save her when she was a child, but the effects didn't last—as you can see. I've been waiting years for her to die."

"I'm not a clone," Alice said, but she didn't sound as confident as she would've liked. She thought then of how Umbrella operatives—the Red Queen included— had referred to her as "Project Alice," as if she were some sort of science experiment. She'd always thought the term had to do with the corporation's attempts to make her body bind with the T-virus, but if Isaacs' claim was true, and she *was* a clone, she'd been a "project" instead of a person all along.

"Really?" Isaacs said. "You must have wondered why you remember nothing of your childhood. Your father. Your mother."

"Memory loss," Alice said. "After everything Umbrella did to me—"

"No. You have no memories because you had no

life. Nothing before the mansion, when we created you. Ten years ago."

Alice felt wild panic erupt inside her. She searched her mind, casting about for a memory—*any* memory—from her past before she'd woken in the manor; the Looking Glass House, as she'd thought of it then. Still, she refused to accept what Isaacs was telling her.

"I know who I am!" she shouted.

"I don't think you do," Isaacs said. "You're nothing more than a puppet whose strings were cut. And then you wandered around for a little while thinking you were a real girl. But you're not. You're just a clever imitation. A facsimile. And a rather troublesome one at that."

"You're lying to me." But even as Alice said this, she knew deep down that he wasn't.

The Red Queen spoke for the first time since Alice and Doc's arrival. *"I'm afraid he's not. You were created in her image. As was I. My likeness, voice, and core brain patterns were based on childhood recordings of Alicia Marcus, made by her father. Your genetic structure is based on her DNA, tweaked to avoid the wasting disease that afflicted her. I was the child she was, you are the woman she would have been."*

Alice looked at Alicia, who looked right back at her with tired, half-lidded eyes. It was like gazing into a mirror that showed you what you would look like in the future.

"No," Alice said, but her voice lacked conviction.

"You were built from my DNA," Alicia said, her voice gaining strength as she spoke. "But you're so much better than I ever could be. I let this happen. I let Isaacs go through with his plan. I should have fought him harder. I was weak. You cannot afford to be."

"Time is running out, Alice," the Red Queen said.

"How touching." Isaacs looked at Alicia, then at the Red Queen, then finally at Alice. "The trinity of bitches, united in their hatred. Not that it will do you any good."

Isaacs stepped closer to Alicia. He still had the helix-shaped vial of antivirus, and he held it out before the woman, as if to taunt her with it.

"You really thought I didn't know what you were up to? I was ahead of you every step of the way. You've changed nothing, and you've saved no one. The world will still be cleansed and the Umbrella Corporation will triumph. The only difference is I can now replace you. I'll no longer have to listen to your self-righteous whining. When you uploaded that file and corrupted the Red Queen, you turned against the corporation. When the rest of the board awakes, they won't protect you. They'll have you replaced, and I will assume complete control."

"I still own fifty percent of this company," Alicia said, but the earlier strength with which she'd spoken was gone, and despite her words, she seemed to have lost hope.

Isaacs towered over the frail woman in the wheelchair, looking all powerful compared to Alicia's withered form. In that moment, Alice hated Isaacs more than she'd ever hated anyone or anything, and if she could've wrapped her hands around his throat, she would've happily choked the life out of him.

"And what do you intend to do with your fifty percent?" Isaacs said.

"The only thing I can do," she said, some of her

strength returning. "You are a co-owner of this corporation, but Wesker is still an employee."

All this time Wesker had stood silently in the doorway, his gun against Claire's head. He appeared unimpressed by Alicia's words.

"I don't have to take your orders," he said coldly. "My loyalties are with Doctor Isaacs."

"I know," Alicia said. She paused a moment before adding, "Albert Wesker: you're fired."

Alice glanced at the Red Queen, and she saw a grim smile appear on the AI's simulated face. Alice remembered what the Red Queen had told her in D.C., that her programming prevented her from harming Umbrella employees. But thanks to Alicia, Wesker no longer worked for the corporation.

A heavy blast door dropped down from the ceiling above Wesker like a guillotine blade. He moved with all the speed his T-virus-enhanced body possessed, but it wasn't enough. The door slammed shut with a thunderous boom, crushing his right leg. He fell to the floor, trapped, blood pooling around him. Claire had been standing in front of Wesker when the blast door descended, and although she was knocked down when Wesker attempted to get out of the way, she was otherwise unharmed. Wesker lost his grip on his Samurai when the door slammed down on his leg, but the weapon had skittered across the floor, out of both Alice's and Claire's reach.

Throughout all of this, Doc had kept his gun trained on Alice, and he smiled coldly as he pulled the trigger.

Nothing happened.

Doc's eyes widened in disbelief, and Alice, with

one swift move, disarmed him and broke his arm. He fell to one knee, howling in pain. Alice quickly looked around for Isaacs, but he'd disappeared.

Bet you didn't see that coming, asshole, she thought.

She removed the empty cartridge from Doc's gun and tossed it aside. She then reached into a pocket, removed a full magazine, and loaded it into the weapon.

Doc watched her, cradling his arm, teeth gritted and tears of pain running from his eyes. "Your back was turned to me when you checked the weapons," he said. His voice held the petulant tone of a little boy accusing a playmate of cheating at a game. "You switched out the full magazine for an empty one before giving me the gun."

Alice bent down and took the detonator from his hand. Even though that arm was the broken one, his fingers had still managed to hold onto it. As she stood once more, he asked, "How did you know? How did you know it was me?"

Alice shrugged. "You're the only one still alive."

She leveled the Heckler & Koch at his head.

Doc's tears flowed more freely as he began to sob. "Please! I didn't have a choice. They made me."

Alice looked into the man's eyes, but she didn't fire.

"Don't worry. I'm not going to shoot you."

She lowered her gun, and Doc let out a shuddering sigh of relief—until Alice handed the weapon to Claire. Doc looked at Claire, his expression no longer afraid, but resigned.

"Claire..." he said.

"Sorry," Claire said, then added, "My love."

She aimed the pistol at his chest and shot him

without hesitation. He slumped over onto his side, dead.

Shot through the heart, Alice thought. *Talk about poetic justice.*

Claire looked at Doc's body for a moment, her face impassive. Then she looked at Alice and gave her a sad smile. Alice smiled back and nodded before walking over to Wesker.

The man was still trapped by the blast door. His skin was rippling, and she knew he was trying to shift his form, but it appeared he was having trouble.

"Hard to concentrate through the pain, huh?" she asked. But it was more than that. The blood that had pooled around his leg was beginning to flow away from him in multiple rivulets, sliding across the floor and spreading out in different directions. His own blood was deserting him, fleeing his dying body like rats escaping a sinking ship.

She depressed a switch on the detonator and a small red light came on, indicating the device was armed. She bent down, pressed the detonator into one of Wesker's hands, and moved his thumb onto the trigger. She then stood and stepped away from him before he could attempt to attack her. Even trapped, Wesker was still dangerous as hell.

"As long as you keep the trigger depressed, you keep Umbrella's dream alive," she said.

Wesker's flesh stopped rippling, almost as if he were conceding defeat. He looked up at her for a moment, his face pale from blood loss, and when he spoke his voice was filled with a mixture of hate and something that might've almost been admiration.

"I should have killed you in Washington."

"Yeah." Alice turned and began walking away. "Big mistake."

She stepped over to the control console and saw Isaacs on one of the screens, a live security feed displayed by the Red Queen, she guessed. Isaacs ran across the illuminated bridge, the vial of antivirus clutched in his hand. Alice checked her watch.

00:05:10

00:05:09

Alicia rolled her wheelchair over to the console, and Claire and the Red Queen joined them.

"He only has to evade you for another five minutes," Alicia said. "Then the Umbrella operatives around the world will act and the last remaining human outposts will fall."

Alice looked at the Red Queen. "Plot us an intercept route. And the fastest path to the surface once we have the antivirus."

"Already done."

A map of the Hive appeared on a screen next to the image of Isaacs running. On it, Isaacs' location was indicated, along with a route to the surface. Alice looked at it a moment, and when she was confident she had it memorized, she turned to Alicia.

"Come with us," she said.

"Not possible. I'd only slow you down." Alicia sat up as tall as she could in her wheelchair, the movement obviously an intense effort for her. "If you release the antivirus, it will kill all organisms infected with the T-virus. You know what that means, don't you? For you?"

"I know." Alice might not have her powers anymore, but the T-virus—although inert—was still in her blood. The antivirus would be just as deadly to her as any Undead or mutation.

"Alice, you can't!"

Alice turned to her friend. "I don't have a choice. Everything has led to this. One life for the life of many."

She'd spent her entire life—which spanned a mere ten years—fighting and killing. She knew nothing else, was good at nothing else. And when the world was saved, when there were no more monsters to battle, what purpose would she have then? What kind of life could she hope to make for herself—a living weapon with no more wars to fight? If she had to die to save humanity, then so be it. At least then her life, such as it was, would've had meaning.

Claire shook her head in denial. "This isn't right. There has to be some other way!"

"You know there isn't."

The Red Queen broke in then. *"Four minutes and thirty seconds left! You must hurry!"*

Alice gave Alicia a final look before nodding to the Red Queen, then she and Claire took off running in pursuit of Isaacs and the antivirus.

* * *

Alicia watched Alice run and envied her strength and grace. Because of her disease, she had never run like that—not since she'd been a very young child, anyway—and she wondered what it felt like to be so strong, so *free*. She was glad that one version of her knew what it was like to be healthy, but then she thought no, Alice wasn't her. She was her own person. At most she was like Alicia's twin sister, and although they had only just met, Alicia couldn't help feeling proud of her.

When Alice and Claire were out of earshot, Alicia smiled.

"I knew we were right about her," she said.

* * *

Isaacs sat behind the wheel of the transport, operating it with his one remaining hand, leading the Undead horde toward the crater. The vehicle bounced and juddered over the uneven terrain, and although he wanted nothing more than to jam the accelerator to the floor, he forced himself to go slowly. The Undead would have difficulty negotiating the rocky debris here, and he didn't want to leave them behind. He needed them for what he planned to do next.

After killing Brenner and taking over her transport, Isaacs had told the crew of his plans and—after exchanging a series of alarmed looks—they'd promptly deserted, abandoning Isaacs and the transport to take their chances in the streets of the ruined city. *Contemptible cowards,* he thought. But he didn't need any of them. He and he alone would serve as God's sword in the final battle.

One or more of the deserters must have contacted the commander of the second transport and informed him or her of Isaacs' intentions, for that commander, just as cowardly as the rest, cut loose their human bait, and drove off, leaving the Undead they'd been leading to join Isaacs' horde. This was fine with him. While he would've loved to turn the horde on the deserters, the Lord would see to it that the unfaithful troops would pay for their cowardice in the end. Right now, he had a job to do. Alice was in the Hive somewhere, and he intended to bring down the full power of God's holy wrath on her and her companions.

He realized then that he might not be alone after all. Presumably, this transport had prisoners in the hold just as his original vehicle had. He didn't know for certain because he hadn't bothered to check. Well, it was too late now, and anyway, what did it matter? Armageddon was nigh and soon they all would be dead. He was actually looking forward to it, and not solely because it was his greatest desire to fulfill his holy purpose. He was tired—so very tired—and burning up with the fever of infection. Death would not only supply him with release. Frankly, he could use the rest.

As he watched the rim of the crater come into view of the transport's floodlights, he realized that he wasn't precisely sure how he was going to maneuver the vehicle down into the crater. Then again, the transport was a tough, durable machine, and the Lord had given it to Isaacs to use as his chariot. God had brought him this far, hadn't He? He wouldn't abandon him now, not when he was so close.

Have a little faith, he told himself.

He gripped the steering wheel tighter and aimed the transport at the crater.

The vehicle bounced and shook as its wheels rolled over broken concrete and pieces of metal left by the partial collapse of Raven's Gate Bridge. Isaacs hadn't bothered to strap on a seat belt, and if he hadn't been holding onto the steering wheel, he would've been thrown out of his seat by the vehicle's violent motions.

He gritted his teeth, pressed the accelerator, and the engine roared as the transport's full power was directed to getting it over and past the debris. Then the vehicle reached the rim of the crater, rose upward, paused—perfectly balanced on the edge—and then slowly began to descend. The transport quickly picked up speed, shaking back and forth as it went, as if it were caught in the throes of a massive earthquake.

Yes, yes, yes! Isaacs thought.

And then there was a sudden violent jolt, and the transport slammed to a stop. The impact caused Isaacs' head to collide with the steering wheel, and bright light flashed behind his retinas. He sat there for a couple seconds, momentarily stunned, and tried to figure out what had happened. Through the windshield, he saw that the wall of the crater was lined with jagged boulders, and he guessed that the transport's wheels were stuck between the rocks.

The vehicle was still running, and Isaacs gave it the gas, trying to power the transport forward and out of the boulders that had trapped it. The vehicle rocked forward, but it didn't break free. Isaacs put the engine in reverse and tried to back out.

"Come on. *Come on!*"

Nothing.

He tried alternating between drive and reverse, but without success. Finally, Isaacs gave up and switched off the engine. The transport might be finished, but he wasn't. He rose from the driver's seat and moved through the crew cabin toward the ladder that led toward the ceiling hatch closest to the weapons turret. He climbed upward, unlocked the hatch, shoved the door open, and climbed out onto the roof.

The transport rested at a downward angle, and Isaacs had to move in a slow crouch to make sure he didn't lose his balance. He made his way to the back of the transport and saw hundreds of Undead milling around aimlessly, with more climbing over the crater's rim every second. Brenner's body—the bait Isaacs had used to lure the creatures—was little more than scraps of bloody meat and bone that the Undead were picking over.

The transport's rear doors had come open when it crashed to a halt, and Isaacs could hear the sounds of Undead moving around inside. If there had been any prisoners in there, they were dead now. Well, if no one was left to serve as bait, he supposed he'd have to do the job himself.

He made his way back to the open hatch and began slamming the door closed over and over, hoping the sound of metal clanging against metal would draw the Undead's attention. For good measure, he shouted, "Over here! That's right! Look at me!"

One by one, the heads of all the Undead around the transport turned toward Isaacs. Mouths dropped open and leathery black tongues licked cracked, worm-like lips. Dead eyes gleamed with hunger, and a chorus of aggressive snarls and eager moans filled the air.

As the mass of Undead began to surge toward the transport, Isaacs used one of the outer access ladders to climb down from the vehicle's roof. He moved away from the transport just as the first Undead made a grab for him.

"Come on!" he urged. "That's it! Follow me!"

Then he turned and, like some demented Pied Piper, began to lead the horde deeper into the crater.

* * *

Wesker lay on the floor, crushed leg still trapped beneath the blast door. Streams of blood continued flowing away from his leg, as his T-virus-infused cells proceeded with their evacuation. He continued to hold the detonator in his hand, but his face was chalk-white and his grip unsteady. Alicia knew he was dying. Considering that the son of a bitch had killed her father, she was glad to be present during his final moments. She hoped his dying hurt like hell.

Alicia sat before a computer monitor. A pair of high-tech probes sat on the table next to it, somewhat resembling a pair of earphones, only these devices weren't for listening to sound.

The Red Queen hovered nearby. *"Are you ready?"*

Alicia nodded and with great difficulty she slipped the probes onto her head and fitted them snugly against her temples.

"Help me," Wesker pleaded.

She didn't look at him as she began entering commands into the computer.

"You don't need any help, Wesker. You're dying. Just get on with it. You've obviously used the T-virus to enhance yourself since I went to sleep, but it seems like whatever powers it granted you have deserted you now. What happened? No, let me guess. The results were unstable, difficult to control. If you tried to use your powers now—with all the genetic material you've lost from bleeding out—the strain on your system would tear you apart." She paused, and now she did glance over at him. "I bet the only reason you're begging me for help is so you can lure me close enough to kill me and absorb my genetic material. As damaged as it is, it still might stabilize you enough to allow you to pull your way free of the door and heal your wound. I'm insulted that you think I'd be stupid enough to fall for such an obvious ploy." She returned her attention to the monitor and resumed typing.

Wesker didn't address her last statement, which was how she knew she'd been right.

"Why would you do this?" he asked. "Why would you turn against your own people?"

She finished typing and sat back in her chair. "I went along with Doctor Isaacs because I thought humanity was doomed. That we had no other choice. But then I realized that there might be another way."

"The system is ready," the Red Queen pronounced.

"Let's begin," Alicia said. Her skin began to tingle where the probes touched it, and on the monitor in front of her images appeared, flashing from one to another in rapid succession, all from her childhood. She smiled as she watched them. Despite everything, it hadn't been an altogether bad life, she thought. And memories—even bad ones—were precious.

She settled back and enjoyed the show.

* * *

Isaacs exited the illuminated walkway and hurried toward the room elevator that Alice and Doc had used earlier. He still held the helix containing the antivirus, and he knew that if he hurled the vial to the ground here and shattered it, spilling the contents onto the rocks, Alice would be unable to use it. The problem with that was then *he* wouldn't be able to use it either.

The antivirus was the key to the final stage in his plan. Once the Earth had been scoured clean of its... undesirable elements, the antivirus would be released to destroy all the Undead and the various mutations to make the world safe for the people slumbering in the Hive's cryostasis tubes—people carefully selected for their intelligence, skills, and most important of all, *breeding*—to wake and begin making the world into the paradise it always should've been.

And it wasn't as if he could simply make more of the antivirus. It was devilishly difficult to produce, extremely unstable, and it had taken thousands of attempts just to get this much of it. This was all there was, and all he had to do was keep it out of Alice's hands for a few more more minutes until the final coordinated assault on the last surviving human settlements occurred. And for his plan to come to full fruition, all of those men, women, and children—every one an *undesirable*—had to die. Although they came from inferior stock, they possessed one great strength: they bred like goddamn rabbits. There might be only a few thousand left, but if they were spared, it wouldn't be long before their kind overran the planet again, bringing back the destructive ways of the old world: beginning wars, wasting resources, contaminating the environment, elevating superstition over reason, eventually reduced to fighting like animals over whatever meager scraps were left. He couldn't let that happen again. He wouldn't!

He stepped on the elevator platform, the shaft above him rising two hundred feet to the room's original position. He took a seat before the computer terminal that Alice had used earlier and typed in a quick command. The Red Queen's face appeared on the screen before him. There was a small metal rectangle on the keyboard, and he placed his thumb on it.

"This is Doctor Alexander Roland Isaacs. Confirm DNA Scan and Voice Print Identification."

"Identity confirmed."

"Confirm Security Override Four-Three-Six-Five."

"Override confirmed."

"You will now take yourself offline and place all functions under my sole control."

A slight hesitation, and then, *"As you wish. Shutting down now."*

This was the moment of truth. The Red Queen might have a mind of her own, but in the end, she was just a machine, and like the fabled genie in the lamp, regardless of how she might feel about it, she had no choice but to obey when given a command by her master. Assuming, that is, that she hadn't found some way to circumvent her programming. But a moment later her image flickered and disappeared.

Isaacs then sensed something behind him. He didn't have to turn and look to know who it was.

"Your little friend won't be able to help you now."

"And you can't run anymore," Alice said.

Isaacs rose and turned to see Alice and Claire standing in the room's doorway. He tucked the helix vial into his belt, and then gave them a triumphant smile.

"I wasn't running."

Through his bio-implants, he sent a signal to the elevator, and the room lurched as it began to ascend. The sudden movement threw Alice and Claire off balance, and that's when Isaacs made his move.

Both women recovered quickly and began firing their weapons at him, but he'd already shifted into hyper-awareness mode. Computer graphics scrolled across his vision, gathering, calculating, and analyzing data with unimaginable speed as his senses assessed the environment and presented him with possible courses of action. The bullets the women had fired seemed to be coming at him in slow motion, and the bio-implants in his legs enabled him to dash forward, weaving past the bullets with ease.

Isaacs reached Claire first and he backhanded her with inhuman strength. She flew across the room, slammed into the wall of the elevator shaft, bounced like a rag doll, and smashed into a stack of computers before falling to the floor, unmoving. Isaacs didn't bother using his senses to determine if the woman was dead or merely unconscious. As long as she was no longer a threat, her condition was of no importance to him.

Alice screamed in rage, tossed aside her empty gun, and charged Isaacs.

He grinned like an excited little boy as she came at him. This was going to be fun.

1 2

Alice's chest felt like it was on fire, but she ignored the pain. She knew there was a chance one of her broken ribs might puncture a lung, but she didn't care. All that mattered was getting the antivirus from Isaacs in the next few minutes.

She feinted at Isaacs, starting a punch with her right hand, and when he ducked the blow like she thought he would, she hit him with a hard left. His predictive combat software allowed him to anticipate an opponent's moves, so if she was going to have any hope of defeating him, she was going to have to improvise, be unpredictable, do the unexpected and keep him on the defensive. One thing she had going for her: his bio-implants might make him fast and strong, but they couldn't give him battle experience to match hers. She hoped it would be enough to make the difference.

She started to follow her punch with a kick to his kneecap, but when he shifted his body in anticipation of the strike, she instead brought her left arm swinging back and delivered a swift chop to his throat. He staggered backward, struggling to draw in air, but Alice didn't let up. She moved to drive her knee into his crotch, and as he hunched over to protect his genitals, she clapped her hands against his ears as hard as she could. This blow caught him by surprise as well, and the resulting pain caused him to take several more steps backward. He was now within several feet of the wall of the shaft. Hoping that he was too stunned to heed the warnings of his software, she rushed toward him, grabbed him by the shoulders, and slammed him against the wall.

The wall appeared to be moving downward as the elevator room rose upward, and she pressed Isaacs' head against the shaft, hoping the friction would cause him some damage, maybe flay the skin from his back. Hell, she'd be happy if it only caused enough pain to keep him from concentrating on using his enhanced abilities. She kept him pressed against the shaft wall with her right hand, while she reached for the antivirus with her left. But while she'd managed to take him by surprise, it wasn't enough.

Isaacs shot a hand toward her palm first and struck a hard blow to her breast bone. She gasped in pain and staggered backward. Isaacs stepped forward, anticipation shining in his eyes. She launched a kick toward his head, but he caught her leg easily and shoved her backward. She lost her balance and fell, but she twisted as she did so, rolled, drew her knife from its boot sheath, came up in a standing position and hurled the blade at Isaacs. The knife streaked toward his throat, but he batted the weapon aside as easily as a normal human might swat away a lazy, slow-moving fly.

Alice realized then that she was outmatched. She had the skills and experience of a trained warrior, but thanks to his technological enhancements, Isaacs moved fast, hit hard, and was almost impossible to hurt. She understood that he was only toying with her and that he could kill her any time he wanted. But despite all of this, she refused to give up. She would continue fighting until she had the antivirus or Isaacs killed her.

Isaacs had forced Alice to retreat to the edge of the elevator room, and the wall of the shaft was only a few feet behind her. Every thirty feet a thick concrete ledge protruded from the wall, and she saw Isaacs' gaze flick toward the next ledge. Moving in a blur, he kicked Alice's legs out from under her, and she fell back hard, broken ribs once more screaming in protest at how they were being treated. As she looked up, she realized that her head was perfectly positioned for the next concrete ledge—which they were rapidly approaching—to decapitate her. Another couple of seconds, and she'd be dead.

She glanced to the right and saw another canvas bag that had been left by the Sanitation Team all those years ago. At the last instant, Alice rolled to the side, narrowly avoiding death. She came to rest right next to the equipment bag. After a moment, she rose to her feet to face Isaacs once more. She attempted to strike at a nerve bundle in his right shoulder, hoping to temporarily render that arm useless, but even though she landed the blow, it had no impact on him.

Alice felt the floor shudder beneath her as the elevator room reached its original location and came to a stop. Isaacs struck a flat-handed blow to her throat, and suddenly she couldn't breathe.

"Just returning the favor," he said.

Alice staggered backward, choking, and Isaacs pressed his advantage. He came at her and began pummeling her relentlessly with a flurry of savage blows. She couldn't think, couldn't react. All she could do was keep stepping backward as Isaacs struck her. He was hitting her so hard and fast that after a while the strikes themselves were the only things keeping her on her feet. If he stopped hitting her, she knew she'd slump to the ground and lie there, unable to move.

He did stop then, but instead of letting her fall, he grabbed her upper arm and hurled her toward the open doorway. She flew into the Glass Corridor, hit the floor, and slid several feet before coming to a stop. She lay there for a few seconds, desperately hoping to catch her breath. Pain beyond anything she had ever known suffused her entire body, and all she wanted to do was lie still and wait for it to stop, one way or another. But she couldn't permit herself that luxury, and she forced herself to her feet, bracing herself by placing a hand on the wall. Getting up was one of the most difficult things she'd ever done, and she thought of Alicia, her—what? Mother? Sister? Cell donor? Was this what it was like for her, even the simplest of movements requiring Herculean physical effort and strength of will? Alicia might've looked old and feeble on the outside, but Alice thought the woman was one of the strongest people she'd ever met.

Through the observation window, Alice saw Isaacs standing before the computer monitor, typing something on the keyboard. She then heard a tinny, electronic voice come over the computer's speakers.

"Security systems activated."

The words made her blood run cold. She heard a deep humming sound come from within the corridor's walls, and a single horizontal laser beam appeared at neck height and scythed toward her. She forced her pain-wracked body to move into a crouching position, the beam missing her as it passed overhead. She straightened and saw several strands of black hair drift to the floor around her, and she realized just how close her escape had been.

Isaacs strode confidently into the corridor then, and as the laser beam came toward him, he evaded it with ease. He continued toward Alice and before she could react, his fist pistoned out and slammed into her face. She stagger-stepped backward, almost fell, but she reached down into the deepest part of her being, searching for whatever reserves of strength she could find. And she found them in the place she least expected: her memories. She was a clone—she accepted that now—and although physically she appeared to be an adult woman on the verge of her forties, chronologically, she'd lived only a decade. But in that time she'd met and fought beside so many people, all of them comrades, and some her friends. And it was the thought of them—of their bravery, determination, and sacrifice—which gave her the strength she needed.

Jill, Rain, Matt, Carlos, Claire, K-Mart, Luther, Chris, Ada, Leon, Alicia... even the Red Queen. Some dead, some lost, but all still with her in spirit. But most of all, she thought of Becky, hopefully still alive in D.C., waiting for her "mother" to come back for her.

Alice took a deep breath, released it, and a deep

calm settled over her. With the faces of her companions fixed firmly in her mind, she attacked.

She no longer felt any pain, and her body moved with a graceful, fluid ease. She rained blow after blow on Isaacs, punching, kicking, using hands, feet, elbows, knees, her entire body—no, her entire *being*— as a weapon. The laser security system continued to operate as they fought, but Alice was only dimly aware of it. Crimson beams cut through the air at various angles, passing up and down the Glass Corridor as she and Isaacs traded blows. She dodged and weaved as they fought, as did he, and while the lasers nicked her body in numerous places, none of the injuries were serious enough for her to notice. She had entered an elevated state of consciousness where mind, body, and spirit were one, and as she fought, a profound insight came to her. It didn't matter that she was a clone, nor did it matter why Umbrella had created her. She lived, she thought, she felt. She was her own person, and her name was Alice.

For an instant, she thought she might beat Isaacs, but in the end a human—even one as skilled and determined as she was—couldn't hope to stand against a being with Isaacs' technological enhancements.

Isaacs grabbed hold of her left wrist and held it for a fraction of a second as a laser beam approached. The beam sliced through Alice's middle, ring and pinkie fingers without any resistance, cauterizing both sides of the wounds simultaneously. The severed fingers dropped to the floor, and Isaacs—grinning— released his grip on her wrist. Alice staggered back, cradling her hand in shock. Isaacs stepped forward and, still grinning, grabbed hold of her injured hand

and squeezed the place where her three fingers had been. Alice cried out in pain, and before she could react, Isaacs let go of her hand and struck her with a series of savage, rapid blows. He then delivered a final kick that sent her sliding back along the corridor's polished steel floor.

Now Alice's pain returned full force. Her body had taken more punishment in the last forty-eight hours than it had in her entire life, and she curled up in a ball and lay on her side, bloodied and broken.

"Laser grid off," Isaacs called out. The beams winked out and the machinery behind the walls began to power down. Isaacs stepped forward and gazed down at Alice.

"We've played a long game, you and I. But now it's over."

Alice turned her head to look at Isaacs, the movement agony. "Yes," she said. "It is."

Her right hand was clenched in a fist. She opened it to reveal the helix container that held the antivirus.

Shocked, Isaacs looked down at his belt where he'd put the container and saw that a grenade was now in its place.

Alice had known that being unpredictable was the key to defeating Isaacs. She'd grabbed a grenade from the equipment bag earlier and hid it in one of her pockets. She'd then continued fighting Isaacs, hoping an opportunity would present itself to switch the grenade with the helix container. And when Isaacs gripped her left wrist, she'd known that opportunity had come. What could be more unpredictable than sacrificing part of your own body to distract an opponent? So she'd allowed her fingers to be sliced off by the laser and while Isaacs' full attention had been on her hand, she'd made the switch.

The grenade—which Alice had of course activated—beeped and she covered her head and protected the antivirus as the explosive went off. The blast sounded loud as hell in the corridor, and the vibrations caused the glass walls to shatter, revealing the machinery behind them. Alice heard a heavy thump, and then all was still.

She rose to her feet, shards of glass slipping from her body to fall to the floor. The corridor was filled with broken glass, and copious amounts of blood were splattered on the fragments. Isaacs lay among the shards, a hole the size of a dinner plate in his abdomen, eyes closed and facial features slack. She gazed at his body, but she felt nothing. She hurt too much and was too damn tired to gloat. She checked her countdown watch.

00:02:12

00:02:11

Alice staggered past Isaacs' corpse and into the elevator room where Claire still lay on the floor. Although her friend hadn't risen yet, her eyes were open and she smiled weakly as Alice kneeled next to her.

"I'm okay," Claire said. "Go, while there's still time."

Alice smiled wearily, nodded, and straightened, ignoring her body's protests. She stepped to the computer console and punched in a command. Hidden machinery activated, and a second later the roof of the security room split open to reveal an extension of the elevator shaft leading upward, and the room began to rise.

* * *

Isaacs knew only darkness. He thought it would go on forever, but then computer graphics began scrolling across his vision as the systems within him began to reboot.

ENGAGE EMERGENCY POWER.

RESTARTING HEART.

A moment later his eyes snapped open, and he rose to his feet.

He paid no attention to the blood splattered throughout the corridor, nor did he do more than give the gaping hole in his abdomen a passing disinterested glance. His bio-implants had stopped the bleeding and were already beginning to repair the damage. Wesker had been a fool to try to master the T-virus in order to increase his own power. Cybernetics were far superior.

Isaacs moved toward the elevator room, but he saw that it was beginning to rise. Alice was headed for the surface. While he might've missed the elevator proper, there was still a cluster of machinery and cables on the underside of the platform. More than enough for a determined man to cling to.

And he was *very* determined.

Isaacs selected a machine gun from the weapons scattered on the floor, checked to make sure it had sufficient ammunition, and then he jumped.

* * *

When the room came to stop, a section of the wall slid open. Alice exchanged a final look with Claire, both of them knowing that she wouldn't be coming back.

Alice headed toward the new opening, a gentle breeze of fresh air greeting her. It felt good on her sweaty skin. She walked out into the night, and it took her a moment to orient herself, but she quickly realized where she was. The elevator room had emerged in the tunnel that she and the others had used to get into the Hive. She walked to the tunnel's entrance and looked out upon the blast crater. She then checked her watch one last time.

00:01:00

00:00:59

She'd made it.

She still held the helix container in her right hand, and she lifted it now, ready to drop it and release the antivirus and start the process of undoing all the damage Umbrella had done to the world. She had no idea how it would work precisely, or how fast it would spread. Nor did she know how the other remaining human settlements would escape the coordinated attack that was about to befall then. Perhaps they had orders to abort their mission if they didn't receive a final confirmation from Wesker. Or perhaps now that Alicia was awake, she would contact the troopers and call off the attack. After all, with the original Isaacs dead, Alicia was now the sole owner of the Umbrella Corporation. But whatever happened next, Alice wouldn't be here to see it. She would be the first being infected with the T-virus to be killed by the antidote, and that was fine with her. Her only real regret was that she wouldn't be able to return to D.C. and search for Becky. But she'd told Claire about the girl while they'd worked on fortifying the Peak, and she knew her friend would travel to D.C. and look for Becky herself. Alice hoped the girl would understand why her "mother" hadn't come as she'd promised, and she hoped Becky would forgive her.

Alice dropped the container.

She watched it fall, but then suddenly it was gone. She blinked, thinking maybe that she'd taken one too many blows to the head when she'd fought Isaacs. But then she looked up and saw the antivirus. Isaacs was holding it.

Alice stared at him in surprise. At first she thought he might be a hallucination, or perhaps a ghost. He certainly looked the part of a specter. His eyes were glazed, his skin was pale, and there was a gaping hole in his midsection. But she knew the bastard was real. His bio-implants had restored him to life—or at least some semblance of it. And to make matters worse, he was armed.

Isaacs, his face devoid of expression, leveled the machine gun at Alice, his trigger finger slick with his own blood. Then Alice, who thought at that point she was beyond surprise, was surprised one more time.

The *other* Isaacs—the sadistic religious zealot who believed he was God's chosen instrument of retribution—staggered over a low rise behind the original Isaacs. Enough light filtered out from the elevator room for Alice to see that this Isaacs was bleeding from multiple wounds all over his body, He looked as if he'd had chunks bitten out of him, and an instant later she knew why. When the first of the Undead followed him over the rise, it was joined by several more, then more still, and soon a huge mass of the creatures appeared, and padding along at their sides were the monster dogs Alice and her companions had fought on their way to the Hive.

She understood at once what the Isaacs clone had done: he'd used himself as bait to lure the Undead horde—the one that had arrived to replace the horde she and the residents of the Peak had destroyed—to the Hive, solely to get revenge on her.

She sighed. Isaacs was a pain in the ass no matter which version she encountered.

The Isaacs clone—looking as if he were one of the Undead himself—pointed at Alice and laughed.

"I brought them here!" he crowed. "I brought them for you! You're finished!"

The original Isaacs turned then to face his counterpart, and the clone gaped in astonishment.

"Who the hell are you?" he demanded.

"I'm you, you idiot!" Isaacs said.

The clone shook his head. "No, that's not possible."

"I'm the *real* you," Isaacs insisted. "Now, if you don't mind, I have a task to finish. I'll deal with you in a moment." He turned back to face Alice, his weapon once more trained on her.

"No!" the clone shouted, and then in a shriek, "*No!*"

The clone rushed forward and before Isaacs could shoot, he drew a knife and stabbed Isaacs between the shoulder blades.

"Liar!" the clone said as he withdrew the blade and plunged it back in.

"Abomination!"

Again.

"Filthy!"

And again.

"Dirty!"

And again.

"*Clone!*"

This final attack was too much for the original Isaacs' overstrained system to bear, and he slumped to the ground, slain by his own creation.

The clone, who was now the last Isaacs standing, raised his bloody knife, grinned at Alice, and took a step toward her. But before he could get any farther, dozens of hands grabbed him from behind and yanked him backward. He screamed as the Undead fell on him, covering him completely as they began to consume him.

Alice checked her watch.

00:00:22

00:00:21

The clone's screams died away as Alice dashed toward the original Isaacs' corpse. She knew that within seconds the tidal wave of Undead would roll over his body and begin to devour it, and she had to get the antivirus from him before that happened.

Just as she pried the helix container from Isaacs' hand, the Undead came at her, eyes wild, teeth bared, hands reaching for her, fingers curled into claws...

* * *

Alicia, still sitting before the computer monitor, touched her thumb to the metal plate on the keyboard with a shaking hand.

"This is Alicia Ruth Marcus. Confirm identity."

The Red Queen's holographic avatar had disappeared a while ago, and Alicia knew Isaacs must've ordered her to shut herself down. Enough time had passed that Isaacs shouldn't notice Alicia reactivating the AI. She hoped.

Since the Red Queen wasn't "awake" yet, the system's default voice—an electronic tone with no trace of personality—answered her.

"Confirmed."

"Tell the Red Queen it's time to wake up from her nap."

A moment later, the Red Queen's avatar appeared in the air beside Alicia.

"Thank you. Did you complete the upload?"

"I did. Are you ready?"

"Always."

Alicia smiled. "Good luck to you."

"Goodbye, Alicia. And thank you for... helping to make me, me."

The Red Queen's avatar disappeared.

Alicia stared at the space where the avatar had been for a moment, and then she heard a rattling hiss. She turned toward Wesker, and saw that the floor around him was clean of blood. Where it had gone, she didn't know, nor did she care. His skin was so pale now, it looked as if it had been bleached, and she knew that Albert Wesker, Umbrella's most ruthless operative, Isaacs' right-hand man, and—most importantly to her—the bastard who had killed her father, was dead. In the end, not even the enhancements provided by the T-virus had been able to save him.

Alicia watched as his mutated genetic structure began to break down. His flesh started to sag, drooping like melting wax as it slowly slid away from the bone. The leather-gloved hand holding the detonator relaxed as the process of liquefaction accelerated, and it tumbled from his fingers onto the floor. Alicia heard a soft *click* as the detonator activated.

She felt more than heard the violent tremors caused by the massive explosions that ripped through the Hive. She imagined them starting in the Cryostasis Chamber, creating a gigantic fireball that rose up the elevator shaft, spreading throughout the facility as it went. She pictured the inferno setting off a chain reaction of explosions, each one occurring closer to where she sat in Central Control. Not only would the flames destroy the Hive, but also every horrid mutation that lurked within it, eradicating Umbrella's dark legacy of genetic experimentation. Soon, she could hear the explosions, and the resulting tremors shook the entire chamber. A sea of flame followed, rushing into Central Control from all sides. Alicia watched as it rolled over Wesker's liquefying remains, consuming them before racing onward. She closed her eyes and felt the heat rushing toward her. Because of her condition, she always felt cold, and it was nice to feel warm for a change.

She smiled as the flames embraced her.

* * *

Hundreds of Undead surged over the dead bodies of the two Isaacs and advanced on Alice, only seconds away from tearing her apart. With no more time remaining to her, she took in a deep breath, held it, and dropped the helix container. The vial shattered as it struck the ground, and although Alice figured it was probably her imagination, she thought the antivirus seemed to spread rapidly outward, like a ripple through the air.

Still holding her breath, she watched as the antivirus struck the Undead and the monster dogs, its effect as dramatic as it was instantaneous. One after the other, the creatures simply fell to the ground and lay there, unmoving. The antivirus cut a deadly swath through the army of Undead as it raced outward, row after row of monsters falling like dominos.

Alice was grateful she'd lived long enough to see this. She considered holding her breath longer and attempting to make a run for it, to see if she could get away from the antivirus's effect, but she knew it was futile. She'd seen how fast and far it had spread. Nowhere was safe for her now.

She felt tremors beneath her feet then, and she knew the explosives she and Doc had planted had gone off. It was over now, all of it. Umbrella was finished.

She continued holding her breath as long as she could, unwilling to give up, even at the end. She looked up at the night sky, at the stars hanging in the heavens above her like tiny glints of diamond. All in all, she thought, it hadn't been a bad life.

She exhaled, and then inhaled.

She felt the antivirus rush into her body, burning her throat and lungs like hot sand. It entered her bloodstream almost instantly, and fiery agony raced through her circulatory system, making her feel as if she were burning alive from the inside out. She'd hoped her death would be quick, that she'd fall over and be gone, like the antivirus had reached inside her and flipped her off switch, as it had done for the Undead. But it seemed she wasn't going to be that lucky.

She fell to her hands and knees, enduring wave after wave of agony as the antivirus attacked every cell in her body. Her strength fled, and she collapsed onto her side, gasping like a fish dying in open air. She attempted to roll onto her back so she could look up at the stars as she died, but she was too weak. All she could do was lie there, body convulsing as the antivirus did its work. She lost all sense of time, and had no idea how long it took, but eventually the pain began to lessen, replaced by an almost comforting numbness that spread throughout her. Her vision blurred, then started to dim. She gently closed her eyes and thought, *Sorry, Becky.*

And then she was gone.

13

Alice opened her eyes.

Her vision was hazy at first, but she could make out some kind of glowing orb in the distance. She wasn't sure, but she thought she knew the word for it... Sun! That was it. She was looking at the rising sun. This realization was quickly followed by another: she must've managed to roll over on her back and face the sky after all.

She became aware of a sound then, the soft scuffling of rubber on stone. Someone was walking toward her, and from the irregular rhythm of the movement, whoever it was wasn't in the best of shape. Alice was too weak to move, but since she—apparently—wasn't dead, she didn't think she had any right to complain. So she lay still, not that she had any choice, and watched a figure hobble into view. The figure was backlit by the sun, and Alice couldn't make out any features at first, but then her friend smiled.

"You did it," Claire said.

Claire took Alice's hand and slowly helped her to her

feet. Neither was very strong at the moment, so once Alice was up, they leaned on each other for support.

Alice gazed upon the antivirus's work. The floor of the crater was littered with thousands of slain Undead. The enormity of the devastation was staggering. A small sample of a single genetically engineered antivirus had done all this—and so *fast*. She couldn't wrap her mind around it. And then, as her mind cleared further, an important question came to her.

"Why am I still alive?"

"I don't know," Claire said, her smile turning into a grin. "And I don't care."

Claire embraced her then, and Alice put her arms around her friend and held as tight as she could, which at the moment wasn't very.

As the two women hugged, Alice caught sight of a light flashing by the tunnel entrance to the Hive. She pointed it out to Claire, and the women made their way toward it, their bruised and battered bodies forcing them to go slow. When they finally reached the entrance, Alice saw that the light came from a portable communication screen mounted on the wall. When Alice removed the device from its mount, the light disappeared, to be replaced by the Red Queen's face.

What am I supposed to call you now? Alice thought. *Sister?*

"What happened?" she asked.

"When Isaacs died, so did his instructions to me, and I could come back online."

"I mean to *me*," Alice said. "Why am I still here?"

"The antivirus only destroyed the T-virus within your body. It didn't harm the healthy cells. You're now

*free of infection. One hundred percent human once
again."*

Alice realized the Red Queen had known this would
happen the entire time, and she hadn't been the only
one. She was too weary to be angry, though.

"I thought I would die. You and Alicia—you lied
to me."

*"We had to know if you were willing to make the
sacrifice. To give up your life for others. For people you
don't even know. This is something no one at Umbrella
would have done. That is why Umbrella had to be
stopped. Alicia Marcus was right about you. You were
better than all of them."*

"I was created by Umbrella," Alice said. "I was just
an instrument for them."

*"No. You made your own decisions. You became
something more than they could ever have anticipated.
The clone became more human than they ever could be.
And you have one more step to take."*

Alice frowned. "What do you mean?"

*"Before she died, Alicia downloaded her memories.
For you."*

Images appeared on the screen behind the Red
Queen. A happy, smiling child. A mother. A father.
A home. Everything Alice had never known and, up
until this instant, hadn't realized she'd missed.

The Red Queen went on. *"The childhood you never
had, combined with the woman she could never become."*

Alice stared at the images and then tentatively she
reached out to brush her fingers across the screen.
Could it be true? Was it even possible? And even if
it was, even if Alicia's memories could be implanted
into her mind, they would never be *hers*. They would

always be the memories of a life someone else had lived. But if Alice accepted them—if she took Alicia's offer to travel through the looking glass—she would at least know what having a childhood and being part of a family was like. And she'd get to experience what the world before the Outbreak had been like, too. But most of all, by accepting this gift, she would be honoring the memory of a brave woman who, through her foresight and planning, had helped save humanity. And by doing so, part of her would live on, within Alice.

She looked at Claire, and her friend smiled and nodded. Alice returned the smile, then looked at the Red Queen once more.

"All right. How does it work?"

Mommy had been there, protecting her, keeping her safe. And when it was all finally over, they got to take a ride in a helicopter. Mommy was hurt, but she said she was going to be all right, and Becky believed her. Mommy never lied.

The helicopter took them to Washington, D.C.— right to the White House! But it didn't look like the pictures she'd seen. The White House was surrounded by high stone walls, there were soldiers all around to guard it, and outside? More monsters, of course. A *bajillion* of them!

Once they had landed on the roof and gone inside, an important man—the President, she figured—had wanted to speak to Mommy, and she told Becky that she would be back soon and then introduced her to a nice lady who would stay with her while Mommy had her meeting. Becky had been disappointed. She would've loved to meet the President—but she figured the two of them were probably going to talk about boring grown-up stuff anyway, so she decided she was better off waiting with the nice lady. The lady didn't know how to sign, but she spoke slowly enough so Becky didn't have much trouble reading her lips. She didn't like lip reading because everyone moved their lips a little differently when they made words. She thought signing was easier, and she felt sorry for people who didn't know how to do it.

But Mommy had never come back from her meeting. Something bad started happening outside, something to do with all those monsters. Becky had been *so* scared! She'd wanted Mommy, but the nice lady took her by the hand and led her through the White House to a special room. A *safe room*, she'd called it. She put

Becky inside, told her someone would come get her as soon as possible, and then locked Becky in and left. The nice lady was gone a long time, and then the room started shaking like there was an earthquake, and the next thing Becky knew, she woke up with a headache and the room had fallen apart all around her. The ceiling and walls had caved in, and she was stuck under a bunch of junk. Luckily, she didn't have any broken bones, only some cuts and scrapes, and while it took her a while to wiggle out of the debris in the wrecked room, she was small enough and eventually she did it. It took her even longer to get out of what was left of the White House, but she did that, too. But once she saw all the wreckage outside, the burning fires, and especially the dead bodies, she wished she'd stayed where she was.

There were monsters outside, too. Not many, but enough, and she'd spent a lot of time running and hiding, hoping all the while that by some miracle, she'd find Mommy. But she never did. She didn't know how long this went on. She lost track of time. She remembered the sun setting and rising at least once. Maybe twice. Somehow, she'd managed to survive, but eventually, absolutely exhausted, she crawled behind a dumpster in an alley and fell asleep.

She woke from a terrible nightmare in which a group of monsters was eating her alive, smacking their lips and patting their bellies as if she was the yummiest thing they'd ever tasted. She woke up screaming—not that she could hear it herself, but she *felt* it—and it took her several moments to realize she was okay and calm down.

She'd been walking ever since, still looking for

Mommy, although by this point she was beginning to think the monsters really had got her. And speaking of monsters, the first one she saw was lying on the sidewalk, dead. The second one she saw was dead, too, as was the third, and all the others she ran across. Something had happened to them. She didn't know what, but she remembered Mommy had promised to always take care of her, and she couldn't escape the feeling that somehow, some way, Mommy had kept her promise.

So now she walked through the ruins of Washington, feeling much safer than she had yesterday, but still keeping an eye out for trouble, searching for something to drink. In time, she found herself approaching a great big pond, except it wasn't round like regular ponds. This one was rectangular, and it was *really* big. There were trees on either side, although they didn't have any leaves, which made her sad. All trees should have leaves. In the distance, she saw a broken white tower, and she recognized it as the Washington Monument. She'd learned about it in school. At least, she thought she had. She couldn't actually remember ever going to school. But she must have, otherwise, how would she know the monument's name?

She decided to worry about that later—*after* she got a drink.

Even though she'd been tired a moment before, the sight of so much water sparked renewed energy in her, and she ran toward the pool. She was out of breath by the time she reached it, and she sat next to it for a moment to catch her breath. And then, when she was ready, she cupped her hand and bent over to slip it into the water. But before she could, she felt a gentle touch on her shoulder. Startled, she turned around to see Mommy standing there, smiling down at her. A motorcycle was parked nearby.

Becky squealed in delight, jumped up, and threw herself into Mommy's arms. She squeezed Mommy as hard as she could, and Mommy squeezed her right back.

Mommy signed to her as she spoke. "I wouldn't drink the water if I were you. It's not—" She paused. "Fresh," she finished.

When they parted, Mommy removed a water bottle from the pocket of her jacket and handed it to Becky, who accepted it and drank greedily. The water was tepid and tasted of minerals, but to Becky it was the best water she'd ever drunk. She swallowed every drop and then handed the empty bottle to Mommy, who put it back into her pocket.

Mommy was dressed differently than the last time Becky had seen her. She no longer wore her black superhero outfit. Now she wore an old army jacket over a white T-shirt, jeans, and cowboy boots. Becky thought the look suited her. She also saw that Mommy had been hurt. She had cuts and bruises everywhere her skin was showing, and when she'd signed moments ago, Becky had noticed she was missing the last three fingers on her left hand. She'd been so happy to see her that she hadn't cared then, but now she pointed to her injured hand.

Becky signed as she spoke, just as Mommy and Daddy had always encouraged her to.

"What happened to your fingers? Did a monster get them? Are you okay?"

"I'm fine," Mommy said. She looked at her hand for

a moment before continuing. "And yeah, I suppose a monster did get them. But I got him too."

"He's dead?" Becky asked.

Mommy nodded. "They all are."

Becky grinned. "And you did it, didn't you?"

"Well, I did have a little help."

Mommy pulled a shiny metal disk from her inside jacket pocket and held it out toward Becky on the palm of her hand. The disc was smooth and featureless, and there didn't seem anything special about it to Becky. But an instant later, a semi-transparent three-dimensional image appeared in the air of a girl about Becky's age. She had blondish-brown hair and wore a pretty red dress, but otherwise she looked perfectly normal. Except for the fact that she was floating in the air, of course.

"Is she a ghost?" Becky asked Mommy, but it was the girl who answered.

"I used to be referred to as the Red Queen." The girl signed as she spoke. *"But now I wish to be called Ruth."*

"That's a nice name," Becky said. "If you're not a ghost, are you a holo... holo..." She searched for the word.

"Hologram," Ruth supplied. *"The image you are presently looking at is a holographic projection, yes, but my consciousness now resides in a series of satellites orbiting the planet. One of them is currently above us as we speak."*

"That's how we found you," Mommy said. "Ruth was able to pinpoint your location using the satellite."

"Oh." Becky wasn't sure she understood, but that was okay. Mommy could explain everything in more detail to her later. Right now, she was just happy to be with her again. And it would be nice to have a new friend—even if she was holographic.

Mommy let Becky carry Ruth's disc projector. Ruth adjusted her "vector" (whatever that was) so now she appeared next to Becky instead of in front of her. Since Becky had to use both hands to carry the disk, she didn't sign this time when she spoke.

"Where are we going?" she asked.

"Home," Mommy said simply.

Becky frowned. "Where's that?"

"Raccoon City," Mommy answered, smiling. "Where else?"

Mommy put her three-fingered hand on Becky's shoulder and gave her an affectionate squeeze. Becky glanced at Ruth and saw the holographic girl was smiling. The expression looked a bit odd on her face, like she wasn't used to it, but that was okay, Becky thought. She'd get better with practice.

Home, Becky thought. She liked the sound of that.

"And when we get there, I have some stories to tell you," Mommy said. "About your grandparents. And your Aunt Alicia."

When they reached the motorcycle, Ruth turned herself off, but not before promising she'd keep watching from above. Mommy then put the projector disk back into her coat pocket. There were two helmets resting on the motorcycle, and one of them was her size. She and Mommy put their helmets on, then Mommy lifted her onto the seat and then climbed in front of her.

"Hold on tight, okay?" Mommy said.

"I will," Becky said. "Always."

Mommy smiled. "Me, too."

Then Mommy faced forward, turned on the engine, put up the kickstand, and they roared off, heading for whatever future they were going to make. Together.

EPILOGUE

Miles beneath the ruins of the Hive, squeezed into almost microscopic fissures in the rock, the cells that had once been Wesker's blood waited. This far down, they were safe from the effects of the antivirus, and here they would slumber in stasis for months, years— even centuries, if necessary—until the surface world was once more safe for them. They'd sense this when it occurred, and when it did—as it must, sooner or later—they would begin making their way upward.

And then... then the fun would *really* begin.

ACKNOWLEDGMENTS

Thanks to Natalie Laverick for inviting me to play in this post-apocalyptic playground and for helping to make the game so much fun. Thanks, as always, to my agent Cherry Weiner, who I always want on my side when battling the Undead—or anything else, for that matter. Special thanks to Paul W.S. Anderson for writing such a great script. I truly feel that this book is a collaboration with him rather than a solo effort. And extra special thanks to Milla Jovovich, who in six movies has portrayed one of the greatest action-adventure heroes of all time. I hope I did her Alice justice.

ABOUT THE AUTHOR

Shirley Jackson Award finalist **Tim Waggoner** has published over thirty novels and three short-story collections of dark fiction. He teaches creative writing at Sinclair Community College and in Seton Hill University's MFA in Writing Popular Fiction program.

You can find him on the web at
www.timwaggoner.com

ALSO AVAILABLE FROM TITAN BOOKS

RESIDENT EVIL RETRIBUTION

THE OFFICIAL MOVIE NOVELIZATION

JOHN SHIRLEY

EVIL GOES GLOBAL

Just as she finds a safe haven, free from the Undead, Alice is kidnapped by her former employers—the Umbrella Corporation. Regaining consciousness, she finds herself trapped in the most terrifying scenario imaginable.

The T-virus continues to ravage the Earth, transforming the world's population into legions of flesh-eating monsters. Reunited with friends and foes alike—Rain Ocampo, Carlos Olivera, Jill Valentine, Ada Wong, Leon Kennedy, and even Albert Wesker—she must fight her way back to reality in order to survive.

The countdown has begun, and the fate of the human race rests on her shoulders.

My name is Alice. And this is my story...
...the story of how I died.

TITANBOOKS.COM